TEXAS LAW: SERIAL MANHUNT

Jennifer D. Bokal

HARLEQUIN
ROMANTIC SUSPENSE

HARLEQUIN®
ROMANTIC SUSPENSE™

ISBN-13: 978-1-335-59373-3

Texas Law: Serial Manhunt

For questions and comments about the quality of this book, please contact us at CustomerService@Harlequin.com.

Harlequin Enterprises ULC
22 Adelaide St. West, 41st Floor
Toronto, Ontario M5H 4E3, Canada
www.Harlequin.com

Printed in U.S.A.

Jennifer D. Bokal is the author of several books, including the Harlequin Romantic Suspense series Rocky Mountain Justice, Wyoming Nights, Texas Law and several books that are part of the Colton continuity.

Happily married to her own alpha male for more than twenty-five years, she enjoys writing stories that explore the wonders of love. Jen and her manly husband have three beautiful grown daughters, two very spoiled dogs and a cat who runs the house.

Books by Jennifer D. Bokal

Harlequin Romantic Suspense

Texas Law

Texas Law: Undercover Justice
Texas Law: Serial Manhunt

The Coltons of New York

Colton's Deadly Affair

The Coltons of Colorado

Colton's Rogue Investigation

Wyoming Nights

Under the Agent's Protection
Agent's Mountain Rescue
Agent's Wyoming Mission
The Agent's Deadly Liaison

The Coltons of Grave Gulch

A Colton Internal Affair

The Coltons of Kansas

Colton's Secret History

Rocky Mountain Justice

Rocky Mountain Valor

Visit the Author Profile page at Harlequin.com for more titles.

To John—the love of my life.

Prologue

Josie Kruger's head collided with a stone as she careened to the bottom of the ravine. The instinct to wrap her arms over her head was stronger than thirst, yet she remained limp. Instinctively, she knew that pretending to be dead was the only way she would ever survive.

Her eyes watered as she realized her first mistake was getting into the car.

Coming to rest on the rocky ground, Josie fought the urge to sob. Every part of her body ached. Her stomach burned. Her throat hurt worse than death. Then again, maybe she was already dead. She'd been choked. Sliced open. Thrown into a trunk. And finally pitched to the bottom of a gully.

Yet, the sky spread out above her in all directions, filled with endless stars. To Josie, this seemed like a nice place to just slip away. Maybe dying would be easiest.

A beam of light cut through the darkness. The illuminated circle danced across the dirt until it found Josie.

She stared, unblinking, into the night.

The light clicked off. From the top of the ravine, Josie heard footfalls on gravel. There was the slamming of a car's door, along with the crunch of tires as the vehicle drove away.

Finally alone, she drew a shaky breath and blinked her eyes. The first tear leaked out, running down the side of her face and into her ear.

After a minute, she slowly rolled to her side and pushed up to her hands and knees. Josie looked up at the hill. Even in the dark, she could see the steep pitch. The rocks that littered the ground. The fact that the hill was long.

Damn. She'd been lucky not to have broken her neck on her tumble to the bottom. But now she had a different problem. How in the hell was she supposed to climb to the top?

Staggering to her feet, she cried out as a bolt of pain shot through her stomach. Her shirt was ripped open, and she peered at her torso. A long cut ran from her chest to her pelvis. It wept gore. Gripping her bloody shirt, she pressed it into the wound. Agony clawed at her middle and stole her breath.

Yet, Josie refused to relent.

Putting one foot in front of the other, she began to trudge upward. Her vision blurred. Her hands trembled. Her head pounded with every beat of her heart. Wind blew down the hill, and she shook with cold.

One more step. Another. Another.

Her foot hit the cool pavement and she dropped to her knees. In the distance, two headlights cut through the dark. Josie lifted her hand against the glare. There was something important about a car, but she couldn't remember what.

The oncoming vehicle screeched to a stop, the grille just inches from her face.

A shadowy figure approached and dropped down beside Josie.

She looked at the man. His face wavered as if he were underwater. Still, she recognized him. "Sheriff Cafferty?"

"Josie Kruger? That you?"

And then, there was nothing.

Chapter 1

Sage Sauter woke with a start, her heartbeat thundering in her chest. She was reclined in her chair. Her TV hung on the wall. The local weather forecast was on the screen. A plate with the remnants of her dinner and glass of wine—half-full—sat on the coffee table. A single lamp lit the room. So, she'd fallen asleep in front of the TV again. The time on an old DVD player glowed. 10:17 p.m.

At least she woke before midnight and could get a restful night's sleep in her bed.

But she'd woken with a fright. Why?

Someone knocked on her front door. That must've been the noise that woke her.

"Who is it?" she called out.

"It's me, Sheriff Cafferty." The voice was male, and she recognized it at once.

Her heartbeat stuttered, skipping a beat. A visit from

the sheriff after dark was never to deliver good news. She rose from the chair and wiped the sleep from her eyes. "Hold on a sec," she called out. "I'm coming."

Built almost a century earlier by Sage's great-grandparents, the house was a hodge-podge of rooms that were added onto the home as needed and not with an eye for aesthetics. The den was connected to the entryway by a narrow doorway. She kicked a pair of shoes toward the wall and opened the front door. Maurice Cafferty, otherwise known as Mooky, stood on the porch. He wore his uniform, a dark brown shirt and khaki pants. Holding his hat, he shifted from one foot to the other. "Sorry to bother you. But I wouldn't stop by if it wasn't important." The gravity of Mooky's tone told her everything she needed to know—even if she hadn't heard the details.

"What happened?" Her ranch, The Double S, employed four full-time hands, along with Bruce, the foreman, and several part-time workers. Good people, all of them, even if they liked to drink. Was that it? A car accident? Bar fight? It had to be something more than one of them getting pulled over. Mooky wouldn't bother her at home with that.

"It's Josie." He paused. "I don't know how to tell you this, other than to say it plain. She was attacked. I happened to find her on the side of the road." He let out a breath that shook his whole body.

The floor seemed to tilt violently. Sage began to slide. Reaching for the wall, she held herself upright. Bile rose from her gut. Drawing in a deep breath, Sage forced her roiling stomach to steady. Much as she wanted to give in to the panic that was trying to break free, she wouldn't. She couldn't. Her daughter needed her. She had to be strong—now and always.

"Sage." He stepped into the foyer and put his hand on her elbow. "You okay?"

"I'm just..." What was she? Shocked? Anguished? Afraid? She was all of that and more. "What happened? Where's Josie? How is she?" Her voice shattered on the last word.

"She's alive. We had her medevaced to San Antonio Medical Center."

"Oh, thank God."

"I don't rightly know what happened to her before I found her, because she doesn't remember a damn thing." He paused and Sage realized she was holding her breath. "I know you want to get to the hospital, but can you spare a minute to give me some information?"

Her heartbeat raced. Her ears buzzed. "If it'll help find out what happened to Josie, you can have all the time you need." Although her words weren't exactly true. She planned to leave for the hospital as soon as she could. She led Mooky to the den and returned to her seat in the recliner. He sat on the adjacent sofa. She asked, "What do you need to know?"

"When was the last time you spoke to Josie?"

"We spoke last night." Josie was in her third year at Texas Midland State University. The campus was nearly three hours from the ranch and Mercy, Texas. "She was at school."

"How'd she seem to you? Anything wrong?"

"She was fine," said Sage, almost automatically. No, that wasn't right. "Josie seemed distracted. Tired, maybe. We only spoke for a few minutes." Sage tried to recall a clue in her daughter's words that she'd missed.

"It's the end of the semester and she complained about tests and papers. Said she was busy, is all."

"Did she say anything about a fight with a boyfriend or an argument with a friend?"

"No."

"Any idea who might want to hurt Josie?" Mooky paused. "Or you?"

The possibility that someone had attacked Josie to get to her left Sage ill. For the most part, she got along with her neighbors. Her customers. Her vendors. In an instant, friends became suspects. She replied, "Nobody comes to mind."

"When was the last time she was home?"

She rubbed her forehead and drew in a long breath, calculating the days since Josie's last visit. "It'll be five weeks on Friday. She was only home for the weekend."

"As far as you know, she wasn't expected this evening either?"

"Are you saying that Josie was found near Mercy? How can that be? She was on campus last night." Sage was afraid to ask for details, but she had to know. "You have to tell me everything."

"I don't know if you actually want all the specifics…"

She could see the look in his eyes. Her child had suffered. But she had to know. How else could she fix the situation without the facts? "Mooky," she said, her tone both a plea and a warning.

"I'll tell you everything that I can, at least." He drew in a long breath. "She was hurt bad. The perpetrator, well—they sliced open her abdomen. Looks like she was strangled and then thrown down a hill. But Josie climbed back to the road. I just happened to be passing by and found her."

Sage pressed a hand to her lips as hot tears flooded her eyes. She wiped her face with her sleeve. Someone had done unspeakable harm to her baby. Josie was a grown woman at twenty-two years old, but she was still her baby.

She stood. "I'm going to San Antonio now. I can't sit around and wait for news about what happened."

Mooky rose to his feet as well. "You're going to have to speak to the campus police—the last place she was seen was near her school. Since they assume that she was taken from campus, they're in charge of the investigation and will most likely ask about her friends."

Sage would talk to the Devil himself if it meant helping her daughter. "Should I call them?"

"No need right now, but I will give them your cell number." He paused. "They're going to want to look at Josie's social media. You wouldn't happen to know any passwords to her computer or phone?"

"She used to use *Rainbowkitty* for everything, but that was when she was in middle school. I can't even guess what she'd use for a password now."

"I'll pass that along to the campus police anyway, just in case."

"Thank you, Mooky." She paused. "For everything."

He regarded Sage and said nothing.

She asked, "What aren't you telling me?"

"It's just…"

She waited. The seconds passed like hours. "It's just what?"

"Well, I was wondering if you planned to call Vance."

The name of her ex-husband stole all the air from

the room, and Sage found it hard to breathe. "I guess I have to…" Her words faded to nothing.

He offered, "If you'd rather, I can reach out."

Mooky and Vance had been close growing up—almost like brothers. Her ex-husband was a brilliant man and Mercy was never big enough for all his talents. He started off as a reporter for the newspaper in Encantador—a town only 20 miles from her ranch. The only thing larger than her ex's talent was his ambition. Vance moved to freelance journalism a dozen years earlier. In a few short years, the trips abroad went from lasting days to weeks to months.

It didn't help that Josie wasn't his biological daughter—a secret that only she and he knew. She always wondered if Vance would have stayed closer to home if Josie had been his flesh and blood. But theirs had been a marriage of convenience and nothing more. Her ex-husband couldn't ignore excitement and fame for a woman he cared about and a child who didn't share any DNA. "Last I heard he was covering some military conflict in Africa. Don't know where, though. Sudan, maybe?" She opened her mouth, ready to suggest that Mooky ask Josie for her daddy's whereabouts. Then she remembered. Sage bit her bottom lip until she tasted blood. "Call Vance if you want. I don't mind."

Mooky nodded. "I'll do that. And Sage?"

"Yeah?"

He hesitated. "Nothing," said Mooky. "It's nothing."

She suspected that was a lie. Which left her with an interesting dilemma. She wanted to press the sheriff for what he wasn't telling her, but she also had to get on the road. Seeing her daughter was the only thing that mattered right now. "I'm going to pack up a few things and then go to the hospital."

"You drive safe, ya hear?"

"Of course," said Sage before adding, "Thanks for taking care of Josie. It means everything to me."

Mooky made a noise that could've meant anything.

She walked with him through the foyer. He pulled open the door and stepped onto the porch. He placed the hat back on his head and took the steps down to the path that led through the yard. His police cruiser was parked next to her truck.

"Hey, Mooky," she called out.

He turned to face her. "Yeah?"

"Call me as soon as you know anything."

He tipped his hat and turned back toward the path.

Sage closed the door and slid to the floor. Pulling her knees to her chest, she fought back the tears that threatened to flood her eyes. Her chest ached and her head pounded with each beat of her racing heart. Yet, sitting on the floor wouldn't help Josie.

She had to get herself up and drive to San Antonio. She supposed it made sense that Mooky had sent Josie there, since it was the closest trauma center to Mercy. The local urgent care was lucky to be stocked with basic supplies on a good day.

She stood. Her legs were weak, but she held onto the wall of the old farmhouse as she made her way to the bedroom at the back of the house.

Sage entered her bedroom and flipped the light switch. Her room was just as she'd left it this morning. Unmade bed. Laundry baskets overflowing with clothes to be folded. Yet, everything was different. When she'd gotten up at dawn, her daughter was whole and healthy—as far as she knew. Now, the world had spun off-kilter.

Sage refused to wallow in self-pity. She had to go to Josie. But who knew how long she'd be gone?

She quickly threw some clothes and toiletries into a duffel bag. On the way to the hospital, she'd call her foreman, Bruce, and tell him to take care of the ranch until she got back.

She had to be strong. There was nobody else who could take care of Josie. But who could Sage look to for help?

Then again, she already knew the answer.

She had nobody. At 44 years old, that realization left her exhausted. With an exhale, she sat on the side of the mattress. From a drawer in the bedside table, she removed a book of poems. The book was always present, yet rarely read. The leather cover was cracked with age and the gilt along the edges of each page had long ago flaked away.

She opened the book to a page she knew well. Yet, it wasn't a verse that she sought. She wanted to see the picture that she'd hidden away years earlier.

In the photo, Sage's legs dangled over the liftgate of a pickup truck. Her skin was tanned by the sun. Her hair, in a tangled bun, was gathered into a scrunchie. She was just twenty-one years old in the photo—and didn't know what turn her life was about to take. Next to her sat a young man with auburn hair. A pair of sunglasses hid his eyes.

Neither looked at the camera. Instead, they were smiling at each other. It was the happiest moment of her life—even if she knew that her summertime romance was coming to an end.

She traced the young man's face. "Michael O'Brien." Her whisper was swallowed by the night. It wasn't often that Sage indulged in the game of what-if. Yet, as she stared at his picture, she couldn't help wondering—what if he'd left three weeks later?

What if Sage hadn't broken up with Michael before he left for the Peace Corps?

They'd argued. Harsh words, spoken out of anger and the passions of youth, still echoed in her mind. "Get the hell out of my town and my life. I never want to see you again."

It had taken her days to calm down after the argument, and by then, he had left the country and it was too late to apologize. But Michael leaving was only the beginning of her troubles.

What if Vance hadn't proposed and promised to be a good father when she found out she was pregnant?

Slipping the picture between the pages, she hugged the book to her chest.

Dr. Michael O'Brien stood at the podium. He stared at the sea of faces in the packed bookstore. The cover of his book, *Let the Dead Speak for Themselves*, had been projected onto a screen at his back. Michael had released the book three years earlier. The sales at the time had been modest, but recently his book had enjoyed a revival when the media learned that Michael had worked on the case of an infamous serial killer, Decker Newcombe. Sales soared and Michael landed on several bestseller lists. His publisher suggested a book tour to capitalize on the newfound popularity, and he'd agreed.

What he couldn't have guessed at the time was how he'd feel after several months on the road. At this moment, he hated that the book was popular because of his connection to the serial killer.

True, Michael's book had been about his job as a forensic pathologist. But he'd written the book for a purpose— to share how medical science was used in conjunction with law enforcement to solve murders.

Yet, it was his connection to the Decker Newcombe case that changed everything.

He was only a popular author because Newcombe was still at-large. His time should've been spent looking at evidence from the murderer, not talking about him.

But he was back home in San Antonio and more than ready to get back to work. He scanned the crowd, as he often did—he'd been told by some of his old colleagues among the feds that, given his subject matter, it wasn't a bad idea for him to keep even a casual eye out for anyone who concerned him. People who hung back at book signings and asked…weird, detailed questions about the methods of a particular criminal, for instance. Or someone who had sent him letters or emails—or in one case, in Chicago, left him voice mails—with increasingly violent threats. Thankfully, security had prevented an incident before the event started.

Today, at the back of the store, he noticed someone he hadn't seen in months. Then again, Isaac Patton was hard to miss. He was taller than Michael and towered over the crowd.

Isaac was the founder of Texas Law, a private security firm that had been tasked with finding Decker Newcombe. Isaac had spent a year working undercover and waiting for the killer to resurface.

Michael had met Isaac when they searched the desert for the missing killer. After a shootout, Decker had escaped into a storm. The two had struck up a friendship. But Isaac didn't strike him as the kind of person to spend an evening at a book signing.

Michael continued to speak. He'd given this talk so many times that he knew the words without looking at his notes. It gave him a moment to study Isaac, who stood unmoving at the back of the room.

The security operative's arms were folded across his chest. His lips were pressed together, and a sheen of sweat covered his brow. As a physician he knew the signs. The man was under some kind of stress—or, make that duress.

Isaac deliberately looked at his watch. Michael took it as a not-so-subtle sign to wrap up the presentation. Still looking at the security operative, he gave a quick nod.

Leaning toward the microphone, he skipped to the end. "Working as a forensic pathologist for more than a decade has taken me to all corners of the globe. And while I've seen the evil that men—and women—can visit upon each other, I am always astounded by the ability of a community to come together to stand in the face of that evil, and how the good overcomes the wicked." He paused. "Thank you for your time."

The applause was instantaneous and if Michael were honest, somewhat overwhelming. A glass of water rested on a shelf. He picked up the glass and sipped as the applause continued. Raising his voice to be heard over the noise, he said, "Thank you. Thank you all. I'm truly flattered."

Before he could step away from the microphone, a woman in the front row, holding a dog-eared copy of the book, lifted her hand. "Can I ask a question?"

"Of course."

She rose from her seat. "Dr. O'Brien, I'm interested in your opinion on Decker Newcombe. Could he have survived being shot and left in the desert?"

He should have been expecting this. Decker Newcombe was a hitman who went on the lam for almost a year after the assassination of a district attorney in Wyoming. Newcombe re-emerged in West Texas. Before being found, Newcombe had killed five people. In a standoff with Isaac, Newcombe was shot in the chest and stumbled into the Mexican desert, where he'd disappeared without a trace.

Since then, there was one question that had kept everyone guessing. Was Decker Newcombe still alive?

Michael had been brought onto the case and examined each of the bodies. One of the female victims had been strangled and then, like the victims of Jack the Ripper, disemboweled post-mortem.

For a moment, he was caught in a flash of memory. Two corpses lay side by side on exam tables in the morgue. Their flesh had been seared beyond recognition. They'd been murdered for no reason—other than Newcombe decided to hide in their home.

The fact that the killer hadn't been caught still filled his chest with hot rage.

"With any case," he began, careful not to offer too many specifics of the investigation, "I need a body to examine before I can say whether that person is alive or not." His comment earned him a few chuckles from the audience. "In all seriousness, I don't know. It would be wrong of me to speculate." He needed to get away from the podium, but several hands were raised. He couldn't ignore the group of readers who came out to see him. Pointing to a man in the back row, he said, "I have time for another question."

"Your book talks about several cases you've worked over the years," said the man. "What's the hardest part of the job?"

In all his years working as a forensic pathologist, Michael had seen murders committed in a variety of cruel ways. It had been his job—still was his job—to find clues that led to the culprit. Sure, he'd helped to put several dangerous people in jail. But he hadn't caught them all. A crime scene photo from a restaurant in Encantador, Texas, was tattooed on his brain. Decker had committed that murder as well. Putting Newcombe in jail would bring a certain level of closure to the victim's family. But there was no way to bring back the dead. Clearing his throat, he leaned toward the microphone. "Even if the killer is arrested, justice is never really served."

"Sounds like a great title for your next book," said the woman in the front row.

He wasn't sure that he had it in him to write a sequel. Yet, he smiled and said, "I'll keep that in mind." Before anyone else could ask another question, he gave a quick wave to the audience. "Thank you for coming."

The applause started again. Michael collected his notes.

The woman from the front row met him as he walked away from the podium. "I just love your book." She held the copy, her arms outstretched.

"I'm sincerely flattered that so many people connected with the work." He removed a pen from the pocket of his suit coat. "Can I sign that for you?"

"Would you? Please?"

Michael scribbled his signature on the title page, trying his damnedest to make it look like something beyond, well, scribbles. "I guess what they say about doctor's handwriting looking like chicken scratch is true," he joked, handing the book back to the woman.

"Can I ask you another question about Decker Newcombe?" the woman asked.

At the same moment, Isaac approached.

He knew that the security operative hadn't come to the signing to be social. But he wasn't going to let his fan know that something was amiss. Holding out his hand to shake, he said, "Hey, man. Thanks for stopping by. Means a lot to me." Then, he remembered his manners. "Isaac, I want to introduce you to…" He turned to the woman.

"Sophia," she said, giving her name.

"Sophia," he repeated. Damn. He should've asked for her name when he signed the copy of her book. "This is Isaac. And honestly, if you have a question about Decker Newcombe, he's the one you should ask."

"Oh sure," said Sophia. "I was wondering how exactly Decker knew he was related to Jack the Ripper?"

Isaac said, "After killing a DA in Wyoming, Newcombe knew he had to disappear. He lived in a Mexican safe house for a year—completely off the grid. After all that time, Newcombe figured the case had gone cold. But to make sure, he hacked into the Wyoming DOC's system." There had been an analysis of the DOC's computer system that led to the library in Encantador, Texas. "On the site, Decker found his own profile and it linked him to Jack the Ripper."

Isaac had given the short answer. But there was more to how Decker had been linked to the Ripper. One time when Decker was arrested, his DNA was taken. From there, it'd been run through the system to see if he was connected to any other unsolved crimes. It was during that search that his DNA was linked to some blood found at a Ripper crime scene.

Michael added, "He stole a book from the library, learning what he could about Jack the Ripper. Then, he imitated a Ripper killing. He murdered five people in and around Mercy before he was stopped by this guy here." He slapped Isaac on the shoulder.

"You know he's a bad guy when he steals books from the library." Sophia gave a little laugh. "Sorry. English teacher joke."

"It's funny," said Michael. "I like it."

And then, there seemed to be nothing left to say.

Sophia lifted her book. "Thanks for the autograph."

Michael smiled. "Anytime."

Sophia walked away and Isaac sighed. "What's the matter with you, man? She's an attractive woman and she obviously likes you."

At 46 years old, he'd been hassled about being a bachelor for years. Still, Michael bristled at the criticism. "What's the matter with me? What's the matter with you?"

Isaac turned to face him. "You're a smart guy. You know what I mean."

Sure, he understood. Michael had been in love once. Since then, a string of bad relationships taught him a single important lesson. Love wasn't worth the hassle. Honestly, he was okay with that—most of the time, at least.

And when he wasn't?

Well, he didn't waste time worrying about what might've been.

He said to Isaac, "If you like Sophia all that much, you ask her out."

"Me? I'm taken."

"You and Clare still together?" Last Christmas, Clare Chamberlain had been running from her former husband and his murderous family. Life on the road had led her to Mercy, Texas. She'd stumbled into the trap that had been laid for Decker and the serial killer had almost made Clare another victim.

Isaac said, "She hasn't kicked me out yet."

Michael was glad that the other man had found some happiness. "She seems like a nice woman."

"You know who else is a nice woman? Sophia, the English teacher."

Michael wondered why he always hesitated whenever someone mentioned him going out with a woman. There was nothing wrong with an evening out with a smart, pretty, funny woman—was there? "Don't tell me you came here just to give me a hard time about my love life."

Isaac asked, "Actually, is there any place we can talk privately?"

Finally, the real reason for tonight's visit. "Follow me. The manager told me I could use the break room." He led Isaac to the back of the store and a door marked "Employees Only." Pushing it open, he wondered what was so important that Isaac would find him at a book signing. Michael's chest tightened with apprehension.

The break room was at the end of the short hallway, the door already open. It was a windowless room with two tables. A single-serve coffee machine and a box of individual snacks sat on one table. The other, covered in a vinyl cloth, was surrounded by four folding chairs. Michael stepped inside and waited for Isaac to follow. He closed the door.

Folding his arms across his chest, he asked, "What's all this about?"

Isaac dropped into one of the chairs. Pulling the phone from his jacket, he placed a call. As the cell began to ring, he turned on the speaker function. Setting it on the table, he said, "I'll let the sheriff explain this from the beginning."

The phone rang three times before being answered. "This is Cafferty."

"It's me," Isaac said. "I'm with Doctor O'Brien."

"Evening, Sheriff." Michael had met the sheriff a few months ago when examining the victims that were linked to the Decker Newcombe case. "Isaac said you needed to tell me something."

"We...we need your help," the sheriff said, his voice a hoarse whisper. "It happened again."

For a long moment, there was nothing but silence. He asked, "What happened, Sheriff?"

"I found another victim from Mercy. She was strangled and cut from neck to belly just like the last one."

There was a lot that the sheriff had said, but even more that he'd refused to say. Was Decker Newcombe killing again? Michael went numb, then anger slammed him back into his body. "Was the body posed like last time? Disemboweled?"

"That's the thing," said Cafferty. "She's not dead."

Michael said, "Tell me exactly what happened, Sheriff."

Cafferty spent a few minutes going over the events

of the evening. Most interesting, of course, was that this young woman was alive—thankfully. But the victim didn't remember anything of the attack and had lost consciousness before the ambulance arrived.

Isaac said, "This attack isn't exactly like the one where Decker imitated Jack the Ripper. But the similarities are striking. What do you think, Doc?"

Michael wasn't sure what to think. "I'd know more if I could examine the victim. Where was she taken?"

"She was airlifted to the trauma unit at San Antonio Medical Center," said the sheriff. "She should be there by now."

That was the first bit of good news he'd gotten since Isaac arrived. As the head of Forensic Pathology at that hospital, he'd be able to investigate the case without any bureaucratic red tape. Rising from the seat, Michael retrieved a leather backpack he'd stored in the corner. "I'll head there now."

"Before we go our separate ways, I think it's best that we keep the possible Decker Newcombe connection as quiet as possible." Isaac rubbed the knuckles of one hand with the thumb from the other. "Once Michael examines the victim, we'll have a better idea what's happening. Until then, there's no use in causing speculation or hysteria."

"Agreed," said the sheriff, "so long as we can get some answers quickly. If Decker's still out there, folks have a right to know and be prepared."

"I agree with you both." Michael paused and pulled his phone from his pocket. After opening a notetaking app, he asked, "What's the victim's name?"

"Josie," said the sheriff. "Josie Kruger."

His finger on the keypad, he paused. Something

tugged at his memory, but he couldn't quite bring it to the surface. With an exhale, Michael typed out the name. He slipped his phone back into his pocket. Then, to both the sheriff on the phone and Isaac in the room, he said, "I'll be in touch."

He walked through the empty bookstore and quickly thanked the manager for hosting his event. He pushed the door open and stepped onto the sidewalk, his heart-beat quickening. There was only one thing that mattered—the truth.

As he walked toward his car, his mind wandered. Decades had passed since that summer he spent in Mercy, Texas. The sun had burned the landscape to a dust brown and the heat made it all but impossible to go outside during the day.

While there, he'd worked at a medical clinic with three other employees—two nurse practitioners and a part-time lab tech. The NPs were an elderly couple, Mildred and Maude, who were incredibly kind and treated Michael as their own. They even said the initial *M* fit with theirs. After his first week of work, they invited Michael over for dinner. It was supposed to be a casual affair to "get the office together."

On the evening of the dinner, Michael leaned against a counter, a glass of iced tea in hand.

Mildred was slicing cucumbers for a salad when someone knocked on the door. "Can you get that? It's probably the part-time lab tech. Her name is Sage Sauter."

"Of course." Michael set his tea on the counter. He walked through the dining room, where a round table was set for four. Beyond the dining room was the living room and the front door. He opened the door and drew in a sharp breath.

Sage Sauter stood on the threshold. She was bathed in a halo of light from the setting sun. Tall with shoulder-length blond hair, she wore shorts, a floral shirt, and no makeup. She smiled at him, and his pulse started to race. Before she'd spoken a word, Michael—at just twenty-six years old—had fallen hard.

Over the next few months, he and Sage spent every day together. Even now, he thought of that summer as the most perfect of his life.

They'd broken up less than a week before he left for the Peace Corps. They'd had a nasty fight that ended in harsh words and wounded feelings.

Three months into his two-year commitment with the Corps, he finally got access to a computer. An email from Mildred was waiting for him. Sage was pregnant and recently married to her childhood best friend. Reading the words brought on physical pain.

His feelings swung from fury to desolation.

In the end, he'd been left with nothing.

Forcing his mind back to the present, he approached his car and pushed a button on the handle. Since the key fob was in his bag, the lock unlatched with a click. He pulled the door open and slipped behind the steering wheel. He stowed his backpack on the passenger seat. Another push of a button and the engine whispered to life. After fastening his seatbelt, Michael pulled away from the curb and drove toward the hospital. Readjusting his hands on the steering wheel, he couldn't help but wonder how different his life would be if Sage had been with him through it all.

The chill of the air conditioning penetrated his skin,

but he didn't turn it down. If anything, it helped cool his emotions. Helped him remember the pain he'd gone through after losing her for good. He knew that no matter what, he was never ever going to give himself to another person again.

Chapter 2

It was after 1:30 a.m. by the time Sage arrived at the hospital. She stood in front of the information desk at San Antonio Medical Center and asked again, "Are you sure you can't tell me anything else?" She didn't know where her emotional gauge was set—somewhere between frustration and sorrow. "Is there someone who can speak with me?"

The intake clerk, a young man with glasses, pointed to a computer screen that Sage couldn't see. "Your daughter arrived an hour ago. She's in surgery and the surgeon will meet with you when they're done."

Since Josie was technically an adult, Sage wasn't authorized to know much about the treatment. And no matter how hard she pushed, the wheels of medical bureaucracy refused to budge.

"What kind of surgery? How long will it take?"

"I don't have that information here, ma'am. I've sent

a note to the surgical team. They know you've arrived. Someone will come to speak to you soon."

Sage wasn't ready to give up. "What can you tell me? You must know more than just that she's in surgery."

"The only thing I can access is what's on my computer." The clerk gestured to a group of chairs that served as a waiting area. "If you could take a seat. There's a line behind you."

She glanced over her shoulder. People had gathered, waiting for their turn at the intake desk. Sure, she understood that many would see her as rude or, at the very least, stubborn. The thing was, Sage didn't care—not when it came to the welfare of her child. "Can I..." she began.

The clerk looked past Sage. "Next."

Refusing to be sidelined, she remained where she stood. A family of three approached. There was a tired mother, along with a father who held a toddler. The child had the glassy-eyed look of someone with a high fever.

She gave the mother a wan smile and walked slowly toward the waiting area. Sage set her purse on the ground before dropping into one of the chairs. She fished her phone from her bag and checked for messages.

There were none.

She opened her contact app and placed a call. Mooky answered on the first ring with a question. "Any news?"

"I just wanted to let you know that I've made it to the hospital." The lights overhead buzzed, and she felt the pinch of tension drawing her brows together. Sage rubbed her forehead. "She's in surgery, but that's all I know. Someone's supposed to come out and tell me what's going on." Mooky was more than the lead lawman for the entire area—he was also a friend. "Any chance you can call? Maybe the hospital will tell you something they won't tell me." She paused, knowing that every second of time he spent on the phone with her was time not spent investigating what happened to Josie. "I mean, if you get a chance."

"I'll see what I can do. Call me if you get an update. I'll do the same."

"Thanks, Mooky." She ended the call and scanned the waiting area. The family with the feverish child sat nearby.

She watched the trio—mother, father and child. A pang of jealousy struck her in the chest. True, Sage sat in a room filled with people but really, she was alone.

She refused to think the unthinkable. Yet, she knew the fear lurked at the edges of her consciousness.

What would happen to her if Josie died during surgery?

The pain in her chest grew. She bit back a sob and rubbed her breastbone.

For an instant, Sage was thrust backward more than twenty years. While sitting in the nursery on the top floor of the farmhouse, she held Josie. The child clung to her neck and Sage could feel the heat as her daughter's temperature climbed. In that moment, she was overwhelmed by a hollow sense of helplessness. It was much the same for her now but a million times worse.

With the resurgence of interest in his book, Michael had taken leave from the hospital for several months to go on tour. True, every place he'd visited was interesting in its own way. Yet, as he walked through the employee entrance of San Antonio Medical Center, he inhaled deeply. The scent of the hospital—disinfectant, coffee, with an undertone of tension—filled him. The only sounds in the empty corridor were the overhead buzzing of the fluorescent lights and his own footfalls.

The smells and sounds were as familiar to him as home.

He took a service elevator to the seventh floor and made his way to the surgical unit. A nurse sat behind a desk. Her cheeks reddened as he approached.

"You caught me." She lifted a copy of *Let the Dead Speak for Themselves*. "Your book is really fascinating."

He pulled a pen from the inside pocket of his jacket. "I can autograph it, if you'd like."

"Sure." She handed him the book. "Thanks."

"As long as you get me information on a patient. Josie Kruger." As he spoke the words, the name felt familiar. True, he'd spent the summer in Mercy—the same place the girl's family lived. Maybe they'd been patients at the medical clinic where he'd worked. He continued. "She's in surgery."

"Give me a sec." She typed on a computer monitor that sat on her desk.

Michael glanced at the nametag the nurse wore. He scrawled a quick note of appreciation, remembering how supportive the nursing staff had always been.

When he looked up, she was staring at the computer's screen. "Lorraine Espinoza is assigned as the hospitalist." Unlike many other hospitals, San Antonio Med used doctors who coordinated all the inpatient treatments. The nurse continued, "Josie is in surgery, but they're just about done."

The fact that Lorraine was in charge of Josie's medical team was good news. Aside from being a top-notch doctor, she was Michael's neighbor and a good friend. He handed the book to the nurse. "Send Lorraine a message. Ask her to text me when the patient's out of surgery." He paused. "Is there anything else in the chart?"

Christine tapped on the keyboard before scanning the computer screen. "Looks like the patient's mom has arrived. She's in the emergency waiting room."

He'd need to speak to the patient's mom eventually. But he wasn't sure if now was the time—especially since Lorraine should speak to her first. Michael rapped his knuckles on the counter. "Thanks for the information."

"Thanks for the autograph," replied Christine. "You're the man."

He took two steps and stopped.

The word *man* was like a splinter in his mind. A memory came to him from twenty-three years earlier. He stood in the examination room of the medical clinic, where he'd spent that summer so many years ago. Holding a chart in his hand, he regarded the patient. An older man with a blond mustache sat on the exam table.

"So, what brings you here today, Mr. Sauter?" Sage's father was a barrel-chested man with broad shoulders. "You told Mildred that you hurt your back last night."

"I told her what I needed to say to see you." His voice was like tires driving down a gravel road. "We need to talk, man to man. It's about my daughter."

Sage had warned him that her father wouldn't approve of their relationship. Still, it was unsettling to see him in the exam room, especially since he lied about an injury to get an appointment.

Michael wasn't willing to give anything away. He said nothing.

Sage's dad continued. "I appreciate that you have tried to be discreet in dating Sage, but we live in a small town. It means we know each other's business. For instance, I know that you're leaving in about a week and most likely won't ever be back this way."

"I might be back, after my time with the Peace Corps is done."

"Can we be honest, Doc?"

Was her father searching for a commitment from Michael?

"It's only been a few months, but I care deeply for your daughter." Michael wondered if he loved Sage. "Like you said, I'll be leaving soon. But it doesn't have to be forever. When I get back to the States, I'd like to see what comes next for me and Sage."

Mr. Sauter shook his head. "You need to break it off before you leave. She's got a life and commitments of her own. For years, she'd planned to marry her best friend, Vance."

Michael felt as if he'd been punched in the face. His head snapped back. "Oh?"

"More than those kids being crazy about each other, our ranches share a property line with the Krugers'. If they end up together, the size of the ranches will double. They go their separate ways?" He shook his head. "Neither ranch will survive for more than a few years. Sage's birthright will be gone. You said you cared about my daughter? Then you know what the Double S means to her."

For Michael, the exam room started to tilt. Holding onto the counter, he asked, "What if I don't want to break it off with her?"

"You have to ask yourself one question. Are you so

sure about your feelings for my daughter that you're willing to waste her future?" Mr. Sauter jumped down from the exam table and crossed the room. With his hand on the doorknob, he turned to Michael. "Think hard on what you do next."

Standing alone in the exam room, Michael didn't need to consider his options. He cared about Sage too much to ruin her legacy. What's more, he was only a summertime fling.

Over the next few days, his unspoken concerns had surfaced as irritability, and he'd been short with her. It led to a fight that ended the relationship. Even now, he looked back on the argument as a warning sign that their future would sour.

The first memory was followed by another. The words from Mildred's email—written more than two decades prior—were somehow still in his mind.

I know you were awfully fond of Sage Sauter and must be wondering how she's doing. Two months ago, she married Vance Kruger. What's more, they're expecting a child. It's happy news for the town of Mercy but I imagine isn't exactly welcome to you...

Kruger…

What were the odds that this patient was also the daughter of his former lover—his former love—Sage Sauter?

He turned back to the intake desk. "You happen to have a name for Josie's mom?"

"Just a sec…" said Christine as she typed on the keyboard. She pursed her lips and shook her head. "No name. Sorry."

Without another word, he left the nurse's station at a

fast walk. At the end of the hall, he pushed the elevator's call button once. Twice. Three times. "C'mon, dammit."

The car stopped on the third floor. He wanted to roar with frustration. Instead, he turned for the staircase, pushed open the door, and began his descent. Each step clanged as his fast walk became a jog. And then a run. On the ground floor, he pushed the door open and entered a long corridor. Wiping a bead of sweat from his lip, he slowed his gait to a walk once again.

Yet, his heart still hammered against his chest. Pushing open a door that led to the emergency room's waiting area, he stopped. Even in the middle of the night, many of the seats were taken. He scanned the faces looking for the one he knew. Sure, it had been years, but he still remembered the deep brown of her eyes. The way her gold hair fell in waves over her shoulder. Or the fact that her bottom lip was bigger than the top. He also remembered how she sighed each time he'd kissed her.

He found her and his heart ceased to beat.

"Sage," he said, whispering her name.

Sage scanned the waiting room. The family with the feverish child were still waiting to be seen. A muted TV hung on the wall. A tall man with auburn hair stood next to a door marked "Employees Only." Her glance passed over the man, then she looked back. Maybe her mind was playing tricks on her, and it wasn't him at all.

But she was already on her feet. "Michael?"

He gave her a small smile. "Hi, Sage. Long time, huh?"

Drawing in a deep breath, she exhaled. "Yeah. Long time." Now, what? Did she shake his hand? Hug him?

Neither option seemed appropriate. At one time, he'd been the center of her universe. Now, he was a stranger.

She let her arms dangle at her sides. "Weird seeing you. What're the chances that we'd both be at the hospital in the middle of the night?"

"It's not so strange when you consider that I work here."

Of course. He'd just finished medical school that summer when his touch burned her hotter than a Texas sun. "Oh. What kind of medicine do you practice?"

"Pathology." Michael regarded her openly and honestly; she didn't mind. It gave her a chance to study him in return. He was the same—and yet, different. There were now streaks of gray in his auburn hair. He was still tall, but the gangly youth she'd known had matured into a man. Now he had broad shoulders, a trim waist and long legs. He wore a navy-blue suit, light blue shirt and no tie. His eyes were the same bright blue she used to love.

"Pathology," she echoed, for lack of anything else to say. Back in the day, he'd wanted to be a general practitioner and work in underserved communities. She wondered what had derailed his plan. "What exactly is pathology?"

"A pathologist is the doctor who reads the results from all of the lab work that's done."

So, that's what became of Michael. He analyzed blood tests all day. To Sage, it sounded boring. "That's nice." When he didn't add anything, she asked, "So, what are you doing in the waiting room?"

"Actually," Michael dropped into a chair next to the one Sage had just occupied. She sat, too. With him so near, his scent surrounded her and for a moment, she was twenty-one years old again. "I was looking for you."

"Me? After all these years, why do you want to see me? And—wait a minute. How'd you even know that I was here?"

"I remembered your husband's name. Kruger. When I saw it on your daughter's chart, I wondered…" His words trailed off, then he drew in a breath. "The authorities want me to look into what happened to your daughter."

"So, you're what? A forensic pathologist?" Maybe Michael was the key to getting answers about Josie's condition. "What did happen? Did you find something in her blood?" Sage never suspected her daughter of partying too hard. Yet, she'd be naïve to assume that Josie never went out. But why did that matter? "Even if she did have booze or drugs in her system, it doesn't explain what happened."

"It's nothing like that." Michael shifted closer to Sage. "I've been asked to do a forensic workup on what happened tonight."

Sage's mouth went dry. She rose from her seat and crossed the carpeted floor. A water cooler with a sleeve of plastic cups stood in a corner. She lifted the top cup from the stack and filled it, then returned to her seat. She looked at Michael and asked, "Is that so?"

Michael nodded. "I'd also like to speak to you about your daughter. Is her father around? I can wait for him."

"Her dad's a journalist. He's out of the country."

He nodded. "Like I said, the authorities want me to look into this case. I really can't say much more about the investigation. But for now, I'd like to get a sense of your daughter's life. Are you okay to talk?"

Sage drank the water in a single swallow. Her mind raced, yet she could find nothing to say. If Michael started poking around in her daughter's life, what would he find?

And if he uncovered the truth, would it ruin all their lives—forever?

All those years ago, Michael had known Sage to be a passionate woman. He imagined that she'd be a fiercely protective mother. Yet she wasn't asking him questions or demanding answers. In fact, she hadn't even told him anything about Josie at all.

"I'm not sure that's the best idea for you to investigate what happened to Josie."

"Why's that?" he asked. "Because we dated in the Stone Age?"

Sage rewarded him with a small laugh. "Among other things."

"I am very good at what I do," he began. It was true. Beyond the book, Michael's expertise was sought by police agencies from all over the country.

She said, "It's not that I don't trust you. You were always a perfectionist, and I imagine that hasn't changed. It's just that you and I have a history that will complicate an already difficult situation."

Sage was right. The situation was complicated. Those complications left Michael with a decision to make. Honestly, he didn't like any of his choices.

It was more than the fact that Sage didn't want him involved in the case—although that was bad enough. Standing next to her left his blood burning. The desire to run his fingers through her hair, just to see if her locks still felt the same, was more of a compulsion than a want.

Yet, there was more.

A pain shot through his chest with each breath. As he rubbed his solar plexus, Michael knew that his broken heart had never truly healed.

His chest burned with another kind of passion—one that was driven by the need to see justice done. He wanted to find Decker Newcombe, not just talk about him.

He was a professional and a physician. What's more, he had a job to do and a duty to humanity. Sheriff Cafferty suspected that Decker Newcombe was responsible for the latest crime. He had to admit that there were similarities between the crimes of Decker Newcombe and what happened to Sage's daughter. If the modern-day Jack the Ripper had attacked Josie, Michael was the person best situated to find the truth. After all, he'd examined all the other victims from Mercy.

Then again, he could pass on the case to someone else.

If he did, Michael could walk away from Sage once and for all.

His cell pinged with an incoming text. He pulled the phone from his pocket and glanced at the screen. It was from his friend, the hospitalist, Lorraine Espinoza.

Heard you were looking for me. I'm checking on a patient in recovery.

He replied.

Josie Kruger?

She texted back.

That's the one.

He sent a final message.

On my way.

"Looks like your daughter's out of surgery and I need to get back to work." He slipped the phone into his pocket and took a step toward the door. "I'll be in touch."

"Wait." Sage reached for him and rested her hand on his arm. Her touch warmed his skin. "What do you know about Josie's condition?"

"That's what I'm going to find out now."

"After, will you let me know what's going on?"

True, Michael was breaking about one hundred different hospital rules. What's more, he knew it was a bad idea, even before he spoke. Yet, he couldn't help himself and he said, "I'll do you one better. You can come with me if you want."

"This place is massive," Sage said, walking at Michael's side.

He nodded slowly. "This is the biggest hospital in the county. It takes up an entire city block. There are seven towers." He used his fingers to hook air quotes around the word. Continuing, he said, "We're headed to the surgical wing in tower five."

They were in a long corridor. White tiles covered the floor and wall. Overhead lights filled the hallway with a yellowish hue. It left her feeling as if she were stuck in rodent tunnel—the kind Josie had in elementary school for her pet gerbils.

When Sage arrived at the hospital, she'd been focused only on her daughter, so she hadn't paid close attention to all the details of the facility. Still, she'd seen enough to know what Michael said was most likely true.

"And you know your way around?" she asked.

"I do," he said with a laugh.

Even after all these years, the sound was music to her soul. Despite the circumstances, her pulse raced.

As they walked through the warren of hallways, Sage admitted to herself that she'd indulged in fantasies about accidentally meeting Michael again. Obviously, her daydreams never included Josie being a patient in the hospital. But she wondered—had Michael ever thought about her over the years?

Probably not. He didn't seem affected by her sudden presence. After all, Michael held his phone, texting as he walked. He sighed and slipped the phone into his pocket.

"Another important case?" she asked.

"I was reaching out to my friend. She's the hospitalist in charge of Josie's medical team."

The fact that he'd been busily texting about her daughter surprised Sage. "What does your friend know about Josie?"

"She's out of surgery and in recovery. Usually, nobody's allowed to see patients until they're moved to a room, but Lorraine's going to pull a few strings for us."

Us. "So, I'll get to see her, too?"

"Sure, you will. But prepare yourself. Josie's going to be sedated, unconscious and unable to speak. She was injured—as you know—and seeing your daughter bruised and battered might be a shock." Michael continued to walk, and she stayed at his side. After a moment he cleared his throat. "Tell me about your daughter."

She's your daughter, too. The thought came unbidden, and she bit her bottom lip. A zing of pain shot through her. "What do you want to know?"

"Friends? Boyfriend? Job? School?"

"All of the above," said Sage, pride filling each word. "She's wanted to be a doctor since she was little." A small laugh crept into her voice. "Before she even started nursery school, she'd gather all her dolls not for a tea party, but a checkup. Then, the teachers noticed she was smart. They called her gifted."

They turned a corner and entered a narrow corridor. A blue plastic sign was affixed to the wall. *Surgical Recovery.* An arrow pointed the way. "Let's start with the basics," he said as they walked down the hallway. "Where does she go to school now?"

"Texas Midland State University."

"That's about an hour from here. Right? What's she studying?"

"Josie's a biology major and plans to sit for her MCATs later this year." The words caught in Sage's throat as she realized that Josie was very much like Michael. For starters, they both liked science and medicine. Josie had her father's auburn hair. His blue eyes.

It didn't matter if the two had never met. Or if they didn't know about each other, for that matter. A part of Michael had been passed on to Josie. There was an inescapable bond of blood and bone and sinew that surpassed any personal history.

After all these years of living a lie, Sage was going to have to face the truth. But how?

Chapter 3

Dammit, Sage. Don't be a coward. Just tell him the truth.

He's a doctor. He knows how things, like pregnancies, work. He'll understand what happened. How it had happened.

She inhaled, then slowly exhaled and glanced at Michael. He was still a handsome man. No wonder she'd loved him so deeply all those years ago. Although it wasn't just his looks that drew her to him. It was his intellect. His sense of humor. There was the fact that he didn't treat her like a hick from the Middle-of-Nowheresville, Texas. And what's more, when she was with Michael, Sage knew she could be anything.

Funny to think that she'd chosen to stay in Mercy and run the ranch after her father died.

Her pulse thundered in her ears. Her stomach churned. It was the same nervous sickness she had felt all those years ago when she realized her menstrual cycle was a week late. She'd taken a pregnancy test from the medical clinic. From there, she'd gone to the only place she could safely take the test—Vance's house. He'd sat in the bathroom with her as the plastic strip rested on the edge of the tub.

A blue plus sign for positive.

She'd cried. Vance had offered to marry her on the spot. He didn't need to tell her that a quick wedding was the only thing to save her from her father's wrath. They both knew how badly Daddy—an old-fashioned man with strict views of the world—would react. Sure, Sage had been terrified of being disowned by her only surviving parent. But she had also been heartbroken that it was her friend who'd proposed and not Michael.

Good Lord, you aren't a dumb kid anymore. You are a grown-ass woman. Tell Michael the truth now. The longer you wait, the harder it'll get.

Still, she couldn't find the right words.

"What can you tell me about her boyfriend?" Michael asked, saving Sage from saying something now she might regret later.

"His name is Ben Ellis. He plays lacrosse for the school and is also a biology major. Last I heard, he plans to join the Army or Air Force or something and then go to med school. Let Uncle Sam pay for his degree."

"Good kid?"

"Actually, he is."

"Roommates?"

"She lives in a sorority house. Josie doesn't have siblings, so I think she likes having a houseful of sisters."

"Whoa." Michael stumbled to a stop. "Your kid joined

a sorority? You are one of the most independent people I've ever met. How'd that happen?"

"Sounds like you're teasing me." Sage kept walking.

He jogged to catch up with her and admitted, "I might've been teasing a little. Josie must be a lot like her dad."

Hadn't Sage just been thinking the same thing? Sage ran her own business—and turned a profit. She managed a group of rowdy ranch hands, and they all respected her. As a parent, she'd taught her daughter to be brave and honest.

What Sage needed was some of that bravery and honesty herself.

Swiping his ID over an electronic lock, Michael said, "This is the recovery area. You'll only a have a few minutes to look in on Josie, but at least you can see her."

A wave of emotion washed over Sage and her eyes started to water. She blinked hard and cleared her throat. "I appreciate you bringing me with you."

"I'm going to speak to the hospitalist now. You can come with me if you want. It'll save Lorraine from having to go over Josie's condition twice."

Want? What Sage needed was to know everything about her daughter. "Thanks."

He pushed the door open and waited as Sage crossed the threshold. A nurse's station sat in the center of the space. Narrow rooms with curtained walls radiated from that central hub. Each room contained a hospital bed, and most were filled with patients. Some people slept while tethered only to an IV. Others were surrounded by machines that beeped, whirred, and glowed.

A woman with short, dark hair stood next to the counter and scanned a tablet computer. She wore scrubs and a lab coat. Looking up as Michael and Sage approached, the woman smiled.

Opening her arms, she said, "Hey, handsome. We've missed you around here."

Michael pulled the woman in for a quick embrace. "It's nice to be missed."

Sage stood back and watched Michael with his colleague. Was the doctor more than a friend? Dropping her gaze to the floor, she wished she didn't care about Michael's personal life. But she was more than a little curious about how he'd spent the past twenty-three years.

He wore no wedding ring, but that hardly meant he wasn't married. Even if he didn't have a wife, he might not actually be single.

Was Michael a father to children other than Josie?

The possibility that her daughter might have siblings struck her like a punch to the face. Swaying where she stood, Sage shook her head to clear her thoughts.

"Lorraine." Michael placed a palm on Sage's shoulder. His hand was strong, and she recalled the soothing feeling of his touch. "I want you to meet Sage Kruger. Josie's mom. She and I worked together at the medical clinic in Mercy about a million years ago."

The doctor held out her hand for Josie to shake. "Nice to meet you, Mrs. Kruger."

She gripped Lorraine's palm and decided that she liked the woman. "Nice to meet you, too. And my last name's Sauter. I took back my maiden name after the divorce. Call me Sage, though." She paused. "How's my daughter?"

Lorraine said, "She made it through surgery, and

that's a big relief. I can give you a rundown of all the treatments she received."

Sage wanted to speak to each and every person who'd been in the operating room. "I'm just thankful for anything you can tell me."

"Josie suffered from multiple traumas and all of those had to be addressed. She has an abdominal laceration." She touched her own middle, placing two fingers on her breastbone and two on her lower belly. "The cut only went through four of the nine layers of skin and tissue, which is good news. None of her organs were damaged."

"None?" Michael asked, interrupting. "Do you have any idea what kind of knife was used?"

"Sorry." Lorraine shook her head. "No." She continued, "Your daughter was also strangled and at some point, lost consciousness. There was considerable bruising to her throat and for now, she's being intubated to keep her breathing. She also has multiple contusions, which are bruises, on the brain. One of those became an intracranial hematoma and that means her brain was bleeding. She had two fractures in her skull and bits of bone from one of those fractures had to be surgically removed." Lorraine paused. In the silence, Sage tried to absorb what she'd been told. It was an impossible task. "The good news is that your daughter is alive. She's getting the best care anyone can get in the world."

"What's her prognosis?" she asked, her voice hoarse.

"I expect her brain to swell, but the magnitude of that swelling can vary and will require different treatments. Best case, the swelling is minimal, and your daughter can be brought out of her medically induced coma within a few days. She may have some neurological delays, loss of skills or even speech. But we won't know for a while."

If that was the best she could hope for, Sage didn't want to hear the worst-case scenario. Of course, she'd deal with whatever came next. It's just that she couldn't handle more bad news. "How long will Josie be in recovery?"

Lorraine blew out a long breath. "That's hard to say. I plan to keep her in this ward for at least twelve to twenty-four hours."

"Where's Josie now?"

"She's in room eight." Michael pointed to a cubby. "I'll come with you. I want to examine her wounds."

Sage followed him to the room. And room was a generous term for the narrow space with thin walls. There was no chair, not that there was a gap big enough to sit. Squeezing in next to the bed, Sage looked at her daughter. A turban of bandages covered Josie's head. Her face was bruised and swollen. A breathing tube was taped to her bottom lip.

Her chest ached at the sight of Josie—bludgeoned and broken. Yet, the fact that she'd survived such a brutal attack was nothing short of a miracle.

Moving closer to the bed, she reached for Josie's hand. For a moment, Sage watched the rise and fall of her daughter's chest, thankful for each breath.

"Hey, honey. It's me. Mom." Talking to someone who wasn't going to answer was harder than she imagined. She continued, "I'm here. I don't know what to tell you—other than you're safe now. Some pretty bad things happened. But we're going to get through the aftermath—physical, emotional, mental—together." She kissed Josie's hand. "I love you so much it hurts."

She glanced over her shoulder. Michael stood near the door and looked at the floor. Sage would be the first to admit that she knew little about forensic pathology—aside from what she'd seen on TV shows. Yet he'd said he needed to examine Josie's injuries for the investigation.

After giving Josie's hand a final squeeze, she stepped away from the bed. As Michael passed her, her shoulder brushed his chest. She ignored the heat of their connection and squeezed in on the opposite side of the bed.

Michael bent toward Josie and peeled back the covers. From where she stood, Sage couldn't see the cut that had been carved into her daughter's middle. As far as she was concerned, that was just fine. What she could see was Michael's profile next to Josie's. The resemblance between father and daughter was remarkable. The nose. The chin. The lips. A bandage was wrapped around Josie's head. Yet Sage knew that her daughter's hair color matched Michael's.

Sure, he was looking at Josie's injuries for clues to who attacked her—and why. But there was more to see beyond the evidence of a crime. Sage knew in her gut that it wouldn't take long for Michael to see that he was Josie's father.

Then, just like living in a castle made of sand, the lies that she'd based her life on would crumble and leave Sage with nothing.

Michael examined both the abdominal laceration and the contusions to the neck. He was looking for similarities between these injuries and those suffered by a specific victim of Decker's. The woman was also from Mercy. The bruising at the neck were the same—

both caused by a belt. The laceration to the abdomen was harder to determine. The location of the cut was similar. But the laceration to the other Mercy victim's stomach passed through all nine layers of skin. Decker had sliced through muscles and tissue. Some of her organs were removed.

Josie only had a single cut. Was it done by Decker or a copycat?

He took a moment to straighten Josie's hospital gown and pulled the covers up to her chest. He lifted his gaze and regarded Sage for a moment. She stood at the bedside, holding onto her purse strap with both hands. "So?" she asked.

So, what was he supposed to say? "Medically speaking, the surgical team did a nice job fixing the injuries." He worked his jaw back and forth, not sure what else to say or share. "I need to make a call. Be right back."

He slipped from the room and opened the door to a set of stairs that led to the ground floor. Leaning against the cinderblock wall, he pulled his phone from his pocket and placed the call. Isaac answered after the second ring. "Tell me what you found."

Michael paused to collect his thoughts. "For starters, I know the victim's mother." He paused again, weighing how much he should share of his past with Sage. "We worked together when I was in Mercy. She was the medical clinic's lab tech. We were—" Another pause as he found the right word. "Friendly."

He didn't have to say anything else for the owner of Texas Law to understand the nature of their friendship. "Is that going to be a problem?"

In all honesty, Michael wasn't sure. Yet, he wasn't about to lay out his troubles to Isaac. "I'm just telling you for the sake of transparency." He glanced over his shoulder. The door was still closed. The circular stairwell was silent. "There are differences between Josie's injuries and those of Trinity Jackson." Trinity was the one person killed in a ripper-style murder. "The cut to her abdomen isn't as deep. She wasn't disemboweled. And the most important difference is that Josie's alive. Trinity's not." He paused a beat. "But there are similarities that can't be ignored. The injuries to Josie could have been made by the same person. They were both strangled by a belt." All that had been shared in the media was that the murder weapon had been some kind of narrow cord.

"Are you saying you agree with Sheriff Cafferty? Do you really think Josie Kruger was attacked by Decker Newcombe?"

Michael couldn't lie. "It's possible."

A nurse with dark hair slicked into a bun entered Josie's room. She wheeled an IV stand beside her. "I need to get Josie started on her meds and take her vitals."

Sage recognized that as a not-too-subtle invitation for her to leave. The thing was, she didn't know where to go next. "Do you know where Michael is?"

"Doctor O'Brien? He said something about making a call and ducked into the stairwell." The nurse pointed to a door that was beneath an illuminated Exit sign.

Sage gave Josie's hand a final squeeze. "I'll be back, honey. I love you."

She left the room and hustled to the stairwell. Her spine filled with steel. She needed to tell Michael that he was Josie's biological dad.

She reached for the handle and opened the door. Michael stood on a landing several steps below the level Sage was on. With his back to her, he had a phone pressed to his ear. Sage backed away, ready to give him his privacy.

Then he spoke—and she stopped. "I agree that this attack is unlike the first one in Mercy because that victim is dead—and this one survived."

One dead victim and one who survived. Was he talking about her daughter?

The person on the other end of the call must've said something because Michael replied with a grunt. Then he said, "The way I see it, Decker Newcombe is a work in progress as far as being a serial killer. We can't conclusively say that because he disemboweled Trinity Jackson and left her body in an alleyway, that's his only mode of killing women."

Sage went numb. She recognized the name Decker Newcombe. How could she not? He'd killed five people right before Christmas. Had her daughter also been attacked by the serial killer? She drew in a deep breath, the air rattling her lungs.

Michael spun around and looked up where Sage stood. His eyes were wide. Their gazes met and held.

He spoke into the phone. "I have to go." And then to Sage, "I didn't hear you open the door."

Taking a step forward, she let the door close behind her with a clang. She felt his deceit in her toes. It started as a spark and the flame grew as it enveloped her in fury. "What the hell, Michael. My only child was attacked by a serial killer, and you don't think that's important information?"

Michael slipped his phone into his pocket. "My examination of your daughter is preliminary. I haven't told you about my findings at this point because there are none to give."

Sage liked to think of herself as a reasonable woman, and what Michael said made complete sense. His words dampened some of her anger—but not all. "It doesn't matter that we used to date. You withholding information from me seems like you've decided to hold a grudge or something..."

She could hear the squeak of rubber-soled shoes on the other side of the door a second before it opened. Lorraine, the hospitalist, stood on the threshold. Her brows were drawn together, the scowl on her face as dark as thunder. "What's the matter with you two? These patients need their rest, and the medical staff needs to focus."

Sage's face burned with embarrassment. "Sorry," she mumbled.

Michael did not seem so contrite. "You need to give us a minute, Lorraine."

"No. No minute. Out," she said, pointing down the stairs "I've heard enough of this conversation to know that you have to take this outside."

Straightening his spine, he stood taller. "You aren't going to kick me out of the hospital."

Sage quickly descended the stairs to the next landing and reached for Michael's hand. "Lorraine is right." She tugged his hand and he let her lead him down the stairs. "We do need to talk. And outside—or at least out of this ward—is best."

Each footfall on the metal steps clanged. She wanted the noise to fill her brain and make it impossible to think. Yet, her mind kept replaying the aftermath of

Decker's killing spree. The first killing happened only four days before Christmas. The community was still in mourning. But the thing that rankled Sage was the media. The TV stations showed up with their caravan of trucks and news people with brilliantly white teeth. Print outlets sent reporters who smelled of coffee and vape juice. They brought a carnival-like atmosphere. People with microphones wanted to speak to anyone who had a connection to one of the victims. All the while, they stirred up more trouble with their questions.

Do you think Decker Newcombe is really dead?

Do you worry that he'll return to Mercy?

Sage would be damned before she let her daughter's life turn into a circus. Then again, maybe that was why Michael had said nothing.

The steps ended at another door. A plastic sign was affixed to the wall. *Patio.*

Sage pushed the door open and stepped outside. Michael followed.

The night was cold, and the air cleared her head. The patio was filled with half a dozen round, metal picnic tables. Yet, with the adjacent cafeteria closed for the night, the patio was deserted.

She exhaled and her breath froze into a cloud. "Tell me everything you know, Michael. Josie is my only child and my life."

"You have to understand that the investigation is ongoing and none of the evidence supports one theory over another."

"I get it," she said. "The case is fluid like a stream, and not set like concrete."

He gave a small smile, and her pulse did a stutter

step. "Sums it up nicely." Holding up his little finger, he continued, "Let's make a deal."

Despite everything going on, she laughed. "Oh, yeah, you and your famous pinky swear. I forgot."

"You forgot about the pinky swear?" he asked, his tone teasing. "I'm shocked."

Stepping forward, she hooked her finger around his. It was nice to be close to Michael—nicer still to touch him. "What's our deal?"

"You can ask me anything you want. From here on out, you and I will be honest with each other. No secrets. Agreed?"

"Agreed," she lied. There was one secret she couldn't—or maybe that was *wouldn't*—tell.

Chapter 4

Quinton Yang sat in the shadows of the hospital patio, praying for the couple to leave. At this time of night, this section of the hospital was closed to anyone other than staff. He was merely delivering food—and not employed at the hospital. So, the last thing he wanted was to be found hanging out where he wasn't supposed to be and get banned from San Antonio Medical Center.

The late-night deliveries to the hospital paid the best in tips.

Pushing his black hair out of his eyes, he leaned against the brick wall. He'd come outside to find a quiet place to think. At twenty-six, he'd spent the last two years of producing his own weekly true crime podcast, Quinton had only a handful of followers and no revenue. With his criminal record, no legitimate media outlet would hire him. It didn't matter that he'd graduated from journalism school.

Maybe now was the time to give up on his dream of being a reporter.

Yet the voices from the couple drifted over to Quinton and he froze.

"Tell me," the woman said. "Why do you think Decker Newcombe attacked my daughter?"

Quinton straightened instantly, his instincts sharpening. *Decker Newcombe? As in, the serial killer?*

The man spoke. "It comes down to a few things. First, both attacks associated with Mercy are similar in their physical profile—the victims were strangled, and their abdomens were sliced open. The victims—Trinity and your daughter—have a similar profile in that they're both the same gender and race."

"Makes me sick to think that Josie was accosted by that animal." Even Quinton could hear the emotion in her voice. "I knew Trinity Jackson. She was a funny lady. Kept me laughing the whole time I got my tattoo."

"You have a tattoo?" His tone was beyond incredulous. "If I remember your dad correctly, he was a strict man. I can't see him liking a tat."

"Things changed over the years. I got a tattoo for my fortieth birthday. It's the Double S brand, just like the ranch."

"Can I see?" the man joked.

"Michael O'Brien," the woman teased in return. "Absolutely not."

Now Quinton knew the guy was named Michael O'Brien. The name seemed familiar, but he couldn't remember where he'd heard it before. But, it was a fact he would commit to memory. Quinton's pulse began to hammer at the base of his skull. Even months after his disappearance, Decker Newcombe was still a hot topic. It's just that there was nothing new to say about the serial killer...until now, that was.

If he could get proof that Jack the Ripper redux was alive and had attacked another woman, then his podcast would get launched into the stratosphere. Quinton would have his pick of lucrative sponsors.

The couple kept talking, oblivious to Quinton sitting nearby. Truth is, he couldn't stop himself from hearing what they were saying, even if he tried.

The man looked over his shoulder. Even in the dark, he could tell the guy was scanning the area. The man's gaze slowed as it passed Quinton. He wanted to scoot farther into the shadows but dared not move. He dared not breathe.

The woman asked, "What do you think? Was it Decker Newcombe? Is he even alive?"

Michael turned to look at his female companion and Quinton relaxed.

He said, "I don't have enough information to form a conclusion, Sage."

Quinton memorized the woman's name as well. She'd mentioned her daughter earlier. Josie.

"I'm not asking for a definite answer. I want to know what your gut tells you."

"My gut," said Michael, "tells me that I need more information."

There was a ping from an incoming text and Quinton's pulse raced. Had it been his phone? Was he about to get discovered?

Pulling a cell phone from the pocket of his suit coat, Michael said, "That's from my lab. Josie's clothes have been delivered. I want to get a look at her belongings before the techs start running tests."

The couple walked to the entrance that led to a staircase. Michael held the door open.

Sage asked, "What kind of tests will you run?"

Before Michael had answered, they both crossed the threshold and the door shut with a *slam.*

Quinton would have paid good money to hear Michael's answer, but the couple was gone. He didn't know everything about what happened in Mercy, but he knew enough to get started. After opening the hospital's app, he scrolled through the tabs until he found a list of the faculty in the pathology department. Within seconds, he had a photograph for Michael O'Brien.

He read the brief bio: Michael O'Brien, MD, is board certified in forensic pathology. He studied biology as an undergraduate at Stanford University and attended medical school at Texas A&M. Upon completion of medical school, he worked at a clinic in Mercy, Texas, before serving for two years in the Peace Corps. After returning to the U.S., Michael specialized in pathology and forensics at Cornell Medical School in New York City. He returned to Texas, and his skills as a forensic pathologist are sought by law enforcement agencies from around the world. He is the author of the book, *Let the Dead Speak for Themselves.*

Quinton whistled through his teeth. *Oh yeah, that's where he'd heard the name before.* Michael O'Brien was a pretty big deal in the medical world.

But he still needed more information—like the full name of Decker's possible victim. He closed the hospital app and pulled up his contact list. He placed a call.

It was answered on the fifth ring by his best friend, Trevor Kane. His voice was thick with sleep. "Quin, this better be important."

"Sorry to wake you up in the middle of the night, but I need you to do me a solid."

The patrolman groaned. "What is it this time?"

Quinton didn't bother answering the question. Instead, he gave his friend the details he knew about the patient from Mercy. He ended by saying, "Her first name is Josie, but I need a last name and any other information you can get."

Trevor cursed. "You kidding me, man? Sharing information like that will get me fired."

"I'm not kidding, and I wouldn't ask if it wasn't important." He paused knowing that he only had one shot to get his friend to cooperate. "You owe me."

And Trevor did owe Quinton. When the two were in college, they got stopped. Trevor had a bag of drugs in the car. He'd always wanted to be a cop, but a drug conviction would end his lifelong dream. Quinton claimed the drugs were his. He never served time in jail, but the conviction followed him around like a shadow. It'd been hard to find a job, and damn near impossible to keep one. The lack of meaningful employment led him to the podcast. As much as he liked the work, sponsors were hard to come by. But if he had a scoop about Decker Newcombe not being dead? Well, that'd change a lot of things.

The line had gone silent. Had Trevor actually hung up the phone?

"You there?" Quinton asked.

"Yeah, I'm here."

"You know I've never brought up that night before and I won't again. But I need this favor."

"You're blackmailing me. You know that, right?"

"Your secret is safe with me. Besides, if I changed

my story now, who'd believe me? I'm just asking you for some return loyalty, is all."

"You know, sometimes you really can be an ass?" Trevor asked. In the background, Quinton heard the swishing of covers and the sound of feet hitting the floor. "I'll ask a few discreet questions and see what I can find. Good enough?"

His heartbeat raced. If Trevor got the information—and he would—then Quinton might have a new episode to drop by tomorrow. "Thanks, man. I appreciate it."

"Don't mention it," said Trevor through a yawn.

"Maybe now I owe you," Quinton joked.

"No, seriously. Never mention what I'm doing for you now. And Quin?"

"Yeah?"

"We are definitely even."

Sage followed Michael into the hospital. Her eyes were gritty, and her vision was blurred. A clock hung on the wall. The time read 3:23 a.m. Only five hours since Mooky's visit pulled her from sleep and now, her life was upside down.

Michael led her down a different hallway that looked the exact same as all the others.

"You know all about me," she said, though that wasn't exactly true. "What about you? What's happened in the last twenty-some-odd years of your life?"

"I wrote a book."

"No kidding. What's it about?"

"My job, mostly," said Michael. "I've worked a lot of cases over the years. Whenever I go to a dinner party or something, people always ask me questions about being a forensic pathologist. I tell them stories, and somebody always says, 'Oh, you should write a book.' And one day, I did." He pointed to a side corridor, and they turned down another hallway. "It came out a few years ago and the sales were so-so. Then, I worked on the Decker Newcombe case and my publicist sent out a press release. It was enough for people to become interested in my book again. The publisher sent me on a book tour. I just got back to San Antonio today."

"Good for you," said Sage. "I'm impressed. Me, I can barely post to social media without a dozen typos."

He chuckled.

"What else?" she asked. "Are you married? Do you have kids?" *Other than Josie?*

"Never married. No kids."

"Never?" Sage repeated. "I find that hard to believe. You're a good-looking guy and a doctor. I'd think some wise woman would want to marry you."

"Over the years, I've dated a few women seriously enough to discuss marriage." He shook his head. "It never worked out. The timing was wrong. Or they wanted things that I didn't. Life. It happens." He paused. "What about you? Mildred sent me an email a few months after I left Mercy and told me that you were married and pregnant. Upstairs you mentioned that things didn't work out."

So, one of the nurse practitioners contacted Michael. It explained why he never reached out to Sage after leaving Texas. Now was the time to tell him the truth. Walking down the hall, phrases swirled through her mind.

She's your daughter.

It was a marriage of convenience.

Tried to contact you directly.

If my father knew I was unmarried and pregnant, there would've been hell to pay.

I'm a stronger woman now...

She tried to string the words together. Even in her own mind nothing sounded right.

Sage had gone for too long without answering his question. "Yeah," she said. "I married Vance Kruger. He and I had always been friends. Well, it seemed like we were going to be stuck in Mercy forever and I figured, why not?" It was a well-practiced lie and one she'd told so many times, it seemed like the truth. But she owed Michael more than her go-to falsehood. "The love was never there, and when Vance got a chance to be a war correspondent, he took it. My dad had a stroke and I started running the ranch. Then, Daddy died, and I filed for divorce. Whatever there was of the marriage was long over, I just made it official."

"And now?" he asked.

"I've run the ranch for years. Now that it's mine, I love what I do."

"I'm happy for you," he said.

This is the perfect time. Tell him about Josie now. "There's something important I need to tell you."

"I think I know what you're going to say."

Sage was stunned. So, Michael had already guessed that Josie was his daughter? Her knees went weak. She stumbled to a stop and held onto the wall to keep her steady. "You do?"

"And it's completely okay."

Now she was in shock. "It is? You aren't mad at all?"

"You don't have to apologize, either. Tonight's been tough on you."

Jogging to catch up with Michael, she had the feeling

that she'd been at the right bus stop but had gotten on the wrong bus. "What do you think I'm trying to tell you?"

"Aren't you trying to apologize?"

Now it was her turn to be confused. "For what?"

"For one, accusing me of keeping information from you about Josie's case."

"The fact that you didn't tell me my daughter might've been attacked by a serial killer isn't an accusation, Michael. It's a fact." Her temperature rose with anger. Then again, she'd accomplish nothing by arguing. What's more, her perfect moment was lost. Sure, it would've been hard to tell Michael that he was Josie's father before. Now, it was impossible.

They continued down the corridor in silence. Michael led her around another corner. After swiping his ID badge over a lock, he pushed open the door. This one led to a metal stairwell that went down.

After several minutes, she spoke. "How can you find your way around this place? The hospital is massive. Everything looks exactly the same."

He gave a quiet chuckle that echoed in the narrow stairwell. "For the first year that I worked here, I was happy to find stairs or an elevator that accessed the basement. Then, after some wandering, I'd eventually find my way to forensic pathology." They took the steps down several flights that ended at a concrete pad with another door. Michael pushed it open. "My lab is this way."

That bone-deep weariness came back. Sage felt like she could sleep for days. "How do I get back to admissions? My truck is in the parking lot. I'll grab a few Z's. Hopefully, in the morning Josie will be in a room where I can visit."

Michael stopped in front of a metal door with a small inset glass window. The room beyond was dark. A sign was affixed to the wall. Forensic Pathology. Michael O'Brien, MD. He looked at his lab door and back to Sage. "I think I can help you out, at least with someplace to rest. I've got an office with a sofa. It's lumpy but only in the best way."

One more swipe of his ID badge caused a quiet click of the lock unlatching. He pushed the door open and allowed Sage to cross the threshold. An automatic light flickered to life.

The lab reminded her of the high school chemistry classroom—that was if her school district had a ton of money to spend on education. It was a cavernous room. Half a dozen lab stations stood in the middle of the floor. There were a variety of microscopes. Beakers. Burners. Lab coats hung on pegs on the wall. There were large machines and Sage couldn't even guess what those did.

"This way," said Michael, interrupting her gawking. "My office is back here."

Several doors stood at the far side of the room. Michael opened the one in the middle. He flipped a switch, and a desk lamp illuminated the room. The office was cluttered with papers, files, and books. There was a desk, along with a computer. Several locked wooden cabinets lined one wall. Pushed up next to the opposite wall was a sofa.

Sage gratefully dropped on to the cushions. "Are you sure I won't get in the way?"

"I'll be doing prep in there." He tilted his head toward the lab. "You rest." He stripped out of his suit coat. "I don't have a blanket to loan you, but you can use my jacket."

Sage stretched out on the sofa and draped Michael's coat over her shoulders and torso. Already, she could feel sleep—an anchor of exhaustion—pulling her under. "Thanks," she said, her eyes drifting closed.

"You're welcome," said Michael.

He flipped the light switch, filling the room with darkness. After slipping through the door, he pulled it shut and Sage was alone. Suddenly, she was awake. Her heart slammed against her ribs, as if it might break free. Cold sweat dampened her brow. She tried to breathe through the panic, but her chest was tight.

Since she wouldn't be able to sleep, she felt along the floor for her purse. From there, she found her phone. The illuminated screen was the only light in the room. She opened her contact app and placed a call.

Mooky answered. "I was just about to send you a message. How's Josie, for starters?"

"She's out of surgery." Sage gave the sheriff a summary of injuries and expected outcomes. She rolled onto her side and turned on the speaker function. "Why didn't you tell me about Decker? You were standing in my living room and told me you had no idea who'd attacked Josie."

"How'd you find out about that?"

"The forensic pathologist who's working on the case is an old friend."

"Oh yeah," he said. "Michael worked in Mercy when I was away on a deployment."

"You never answered my question. You said nothing about a serial killer attacking my daughter. Why?"

"First and foremost, I don't know anything. Until I

do, all I have is speculation. It doesn't do any good to present you—or any other family—with a bunch of rumors and half-baked theories."

It was what Michael had said to her already. Much as she hated not being involved, Sage supposed that she had no choice but to let the professionals do their jobs. "You said you were going to send me a message. What for?"

"I've spoken to the campus police chief. She wants to talk to you. I can help arrange a call."

"No." Sitting up, her head swam but her mind was racing. Josie would be out of school for the rest of this semester and possibly the next. If Sage couldn't sit at her daughter's bedside, then at least she could collect some of her daughter's belonging. "I want to go to campus. I'll head there first thing in the morning."

"I'll let them know. Bernadette Hayes will be expecting you." The call stretched out in the silent office. Mooky asked, "Anything else?"

"Are there any updates on the investigation? Any more clues?"

"Nothing yet. Please remember that I'll tell you what I can—when I can. It doesn't do you any good to hear every blessed detail. Lots of ideas will arise and not all of them will be right or lead to justice for Josie."

She didn't care for the mini-lecture and worked her jaw back and forth. She also didn't care for what Mooky had said—that she wasn't going to be apprised of the ongoing investigation until police had a solid lead. Then again, she was keeping secrets of her own. "Got it."

"Try to get some rest. You sound exhausted."

Sage grunted a reply. "Find out who did this to my child, Mooky."

"I will."

She ended the call and lay in the darkness feeling suddenly exhausted again. Closing her eyes, she hoped to fall into the deep and dark pit of sleep. For her, a few hours of oblivion would be fine. Yet, she now had a whole new set of nightmares to haunt her dreams.

Chapter 5

Without windows in the basement lab, Michael often lost track of time. Morning. Noon. Night. With only the overhead lights, it was all the same to him. What's more, he often got sucked into the mystery of an unexplained death and the passing of time ceased to matter.

He loved that there was only one thing he needed to do in his job—and that was to find the truth.

Sure, he hadn't always wanted to be a forensic pathologist. But during his first few months in the Peace Corps that changed. He could still remember the young mother's screams as she rushed into the hospital with her son in her arms, her husband in tow. She held the limp body of her child as blood dripped from his fingertips and onto the hospital corridor.

"He cut himself playing with a knife," the father said.

The mother gave the father a side eye but said nothing. Michael was suspicious of the look. He treated the boy. The gash was long, deep, and needed an amazing fifteen stitches. As was protocol, he questioned the mother separately from the father. She was nervous but said nothing that incriminated her husband.

He called the local police and told them he suspected the father of cutting his son. The police chief needed proof. What did Michael have?

At first, he admitted he didn't have much. But that wasn't right. In his mind's eye, he saw the laceration. The boy was young—maybe three or four years old. He didn't have the strength or dexterity to wield the heavy blade. The cut itself contained clues. A child may accidentally get a hold of a knife, sure. But once they cut themselves, they instinctively dropped the blade.

This cut was deliberate.

Armed with Michael's findings, the police interrogated the boy's mother. She told them of years of abuse. The father was taken into custody and at that moment, Michael discovered his life's goal.

Over the remaining two years of his service with the Peace Corps, he helped the police solve several crimes. When he returned to the US, Michael became board certified in pathology and then studied forensics.

He checked the wall clock for the time. He had lost fifteen minutes in thought. Being unfocused was totally out of character for him. Then again, the past few hours had been eventful. He needed time to process.

More surprising than the possible resurfacing of Decker Newcombe was the reappearance of Sage Sauter. He had to admit she still looked good. Working on a ranch kept her muscles toned. Her arms were well-defined and her butt, well, that was thing of beauty. He was still drawn to her honest and open personality. But he was also still wounded that she'd been planning to marry Vance all along. She'd never considered Michael as anything more than a diversion.

Oh sure, it was more than twenty years ago.

But just looking at her left his jaw aching and his chest sore.

Rubbing his eyes, he shoved his emotions aside. He had to get to work.

After donning a pair of surgical gloves, he opened the evidence bag that contained Josie Kruger's clothing. Shirt. Pants. Shoes. All of it covered in blood.

Bag in hand, he moved to a lab table with a magnifying light. After removing the shirt, he set it on the tabletop. Turning on the light, he stared through the magnifying lens. When the lab techs arrived in the morning, they'd begin the arduous task of testing the blood on the clothing.

He'd seen the victim's wounds and assumed that most of the blood would belong to Josie. But there was a chance that the attacker had been wounded as well. If their blood was also on the clothing, a DNA sample could go a long way in finding the perpetrator.

Until then, there was plenty of work to do. Adjusting his focus to the lens, Michael searched Josie's top for hairs and fibers. On the shoulder was a single, long blond hair. Pulling the strand off with a pair of tweezers, Michael placed the hair into an evidence bag.

He recalled Vance Kruger. He was a broad-shouldered guy, a whole head shorter than Michael, with white-blond hair. Sage had golden hair. He assumed that blond hair belonged to Josie. Then again, assumptions were dangerous. What he needed was proof.

A computer sat on a desk in the corner. Michael moved to the seat and powered up the device. He entered Josie's name into the hospital's search engine. It took only a minute for her file to appear on the screen.

The first page of the e-file was an intake form.

Patient's name. Address. DOB.

Physical description: Josie Kruger is a 22 y/o college student. 5′ 9″ tall. Weight 140 lbs. Eye color: Blue. Hair color: Red.

Leaning back in the chair, his gaze traveled to the door of his office. How had Sage and a stocky blond guy ended up with a tall, red-haired child? He looked back at the screen and found Josie's date of birth. He didn't have to do the math to know that Josie was born nine months after he left Texas.

He also didn't have to be a practicing OB/GYN to know that the nine-month time frame for gestation starts on the first day of the mother's last menses. Which meant that Sage got pregnant two weeks before he left Mercy.

Could be that she and Vance were more than the friends they claimed to be. But in Michael's final weeks in Texas, he and Sage had been inseparable—at least, until the fight. He wondered when she would have snuck away for a liaison with another man.

But there was another possibility.

That *he* was actually Josie's father.

The tips of his fingers turned cold. Glancing over his shoulder, he looked at the closed office door. Filled with the need to go to Sage and demand the truth, he rose from the seat and strode across the floor. He opened the door. A wedge of light cut across the floor. He could see Sage, asleep, on the sofa.

She'd had a horrible night. No matter how much he wanted to know the truth, he had to push his feelings aside—for the moment. She was a mother, and she was in pain, watching her child suffer. No, he wouldn't interrupt her rest.

After pulling the door closed, he returned to the computer. Sitting in front of the monitor, he tried to focus on work. It was impossible. For Michael, there was now more than one mystery to solve.

Sage woke. Trembling in the darkness, she lay without moving. Her heartbeat raced and the sound of her pulse echoed in her skull. The remnants of a nightmare still clung to her like walking into an unexpected cobweb.

She tried to shake free of the terror. But Josie's battered and bruised face was fresh in her mind.

Sage was filled with guilt that gnawed on her from the inside out. Pulling her knees to her chest, she breathed deeply and reminded herself of the facts that she knew. Her daughter had been brutally attacked, but she'd survived. Josie was in the hospital and getting all the right kind of care. The police were investigating and eventually they'd know the truth.

She had lots to be thankful for. Yet, until her daughter was home—and the culprit was caught—Sage wouldn't rest easy.

She sat up. Michael's suit jacket slipped from her shoulders and pooled in her lap. She brought the coat to her nose and inhaled. The fabric smelled like him—soap clean and juniper. She remembered the sleeping bag they used to use in the bed of her old pickup truck and how for years, she kept it stored in a hallway closet just so it could preserve the smell.

Sage rose from the sofa. Taking both her purse and Michael's coat, she crossed the floor and opened the door. She stepped into the lab. Lights shone down from the ceiling and reflected off the metal tables and white equipment. She blinked at the glare.

"Hey," said Michael.

She scanned the spacious room. He sat at a desk in a shadowy corner. The light from a computer monitor illuminated him in a silvery light.

"Hey yourself." Her throat was thick, and she coughed into her shoulder. "Thanks for loaning me your sofa. It is a great place to catch a nap." She held the coat up. "Thanks for loaning me this, too."

He rose from his desk and took the offered jacket. "Glad you got some rest. How're you feeling?"

"Exhausted—emotionally and physically both." She paused. "Any news on the case?"

Michael walked to a lab table. Spread out on the surface was a bloody shirt. Sage recognized it at once.

Her throat squeezed closed like a fist. "That belongs to Josie." She recalled the back-to-school shopping trip in San Antonio. They'd gone to a discount store that specialized in name brand clothing but in last year's styles.

Josie had lifted the top from the endless line of similar tops. "I love it."

There was a thin band of lace at the end of the short sleeves. A pouf to the shoulders. Small buttons up the front made to look like pearls. Sage slipped her hand under the fabric. The outline of her palm was visible.

It's a little thin, don't you think?

That's the whole point, Mom, Josie had said. *It's sexy but not too sexy.*

If this shirt wasn't too sexy, Sage wasn't sure what was…

C'mon, Mom. I love it.

Sage had glanced at the price tag and her stomach lurched. Even with the deep discount, the top chewed up almost 20 percent of the money set aside for clothes. *Let's think about this one.* She handed the shirt back to her daughter. *If you really want it, we can come back.*

I have money saved from tips.

That's for med school, though.

If I get into med school, I'm going to have to take out loans. Besides, I worked hard this summer. I can splurge on a little something. She dumped the top into the cart.

As a single parent, running a ranch in South Texas, there wasn't a lot left over for the nicer things in life. In the moment, Sage had been torn. Did she give her daughter what she wanted or save the precious resources for something more important?

In the end, Sage paid for everything. What's more, she'd do it all over again.

"There are a few things I found," Michael began, his voice drawing her from her reverie. "Maybe you can help."

Finally, she was useful. "If I can."

He pointed to two different bags. Both were translucent and had black lettering on the plastic. Evidence. As far as Sage could tell, they were empty. "There were two distinct hairs on this top. One is long and reddish. The other is blonde. They still need to be tested for

DNA..." He held up the bag and she could see a single strand of hair in each one.

Sage pointed to the bag with the red hair. "That's Josie's hair." And then, "The other is probably from her roommate, Corrin. They're always sharing each other's clothes." There was something she wanted to ask—but wasn't sure she was ready for the answer. "Did you find anything connecting Josie to Decker Newcombe?"

Michael set the bags on the table and shook his head. "If Josie shares her clothes with her roommate, then that may account for the hair we found. Aside from the hair, I found some fibers on her clothes. The fibers are consistent with automotive carpeting. It could be from the car used to transport her. But it's common stuff so it won't help us narrow down a specific vehicle. It'll just be one more piece of evidence once we have a suspect."

Sage had to admit she'd seen her share of crime and murder documentaries over the years. In many ways, it helped because she'd watched the unraveling of so many cases that she could follow what he told her. Still, she knew there was a lot she didn't know. "Would you expect to find hairs from the person who attacked Josie on her clothes?"

He exhaled. "I try not to have any expectations. Some killers leave behind a trove of clues. Others are more careful and there's nothing obvious to be found. Decker's a professional and in the case of Trinity Jackson, there were no hair fibers or fingerprints on the body. We did find his DNA under her nails from a defensive wound. In the case of the couple he killed who lived outside of town, he burned down their house after. The fire destroyed whatever evidence we might've found. Swabs were taken from Josie before she was medevaced here. Our lab will process them. I'll call in whatever favors I can to try and expedite the results. At best, we'll know something in a few days. At worst..." He exhaled. "It could be a few weeks."

A few weeks? "Did you find anything else?"

"The blood on this shirt needs to be analyzed. If Josie's attacker was also wounded during the assault, their blood will be on her clothing, too."

"Will those tests take weeks as well?"

"This lab processes a lot of evidence, and we usually have a backlog. Aside from that, each test takes time to run. I wish I could give you a different answer. All I've got is the truth." He turned back to the lab table. Without looking in her direction, he said, "I was surprised that Josie is a ginger."

Her pulse began to race. *Tell him now. He obviously suspects something—otherwise he never would've brought up her hair color.* Sage knew her inner voice was right. And yet, she asked, "Why's that?"

"It's just I remember Vance. He was blond—like you. I'd expect your kid to be a towhead."

"My mom was a redhead," she blurted out without thinking. Had her voice quavered? Damn, it had. Then again, she'd been protecting her secret for decades. Sage continued, "Josie takes after my mom—or that's what we always say." It wasn't a lie, either. Sage's mother had strawberry-blond hair. Sure, it was a different shade from Josie's—or Michael's. All the same, it was close enough for people to make their own assumptions.

She had to tell him the truth. Sage tried to find the right thing to say, but the words were jumbled in her mind.

Before she could speak, Michael said, "Sorry, I didn't know. I never met your mom."

He hadn't. Sage's mother had died when she was a child. Clearing her throat, she said, "Don't worry about it. What are you going to do now?"

"I've done as much as I can for now."

He slipped into his jacket and opened the door for Sage. She walked to the door and crossed the threshold. The back of her hand grazed the tips of his fingers as she passed. Her heart skipped a beat. *Grow up, Sage. You aren't some dumb kid who's in love for the first time.*

In the hallway, she glanced in his direction. He watched her. Had the accidental touch left him rattled, too?

Folding her arms across her chest, she knew that she really needed some time alone—and time away from Michael. True, he'd been helpful and kind. But she couldn't trust herself to be alone with him.

She ran a hand through her hair. Her tresses were stiff with sweat from yesterday's work on the ranch. She couldn't show up at Josie's school looking the way she did. "Is there a shower around here I can use? I'm supposed to talk to the campus police this morning."

He walked down the hallway. "I'd like to speak to the campus police as well. You can come with me to my apartment. I have a shower in the guest room. I can't promise breakfast, but I do have coffee. Then, we can drive together to campus."

Sage slowed her pace. She could still feel his fingers on her hand and the old emotions his touch had awakened. "I'm not sure that's a great idea..."

Michael stopped abruptly. "You are welcome to come over to my apartment, grab some coffee and get a shower. But I'm not going to beg. What's more, it makes sense for us to go to campus together. If you don't want to, that's fine. I won't ask again."

Sage was many things. But she prided herself on being pragmatic and practical. If that were the case, she couldn't say *No* to Michael. Then again, she couldn't exactly trust herself around him either.

More than not knowing what to tell him about Josie, Sage knew that it would be easy to develop feelings for Michael again. He was still handsome, charming, and the chemistry between them was so intense that a simple touch made her fingers tingle.

Sure, it made sense for her to grab a shower and a coffee at his place. She'd also get more information from the campus police with Michael at her side than without him.

But, none of that really mattered—not when she realized what was at stake. If Michael discovered the truth, that he was really Josie's father, it could destroy her entire life. She had to refuse his offer. It was the only way to keep her secret and her emotions safe.

"Thanks. I'd love to come over to your apartment."

Now why in the hell did I say that?

Chapter 6

Before leaving the hospital, Sage had spoken to the doctor in charge of recovery. Josie was stable and would be kept in her medically induced coma. After that, she'd be moved to a room and Sage would have limited visits. Having given her contact information to the doctor, she and Michael left the hospital. They stopped in the parking lot, where Sage collected her truck.

"Follow me." He pointed to a sleek blue car. "My apartment's not too far. You can park in the lot next to my building."

At 6:00 a.m., the traffic in downtown San Antonio was light. She followed him for a dozen blocks before he pulled into the parking lot of a high-rise. Sage pulled into a spot, turned off the engine and grabbed her overnight bag.

A man in a gray-and-red uniform stood on the sidewalk. He opened the door as Michael approached.

"Good morning, Doctor O'Brien. It's good to have you back."

"Thanks," he said with an easy smile. "It's good to be back."

They stepped into a lobby. High-backed chairs sat around a wooden table. Marble floors gleamed. The elevator doors were brass. A coffee shop was near the bank of elevators.

"You have a coffee shop in your building?" she asked.

"I never go there. The coffee's overpriced."

Overpriced? Who lives in a place like this and worries about money?

Michael pushed the call button and the elevator doors slid open. They stepped inside and he hit the button for the ninth floor.

"Nice building," she said, trying to keep the awe from her voice.

"I moved in when this building first opened. It was part of the downtown renaissance. Since then, several other buildings like mine have been built."

The elevator doors opened, and they stepped into a hallway that was just as opulent as the lobby. The walls were covered with golden paper that had a subtle damask print in the same shade. The floors were made of wood and a navy runner ran down the middle of the hallway. Michael stopped in front of a door and used a key to open it.

"Home sweet home," he said, pushing the door open.

Sage crossed the threshold.

Michael's apartment had hardwood floors throughout, and the rising sun reflected off the planks. In the living room, the furniture was leather and dark wood.

Paintings and sketches of birds hung on the walls. Aside from the consistent subject matter, there were no personal touches. No trophies. Or certificates. Or even a family portrait. To Sage, it looked more than tidy. It was almost like the room had been staged for a photoshoot.

It was at complete odds with her home. The main house sat at the end of a long, dirt road. Built by her great-great-grandparents, every inch of the house was covered in clutter that went back for generations. In the spring, the breeze smelled of manure. In the summer, the sweet scent of freshly cut hay hung in the air. This place smelled of, well, nothing.

"The guest room is the first door on the left." He pointed to a door. "There's shampoo, soap and towels. Help yourself to whatever you need."

For a split second, her imagination took hold.

In her mind, she could see Josie coming through the front door. She wore expensive clothes, and a pricey backpack was slung over her shoulder. "Hey," she said brightly to a woman who stood in the kitchen. "How was your day?"

The woman looked up at Josie and smiled. "It was great, honey. How was yours?"

Josie said, "You won't believe what I learned in chem class today..." And then the vision vanished, and Sage was back in reality.

Josie would've flourished in this world. But even in her daydream, the woman in the kitchen hadn't been Sage. Without question, she knew that she'd suffocate under the veneer of expensive brands and a spotless home.

It brought up an interesting question. If he'd known about the pregnancy and proposed, would she have actually married Michael? Well, she knew the answer to that question—she would have married him for the sake of the baby.

Would the marriage have lasted?

Even now, she had her doubts.

Michael placed his hand on her arm. "You look like you're a million miles away."

With Michael, she realized that her life was a tapestry and parts of her past were left undone. She wanted to pick at the loose thread.

"Sage?" He regarded her. "Are you okay?"

She sighed. How could she tell him everything she'd just been thinking—especially since she couldn't make sense of her own feelings. "I'm just tired, I suppose."

"Do you want me to make a pot of coffee?"

"I'll have some later. For now, I'll settle for a shower. Where was the guest room again?"

"It's the first door," he said, pointing.

Sage gave him a weary smile and carried her bag into the guest room. After closing the door, she sat heavily on the bed. Rubbing her gritty eyes, she knew one thing. She had to tell Michael the truth about Josie. But even more than that, she owed Josie that truth as well.

Then it all became so simple.

Once Josie was recovered and well enough for a serious conversation, Sage would tell her the whole story. After all, Josie was her daughter. She deserved the truth first. Michael was well-meaning but after all these years, she couldn't even count him as a friend.

Yet, there was a tickling at the back of her neck that made it hard to relax and impossible to congratulate herself. Because with the tickle came a single fear; that Sage was going to fool nobody but herself.

* * *

Michael stood in the shower longer than necessary and watched the water swirl around the drain. He was transfixed by the movement, and the more he stared, the more certain he became. There was something important he'd missed. Memories, like snapshots, flipped through his mind. Some were new, like the clothing worn by Josie Kruger, and the hair he found on the shirt. The instant he saw Sage sitting in the waiting room, the light shining down from the ceiling, and her golden hair becoming a halo. Or the moment she passed him in the doorway and her hand brushed against his own.

Others came to him from years before. Just like an old photograph, the memory was faded and frayed at the edges. He stood in the foyer of the Sauter's farmhouse. On a table was a framed picture of Sage with her mother.

Sage picked up the photo and brushed her fingers over the glass. "My mother died in a car wreck when I was eight years old. My dad was heartbroken. I think that's why he's always so strict. Somehow, he thought he should have been able to protect her."

He took the frame and glanced at the picture. So, he had seen a picture of Sage's mom. In it, Sage sat on her mother's lap and their heads leaned toward each other. Both women had golden hair, but the mother's locks had a reddish tint. But she definitely didn't have the same hair rich color as the strand Michael had found.

There was another memory. Michael and Sage stood in the breakroom of the medical center. They were discussing his departure later that week. It was before the fight that ended it all. Tears filled her eyes. His chest ached at the thought that they might not ever see each other again.

He placed a ready-made meal in the microwave.

"The smell," she groaned as the scent of meat, potatoes and gravy filled the room. "It's making me sick."

She'd turned for the door and rushed from the room.

At the time, he assumed that Sage felt ill because of his upcoming departure. Now, he had to wonder—was she pregnant before he left?

Turning off the water, he reached for a towel and stepped from the shower. He dressed quickly in jeans, a T-shirt, and loafers. As he reached for the door handle, he stopped. Sure, he wanted to speak to Sage, but first he had to ask himself a simple question.

What did he want to hear?

Hell, he didn't know. All he wanted was the truth.

He had to wonder how he would feel if Josie turned out to be his kid. Honestly, he'd be pissed at Sage for not telling him. But there was more. It was a small sense of wonder, like a cool rain on a hot summer's day.

He pulled the door open and walked down a short hallway that led to the kitchen. The nutty aroma of fresh coffee filled the apartment. Sage was sitting on the sofa, scrolling through her phone.

She looked up as he approached, and his mouth went dry.

"I made coffee," she said.

He strode to the kitchen. After removing a cup from the cabinet, he filled a mug. He should offer Sage something to eat. But what? "I'd make breakfast…" he began.

"But you don't have any food. I looked when I made the coffee." She lifted her mug to her lips and took a sip. "Hope you don't mind."

"Not at all." He took a swallow of coffee and waited as it warmed his gut. For his entire career, he'd had tough conversations with families. In all that time, he'd learned that truth was always best. Straightening his spine, he turned to look at Sage. "I need to ask you some questions."

At the same moment, she lifted her phone. The cover of his book, *Let the Dead Speak for Themselves*, filled the screen. "I found this online."

She laughed after they'd both spoken. He couldn't help but smile.

"I'm flattered that you found my book." He paused. "Did you have a question about it?"

"No, you go ahead. What's your question?"

The moment to ask her about Josie was gone. He shook his head. "It's nothing. What do you think of the book?" True, readers and reviewers alike had good things to say about his writing. But Sage's opinion mattered on a personal level.

She closed her reading app. "I like it. Did you write it yourself?"

Michael had been asked that question more than once. He knew that many people had ideas for books, but not the ability to write them. So, they hired ghost writers. "For the most part, I did. I had an agent who worked with me first and once the concept was picked up by a publisher, the editor helped me along." He paused. "I wish you hadn't bought the e-book. I have some hardcover copies around here. I would've given you one."

"I just downloaded the free sample. But it is good. I'll buy it."

A bookcase stood next to the TV stand. He'd stored

several promotional copies on the shelves. Removing a book, he held it out to Sage. "Here, you can have this one."

She rose from the sofa. "Thanks." Holding the book to her chest, she continued. "What was your question?"

"Breakfast," he said, without thinking. "Do you want to get breakfast before we leave for the university?" Okay, fine. He hadn't asked Sage about Josie. But it didn't mean that he wouldn't press her for the truth.

For Michael, there was more than one mystery to solve. First, he wanted to find out who attacked Josie Kruger—and why. He also needed to know if Decker Newcombe was alive—or not. And yet, there was one question he wanted to answer more than the others. Was he Josie's biological father?

One way or another, he'd discover the truth.

The doorman pulled the door open as Sage and Michael approached. He tipped his hat. "Have a nice morning."

"You, too," she said, stepping onto the sidewalk. The morning air still held some of last night's chill and she breathed deeply.

"The diner's only a few blocks away," said Michael. "I can drive us there or we can walk."

Sage started every day before dawn in her office doing paperwork. She finished off the day in her office as well. Beyond those times, she was either in the barns or on the range. Her body craved movement—even if it was in a city and not on her ranch. "Definitely a walk."

He pointed down the street. "It's that way. You can see the blue-and-white awning from here."

She nodded and started walking toward the restaurant. At the corner, a crosswalk light hung above the sidewalk. The figure of a person mid-step was illuminated, and Sage stepped off the curb. At the same moment, a car sped around the corner.

Michael grabbed her from behind, pulling her back. Her ankles hit the curb and she started to fall. He held her tight, keeping her steady.

Her heart slammed against her chest, and she cursed. "Where in the hell did that car come from?"

"Sometimes people are jerks. Are you okay?"

His words washed over her shoulder. Her back was pressed into his chest. His arm was around her middle. The heat from his body warmed her. Her chest was tight, making it hard to breathe—and it had nothing to do with the accident she'd barely avoided.

It was Michael. His touch. His scent. The way she felt completely safe in his arms.

She regained her footing and turned to face him. He was so close she could see the flecks of gold in his dark blue eyes. The strands of gray in his hair. The cleft in his chin. The pulse at the base of his neck. She could also see the fact that his mouth was very kissable.

His hand still rested on the small of her back.

Rising to her tiptoes, she placed her lips on his. He held her tight but didn't kiss her back. Sage's face flamed hot with embarrassment. She dropped to the soles of her feet.

Sure, Sage could tell herself that kissing Michael was a reaction to everything that happened last night, mixed with nearly being hit by a car. Or maybe it was because she had virtually no sleep since the night before, and she wasn't thinking straight. Or maybe she just wanted to remember what it felt like to be alive.

But there was another important truth—Michael didn't kiss her back.

Her cheeks stung, as if she'd been slapped.

Honestly, Sage couldn't remember the last time she allowed herself to be vulnerable. What's worse, he'd rejected her without a thought.

"I…uh…" She shuffled backward and he let his hand slip from her back. "Sorry about that. I lost myself for a second. Won't happen again." She stood at the corner and scanned the street left and right before hustling to the next block.

Michael was on her heels. "Sage, wait. We need to talk."

The last thing she wanted was a conversation about how he liked her and all—but they couldn't be romantically involved. Of course, he'd be right. Michael was part of the team investigating Josie's attack. She shouldn't blur the lines of their partnership.

He was right behind her. Sage walked quicker, putting distance between the two of them. At the next corner, he grabbed her wrist. "Sage, wait."

She turned to face him. Her breath was ragged and sweat covered her brow and upper lip. Michael appeared calm and collected. *Damn him, his long legs and his cool demeanor.*

"Are you okay?"

She shook her head. "Just embarrassed, is all. I definitely don't want to talk about what happened."

He let go of her arm. "Don't be embarrassed."

Was that all he had to say? Shoving her hands into her pockets, she gestured with her chin to the diner's blue-and-white awning. "Let's go. I'm starving." The truth was, she wasn't hungry in the slightest. In fact, her stomach had twisted itself into a knot over her ill-timed kiss. But she was determined to forget all about it and make sure that Michael did, too.

She kept walking. Her footfalls slapped against the sidewalk, like the crack of a pistol being fired. Now there was only one thing to do. She had to focus on Josie and ignore any feelings she had for Michael.

Way to go, O'Brien.

Not only had he failed to kiss Sage back, but now she was mad as hell. How was he supposed to make this right? Especially since he was interested in her. In fact, it had taken all his strength not to wrap Sage in his arms and lose himself in the embrace.

She was halfway up the block. He called out, "Sage, wait up."

She glanced over her shoulder but kept moving. "Yeah?"

"You're mad at me, I get it—"

She interrupted. "I'm not mad at you and I won't be, so long as you drop the subject." At the corner, she looked for traffic and then crossed the street at a trot.

He ran after her. "Will you at least hear me out?"

"I don't need to hear you say that you don't find me attractive. Or that a physical relationship will make a complicated dynamic weird as hell. Honestly, I get it."

He reached for her hand, stopping her. "You don't get it at all, Sage." She tried to pull her hand away and he tightened his grip. "I didn't kiss you because I knew if I started, I wouldn't want to stop." There, he'd said what he needed to say. He let go of her fingers and took a step back.

"Oh, I didn't realize..." He waited to see if she had more to say. She didn't.

"But you are right about one thing. This is a complicated situation. You and I have a past, but we also have a common goal. We both want to find out what happened to your daughter. I don't want to jeopardize the case by making things...what did you call it?" *Oh yeah.* "Weird as hell."

She gave a terse nod. "You're right. Finding out what happened to Josie is what's important."

He paused. Was now the time to ask if Josie was actually his kid? No. He needed to find another moment. Although, if Michael was being honest, he still didn't know how Sage would react to being asked about Josie's paternity. Or maybe he did know. It would end whatever truce they had that allowed them to work together.

Reaching around her, he pulled the diner's door open. "After you," he said.

"Why, thank you." She smiled and his heart skipped a beat. What's more, he could still feel her lips on his. She crossed the threshold and he followed, his gaze skimming her back and the place where he'd rested his fingers.

Over the years, he'd forgotten how good it felt to touch Sage. No, that wasn't entirely true. There were late nights, when Michael was alone and lonely, and he'd remembered all those stolen moments in the back of her pickup truck. And then, he took matters in hand.

Sure, Michael had his share of casual flings. But nobody had ever awakened his desires the way Sage had done all those years ago. Besides, he had his work. With his schedule, he figured he was destined to be alone.

It was more than the erotic memories of their one

summer together that drew him to Sage, though that'd be more than enough. It was the fact that she was unassuming and unpretentious. After years of working in a hospital and dealing with over-the-top egos, her down-to-earth manners were like, well, like the first breath of fresh air after being in the basement lab for hours.

Now Sage was back, and he was suddenly unsure that a life of solitude was what he wanted.

Chapter 7

The scent of coffee wafted through the restaurant. Michael inhaled deeply. "Now, that's what I'm talking about."

"Smells heavenly," said Sage. A server walked past with a tray of food balanced on her shoulder. "Look at those pancakes. They're bigger than the whole plate."

The diner consisted of one room. Booths sat on one side, near the door and wall of windows. Tables filled the middle. There was a counter at the far end of the restaurant, with the kitchen at the back.

At 7:12 a.m. the restaurant was already busy, and most of the seats were taken.

"Popular place," said Sage.

"The food's good. It's close to the hospital and we've stopped in just as the overnight shift is ending." He raised his voice to be heard over the din of conversation.

A hostess approached. "Just the two of you?" she asked.

"Just the two of us," Sage echoed.

"This way." The young woman grabbed two menus and led them to a table set for two. She filled their cups with coffee. "A server will be with you in a moment."

Sage looked at the front of the menu. "New York Diner." On the window a skyline of Manhattan had been etched into the glass. "You ever been? To New York, I mean."

His book tour had taken Michael to several bookstores in Manhattan and the surrounding boroughs. "A couple of times."

"Is it nice?"

"Define *nice*." She gave a quiet laugh. He smiled. "The city pulses with its own energy. There're people everywhere. Noises. Lights. Smells. You either love it there, or you hate it."

She opened her menu and dropped her gaze to the pages. "I bet I'd hate it."

"I bet you would, too."

"Still, I'd like to visit and see for myself."

Michael looked at his own menu as he imagined Sage in New York. If Josie was his daughter, they could travel together as a family.

Family.

The word struck him in the chest. He took a sip of coffee. It wasn't emotionally healthy to get wrapped up in a fantasy that might never happen. After setting down his cup, he dropped his gaze to the breakfast options. "I hope you make it there one day."

A waitress approached the table. "You two ready to order or do you need a minute?"

"I'll take pancakes, sausage links and a side of fruit," said Sage.

Michael closed his menu. "Western omelet. Wheat toast."

"Got it," said the server.

Sage stirred a packet of sugar into her coffee and took a sip. "Ahh, almost human."

Michael drank his coffee black. The additional caffeine began to buzz through his system. Or maybe it was Sage and the kiss. He had to think of something else beyond her lips.

He asked, "Have you ever met with campus police before?" It was a weak segue, but it was all he had to change the subject.

"Never needed to," said Sage with a shake of her head. "Josie's never been in trouble."

He needed to ask her something else. But what? "What about her sorority sisters or boyfriend? Have any of them been in trouble?"

"Nothing that Josie's ever mentioned," she said. "I'm not going to say that my daughter tells me everything—mostly because there's certain things I don't want to know. But I think if she was close with a person who got in big trouble, she'd tell me."

"Earlier, you said that you liked Josie's boyfriend. What about Corrin, or the other girls in the sorority?" Michael could feel the conversation taking on a rhythm of question and answer. He was looking for something but not sure what he needed to find.

"There are so many girls in the sorority. There's got to be one hundred or more sisters, even. I can't say that I know all of them, but she's never complained."

"That seems odd to me. I have two sisters and at

least one of them always has a complaint about the other," he joked.

Leaning forward, she picked up her coffee and took a sip. "I guess she does complain a little, but it's typical girl stuff. There are arguments if one girl gets overly friendly with another girl's boyfriend at a party. Or everyone gets mad if someone hogs all the hot water in the shower." She set her cup in the saucer. "Typical."

It seemed like his search for something useful had hit a dead end. He tried another topic. "Did anyone in Mercy ever mention seeing Decker Newcombe in the area after the holidays?"

"There was a while when it seemed everyone saw him everywhere. Those first few days after Decker went on his killing spree were the worst. Shoot, I couldn't see my own shadow without having a heart attack."

Michael chuckled, although he imagined it wasn't amusing at the time.

"Eventually, most everyone calmed down." She moved the silverware around as she spoke, so that the bottoms were all in a line. "It happened around Christmastime and Josie was home for the holidays. It freaked her out. She slept in my room every night. Couldn't wait to get back to school. You want to hear the funny part—well, not exactly funny but ironic. By the time she went back to campus, everyone had heard about Decker Newcombe. Because Josie was from Mercy, she got a little celebrity status."

"I understand how a connection to Decker can make you a tiny bit famous," he said, trying to make a joke. After all, his connection to the case had made Michael a bestselling author. But really, it was dark humor. On a basic level, Michael wasn't proud that he'd turned such a tragedy into personal fame.

"Damn. I left the copy of your book at your apartment."

"You can pick it up when we get back." He continued, "So everyone was interested in what happened with Decker..."

"All Josie's friends had listened to the podcasts. Or they'd watched documentaries. Everyone was sort of obsessed after break. They'd come to Josie with questions—mostly about Trinity because the two knew each other in passing."

There seemed to be another question to ask, but Michael couldn't find it. Then again, he hadn't slept in a day and a half. Fatigue was setting in. He took another sip of coffee and scanned the restaurant.

The server approached with two plates balanced on her forearm. She set them down.

Sage pulled her plate closer.

Using the side of his fork, Michael cut off a wedge of omelet. Until that moment, he hadn't realized how hungry he was. For several minutes, they ate without speaking.

The food helped revive Michael. The fact that Decker Newcombe might be alive—and, worse yet, still trying to copy the murders of Jack the Ripper—was one theory of what happened to Josie Kruger. But he couldn't be so single-minded as to ignore other possibilities. Like with many crimes, the victims most likely knew the perpetrator. Statistics proved that most murders were committed by a *loved one.*

He asked, "What about Josie's boyfriend? Was he interested in Decker Newcombe?"

That question seemed to give Sage pause. She dragged her sausage through a puddle of syrup and was silent for a moment. "He called every day over break, which was sweet. He asked Josie lots of questions about what happened, but so did everyone else."

"Would you say he was one of those people obsessed with Decker?"

"I don't think I would." Sage pushed her plate away from her. She'd eaten all the fruit and sausage and half of the pancakes.

Michael pressed with another question. "How would you characterize him?"

"At the time, he seemed worried about Josie but also curious about the crimes."

The server returned with the bill. "You need anything else?"

Michael glanced at the balance. He removed his wallet and took out enough money to cover the tab and a generous tip. He handed the cash to the server. "Keep the change." He moved to the edge of the booth before rising to his feet.

Holding out his hand to Sage, he said, "C'mon. The campus police are expecting you."

She placed her palm in his and he felt it. An electric charge filled his palm and raced up his arm. Did she feel it, too?

At 8:12 a.m. Quinton sat at the kitchen table with his computer at his elbow. The microphone was already installed. He'd spent a sleepless night doing research on Decker Newcombe and writing a script for his next podcast.

But he was far from ready to record his latest episode.

He wiped grit from the corner of his eye, then rose from the table and took his empty mug with him. At the kitchen sink, he rinsed out the cup and poured some coffee. He leaned on the counter as he sipped the coffee and checked his watch for messages.

There were none.

Trevor had promised to find out what he could about the mystery patient who'd been brought to the hospital. It'd been hours and still, nothing. He moved back to the computer and opened a new tab.

He found a YouTube video of Michael O'Brien at a recent event for his book. The doctor was on the stage of a community college in Virginia's Tidewater. Michael stood behind a podium under a spotlight from above. He was talking about his involvement in the Decker Newcombe case. "It was late December and the promised storm brought with it rain, sleet, wind and an unseasonal tornado to downtown San Antonio. The twister had tossed cars and trucks along the city's streets like a child having a tantrum with their toys.

"We were all gathered in the FBI's downtown office as rain pelted the windows. The Supervisory Special Agent stood in the middle of the conference room with a cell phone pressed to his ear. 'Can you hear me, Isaac?' he asked, speaking to Isaac Patton, the founder of Texas Law, and the man tasked with finding Decker Newcombe.

"Jones took the phone from his ear. He glanced at the screen and cursed. 'I lost service.'

"'Cell service must be down,' said one agent as the overhead lights flickered.

"Then Jones said the one thing we were all thinking.

'We can't just stay here with a killer on the loose. I don't give a damn about the storm. We need to get to Mercy.'

"The lights flickered once more. There was a pop, like a firecracker, and the room filled with darkness. Sure, we had to get to Mercy. But we didn't even have a way out of San Antonio."

Quinton stopped the video. He admitted the doctor had a way with setting a scene. He took another sip of coffee, and his head began to pound. Closing the lid of his laptop, he pinched the bridge of his nose.

The headache hadn't been brought on by his fatigue, or even knowing that if he wanted to make money today, he'd have to sign into the delivery app and work. It wasn't that Trevor had ghosted him—though that was bad enough.

It was his damn sink.

The faucet in his kitchen drip-drip-dripped. The constant percussion beat into his skull.

He rose from his seat and returned to the galley kitchen. He jiggled the handle and the water stopped dripping. He sighed with relief and returned to the table.

Drip-drip-drip.

"Effing faucet." How many times did Quinton have to beg his landlord to fix the damn sink? He sent a quick text. Faucet's leaking. Again.

It was met with a quick reply. I'll send someone over today.

That was as good as Quinton was going to get, even though he knew the landlord was lying. There was no way a repairman was going to show up today. Or this week. Or probably ever.

The phone pinged with another text.

The message was from his buddy, Trevor.

Josie Sauter, age 22. College Jr at Texas Midland State University. Picked up by medevac and brought to San Antonio Medical Center. Wounds: Stabbed. Choked. Beaten. Thrown down a hill and left for dead. Found by local sheriff Maurice Cafferty.

Yes! Quinton had what he needed to finish his newest episode.

He sent a quick reply. Thanks, man. You're the best.

Another text showed up on his phone as he hit Send. It was also from Trevor. Now we're even. Don't call me again.

Quinton's throat tightened. Did Trevor plan to cut off all communication—as in forever?

Wiping his eyes with his sleeve, he read the text again.

Now we're even. Don't call me again.

Tossing the phone on the table, he slumped in his seat. He had the information he needed for his story. But could he use the tip if it meant losing his friend?

Looking around the dingy apartment, a hard knot of despair dropped into his gut. Quinton's place consisted of one room. He had a sleeper sofa by the door. A recliner sat in a corner. In the opposite corner was the kitchen table that also served as his recording studio. Behind the table was his kitchen with a small fridge, two-burner stove, microwave, sink and toaster oven. At the back of the room, a single window looked out over the alley behind the building and the brick side wall of a closed laundromat. The window was flanked by two doors. To the left was a closet, barely big enough to hold a chest of drawers and the few clothes Quinton owned. To the right was the bathroom, which wasn't much bigger than the closet.

He couldn't keep living like this. No money. No real job. No hope.

Trevor had gotten lucky. He lived in a nice apartment. He had a beautiful girlfriend, along with the career he always wanted.

Pulling the laptop toward him, Quinton opened the recording app. Leaning toward the microphone, he began to read his script. His baritone voice was his best feature, he knew. It was perfectly suited for podcasting. And that was lucky for him—Quinton had been born with a "face for radio," as his father used to say. A backhanded compliment for sure—until he'd found a way to try and capitalize on it. Now—now, he just had to hope his big bet paid off.

"We've all heard the name Decker Newcombe. For years, Newcombe committed murder for hire, and is suspected of killing over two-dozen people. The murder of a district attorney in northern Wyoming sent Newcombe into hiding for a year. When he re-emerged, the hitman was deadlier than before.

"DNA testing proved that Decker Newcombe is a direct descendant of the man who science proved to be Jack the Ripper, the Victorian-era serial killer. Following a killing spree in and around Mercy, Texas, Newcombe was shot by a lawman. Newcombe escaped into the Mexican desert. To this day, his whereabouts is unknown.

"That's a tale we all know well. But what if that's not the end of Decker Newcombe's story? What if Newcombe survived? What if he's still in Texas—and killing again?"

Pressing the headphones against his ears, Quinton listened to the recording and smiled. The rest of the episode would explore what happened to Josie Kruger, but for now, his introduction was perfect.

If all went well—and how could it not—he'd be able to upload his podcast soon. Then at lunchtime, the story of Decker's resurrection would go live, and Quinton's career would be launched.

Chapter 8

The campus of Texas Midland State University was an hour northwest of San Antonio, and three hours away from Mercy. The school, with six thousand undergraduates and twenty-five hundred graduate students, was the centerpiece of life in Greenwood, Texas.

The college was located two blocks from the downtown. Main Street was filled with cafes, bookstores and shops—all of which catered to the students. Most buildings were made of red brick and surrounded by lush green lawns with mature trees. In the center of campus, a fountain shot water into the air. The droplets glistened like a thousand diamonds.

Since Josie was well into her third year of school, Sage knew her way around campus. She directed Michael to the visitor's parking lot that was closest to the campus police building.

"Nice place," he said, easing his car into a spot.

"It's been a good home to Josie." She looked out the window and everything she saw reminded Sage of her child. There was the tree they'd hidden under on parents' weekend during an unexpected thunderstorm. And the bench where they'd sat when Josie was still in high school and on a tour of the college. At the far edge of campus, she saw the roofline of the dorm where her daughter lived during her first year. Her eyes stung. "It was good until, you know."

Michael asked, "Do you need a minute?"

"No. I'm okay." As if to prove her words weren't a lie, she unlatched her seatbelt. Then, she opened the door and got out of the car. Michael turned off the engine and followed suit. She pointed to a one-story brick building. "That's the police station."

"Alright, then. Let's go."

They walked without speaking. Sage tugged on the front door. It didn't budge. A call box with a buzzer was attached to the wall. She pressed the button. A moment later a female's voice crackled through the speaker. "May I help you?"

She spoke into the call box. "Hi, I'm Sage Sauter. Josie Kruger's mom."

The door clicked. "Come in, Ms. Sauter."

Michael pulled the door open and followed Sage across the threshold. They entered a small, windowless office with five workstations. There were two desks on each side of the room and one at the back. A Black woman with her hair in a bun and wearing the uniform of campus police officer stood next to the back desk.

She walked toward them with her hand extended. "Ms. Sauter. I'm Bernadette Hayes, Chief of Police at

TMSU. I'm so sorry to meet you under these circumstances." She paused. "How is Josie?"

"Right now, she's stable." She tried to keep her voice steady. "We'll know more this afternoon."

The police chief let her gaze drift to Michael. "Bernadette Hayes," she said, holding out her palm to shake. "And you are?"

"Doctor Michael O'Brien. I'm a forensic pathologist at San Antonio Med."

"I read your book," she said, shaking Michael's hand. "It's very good." And then, "Can I ask why a forensic pathologist is with the victim's mother—or even here at all?"

Michael answered, "I'm an old family friend."

The chief gave a quick nod. "Thank you both for coming. Before we get started, can I get you anything? Coffee? Water?"

Sage shook her head. "No, thank you."

"First, I'd like to let you know everything I can about the investigation. To begin with, we really are devastated about what happened to your daughter and will cooperate with anything you need." As she spoke, Chief Hayes pulled chairs out from behind desks and set up a cramped triangle of seats in the aisle. Sage and Michael both took a seat and the police chief dropped into the third chair. They all sat knee to knee as Bernadette continued. "The first we knew that Josie was missing, much less hurt, was when we were notified by Sheriff Cafferty that she'd been found. I'm sorry to say that none of her sorority sisters called us. It seems they thought she was with her boyfriend. And her boyfriend thought she was mad at him and was staying at the sorority house. Have you spoken to any of Josie's friends?"

"Not yet," said Sage. "I'm going to stop by the sorority house before we go back to San Antonio. I want to get some of Josie's personal belongings now because she clearly won't be back for the rest of the semester."

Chief Hayes nodded. "Her room has already been searched and some things were taken for the investigation."

"Really?" Sage was surprised, though she shouldn't have been. Hopefully, something that Josie left behind was a clue to what had happened. "What was taken as evidence?"

"The state police have her laptop. They're looking at her computer's memory and the hard drive for something that raises a red flag."

All of this was new to Sage. "What would you consider alarming?"

"Messages that indicate she'd been fighting with someone. Or that she was being harassed—either from the stalker themselves or because she shared an incident with a friend. Or even that she'd made a new friend who she might have been meeting."

"And what have the state police found so far?" Sage asked, not sure what answer she wanted to hear.

"So far, nothing. But they'll keep digging."

Michael said, "I'd like to get back to something you said earlier about Josie's boyfriend. He claimed that she was angry with him. What's that story?"

Chief Hayes let out a slow breath. "According to Ben Ellis, he states that he and Josie had broken up a month ago over an argument. During that time, he had a sexual encounter with another female. When Josie and Ben reconciled, he didn't mention the hookup." The chief used air quotes on the phrase. "Somehow, Josie got wind of what had happened between Ben and the other girl and there was another fight." She paused in her story. "Has Josie shared any of this with you, Ms. Sauter?"

Sage's heart shriveled in her chest. "She hadn't mentioned a word." She'd always assumed she and Josie had a good relationship. Shoot, they spoke on the phone or through a video chat twice a week. Why hadn't she shared something so monumental as a breakup?

The police chief must've guessed what Sage was thinking. Placing a hand on her wrist, Hayes said, "We see this all the time on campus. Kids are trying to make their own decisions without parental guidance. The fact that she hadn't told you any of this doesn't mean anything other than Josie was an independent young woman."

Sure, Sage understood that the police chief was trying to soothe her, but it wasn't working. "Have you talked to Ben? What did he have to say? And who's the girl he slept with?"

"We asked Ben for the name of his liaison. He declined to name the girl and said she wasn't anyone he knew well. He's also been instructed not to contact you or Josie."

"Who told him not to reach out?"

Chief Hayes sat up taller. "I did. Until we know what happened, I don't want rumors becoming facts."

Bernadette's explanation seemed simplistic. She glanced at Michael. He must've guessed at her displeasure because he nodded once.

Sage shrugged. "If I can't talk to Ben, can you at least tell me what he said?"

"He and Josie were supposed to meet and discuss their relationship yesterday evening. When she didn't show up, he assumed the relationship really was over," said the police chief.

"A rejected lover," said Michael. "Sounds like a prime suspect."

"I can't comment on if the police do or don't have any persons of interest," said the chief. "But he has been asked to stay in town for now."

Aside from the shadowy Decker Newcombe, Josie's boyfriend was the only other suspect. "Is that it?" Sage asked. "You aren't going to do anything other than ask him to stay put? There has to be more that you can do. I'm not breaking any law if I talk to him myself..."

"Whoa, whoa, whoa." Chief Hayes held up her hands. "I understand that you want answers, we all do. But you can't contact this young man. It'll jeopardize the investigation."

Michael said, "She's right." And then he asked, "What about an alibi? Is there anything to prove Ben's not involved."

Hayes rose from her seat. She settled behind a desk with a computer monitor and tapped on the keyboard. "If y'all want to come over here, I'll show you what we found."

Sage and Michael got up from their chairs and stood behind the police chief, looking at the computer from over her shoulder. The screen was filled with a black-and-white image. "This is the first camera that picks up Ben." She touched the screen's time stamp. 7:56 p.m. "It's at the edge of campus."

From there, his path was easy to follow. He walked past several buildings on his way to the library. At 8:04 p.m. the camera outside the library captured a clear picture of Ben's arrival. Hayes fast-forwarded the video from the front of the library. "He's seen leaving an hour later." Time stamp read 8:59 p.m.

Michael leaned toward the screen. His shoulder brushed Sage's arm and she sucked in a breath. He asked, "Are there other entrances or exits to the building?"

"Sure are," said Hayes. "Each one's covered by a camera. Ben Ellis did not leave that building for an hour. What's more, the librarian recalls him being there. She remembers him because he took a table by the checkout desk and watched the door. He didn't study and looked miserable the whole time."

Michael asked "What about Josie? Do you have video of her as well?"

"This is the real mystery." Hayes brought up another video. "Josie's first picked up coming toward campus from the Greek Row."

Sage watched the video of an empty street. A figure appeared at the far edge of the screen. As the person came into focus, her pulse started to race. "That's Josie." The time stamp read 8:01 p.m.

"Watch this," said Hayes, her voice low.

On the screen, Josie turned to look over her shoulder. What did she see? With all the people wandering past, it was hard to guess what caught her attention. Whatever it was, she walked back across the street. A bus pulled up next to campus and Josie was blocked from the camera. When the bus drove away, Josie was gone.

Michael stared at the screen. He worked his jaw back and forth, trying to make sense of what he'd just seen.

"Where'd she go?" Sage asked, the pitch of her voice rising. "It's like she just disappeared."

Hayes said, "That's the question we've all been asking."

Michael knew there must be more evidence. "What about video from the bus?"

"Bad luck but the exterior camera on the driver's side is broken. The driver put in an order to get it fixed two weeks prior," said the chief.

He wasn't willing to give up yet. "Any of the other buildings have cameras? What about traffic cameras?"

"There's no traffic signal for blocks," said Hayes. "As far as other buildings with cameras..." She closed the window and opened another. "We have this, taken from a doorbell camera." The video showed a person with long hair walking down the sidewalk. "We think that's Josie," Hayes said as she manipulated the speed of the video. The time stamp began at 7:52 p.m. "As you can see, the quality of the image isn't great. But the build and the clothes are a match. The timing is also right."

"That's Josie," said Sage. "I can tell by the way she moves."

"Thank you for that verification," said the police chief. She turned off the computer, a sure sign that there was no more evidence to be shown. "I'd like to share with you our next steps. The university's' president has canceled classes for the rest of the week. More than giving students time to come to terms with what happened is our desire to cut back on gossip and wild speculation. There's a call out for any pictures or video footage taken from that entrance to campus. People have been helpful, but so far, we haven't learned anything new."

Over the years, Michael had participated in many of these types of meetings with families. The police wanted to keep the victim's family informed—while never giving away anything that would jeopardize the case.

"Do you have any other questions?" Chief Hayes asked, wrapping up the interview.

With a shake of her head, Sage said, "None that I can think of."

The chief removed two business cards from the breast pocket of her uniform and held one out to Sage and the other to Michael. "Call me if you think of anything. Please, keep us informed of Josie's condition."

After glancing at the card, he slipped it into his wallet.

Sage tucked the card into her purse. "I will. Thank you."

The police chief led them back to the same door they'd entered. They walked outside and Sage let out a long, slow exhale.

"What am I supposed to believe now?" she asked. "Decker randomly pulled my kid off the street or did someone else attack Josie?"

"I want to make a call." He looked around. The campus really was deserted. It seemed like the police chief was right and all the students were staying away. He doubted that he'd be overheard, but with a topic this sensitive, he needed some privacy. "Come with me. Let's go to my car."

The car was parked in a lot adjacent to the police station. Once they were inside the vehicle, Michael started the engine. Taking the phone from his pocket, he placed the call.

Isaac answered. "Hello?"

"Hey, man. I need some help." He turned on the speaker function. For the sake of transparency, he added, "I've got Josie Kruger's mom with me, and she can hear what you're saying."

"Got it," he said. "What do you need?"

It's one of the things he liked about Isaac—he was always ready to help. "I need to know what the police are thinking. They have video of Josie walking down the street and then, she's gone. It's like a damn magician's trick or something." He glanced at Sage. She watched the phone, not seeming to mind his glib comment. Still, he had to watch his offhand remarks. He then spent a few minutes outlining the entire video—along with the video of Josie's boyfriend and the fact that the couple was having troubles.

"A jilted boyfriend would be my first suspect," said Isaac.

"Mine as well. But we also need to consider a copycat killer—someone who's trying to imitate Decker's crimes."

"But why is Josie the victim?" Isaac asked.

"She's from Mercy—the same place that Decker found Trinity. The couple he murdered lived outside of Mercy, too," said Sage. "I heard that serial killers usually find their victims in the same place."

Isaac said, "Except Mercy might be Josie's hometown, but she wasn't attacked at home. She was kidnapped at school. To me, it means this crime wasn't random—it was personal."

Sage sucked in a sharp breath and looked away. After a moment, she turned to Michael. "Which leaves us with who as a suspect?"

He shrugged. "The ex-boyfriend."

Sage spoke. "If Ben did this to Josie, he needs to be

held accountable. But…" She shook her head. "I just don't see him getting violent."

He knew that even the nicest people could commit serious crimes when properly provoked. "Even if she'd broken up with him?"

"I assume she was on the way to meet with him, but never got to the library. They never spoke, so she never broke up with him." She paused and asked a question of her own. "How do you explain the video that has him going to the library and not leaving for an hour? Or the witness who saw him there the whole time? Ben was in the library at the exact time Josie was taken off the street."

"Those are good points," said Isaac. Then, he asked, "You got any answers?"

"No," Michael said, "not yet at least." He continued, "But I intend to find out."

The faucet in the kitchen continued to drip-drip-drip. Pressing the set of headphones tighter to his ears, Quinton listened to the final seconds of his podcast.

"A girl has been attacked and left for dead. Decker Newcombe is the prime suspect. It seems like the modern-day Jack the Ripper is alive, well, and hunting his prey again. You've been listening to Crimes with Quinton. I'm your host, Quinton Yang, and don't forget to lock those doors…"

Leaning back in his chair, he looped the headphones around his neck and smiled.

This episode was going to be his breakout.

He checked his file to make sure it was formatted correctly. It was. He was ready. With the click of a key, Quinton uploaded his podcast. It was 10:02 a.m.

Now all he had to do was wait for his life to change. He slipped off his headphones and moved to the sofa. Grabbing a pad of paper and pen, he began to write.

His next podcast would focus on Newcombe's past.

Michael O'Brien, the forensic pathologist, could be the subject of another episode.

Hell, there were so many angles that Quinton could drop a podcast a day for an entire month and not cover the same subject twice.

After nearly half an hour, he had a page full of ideas. His phone began to ring, the watch on his arm vibrating with the call. He glanced at his wrist. It was a Chicago area code—probably telemarketers. Or worse yet, debt collectors. He should ignore the call, yet he hit the phone icon. "Hello?"

"Is this Quinton Yang?" a female asked.

"Who's this?"

"My name is Gabrielle Dubois, and I represent Windy City Media. Our group sponsors many podcasts like yours. I noticed the episode you just dropped." She paused. "Unless I'm not talking to Quinton."

"No. No. It's me, I mean, I'm Quinton." He was more than a little familiar with Windy City Media, the group Gabrielle represented. What did the call mean? His mind started going a million miles an hour and his pulse kept pace. He drew in a deep breath and blew it out in one gust of air. Calmer, he started again. "I just uploaded that episode." He glanced at the time on his watch. "It dropped like twenty-nine minutes ago. How would you even know about my podcast?"

"What?" she said, with a laugh. "You haven't been watching the numbers? You're trending."

Quinton grabbed his phone from the table and

opened his podcast's app. Two thousand listens already. "Holy crap," he said.

"Obviously, you have a hot topic and a major scoop. There's even some chatter that you're going to get mentioned in the next hour on some cable news shows." She paused a beat. "You have proof that your story is real, right?"

"Of course, I do." Was he going to have to tell the world that Trevor had helped? Or that he'd been eavesdropping on Dr. O'Brien and Sage Sauter? Quinton hoped like hell it wouldn't come to that.

"Can you give me your sources?"

Damn. "Listen, lady, you might be who you say you are. But how am I to know? You just randomly call me up and say you represent this media company. But you might be lying to me."

"That's a great answer." It sounded like she was smiling. "I really do need to know where you got your information."

Was this a test? "I'm a journalist," he said. "I won't divulge my sources."

"Now," Gabrielle continued with a sigh, "you might get calls from other media companies. You are under no obligation to let me know who calls or what they say, but I'd take it as a sign of friendship if you did."

Quinton was no idiot. He'd stumbled onto a huge story. What's more, he was the hot commodity, not just to Gabrielle or those she represented either. Other networks would be interested in acquiring his podcast, too. "Until we have an agreement, I won't commit to anything. But I'd like it if we could be friends."

She chuckled. "To be honest, you're savvier than I thought. Can I ask a favor?"

"You can ask, sure."

"Don't make any commitments until you hear from me again."

His mouth went dry. This was his big shot. He couldn't mess this up. "I can wait an hour, but I need to know what kind of money we're talking about."

His watch pinged with an incoming message. He scrolled through the tabs. It was a text from the same number as the call. Just a series of numbers with a dollar sign. The payout was more than he'd made over the past five years combined.

Quinton gasped. "Damn."

"One hour to consider my offer," said Gabrielle.

"You got yourself an hour. Hey, maybe if I'm generous, I'll give you an extra fifteen minutes."

She chuckled again. "Save the jokes for the podcast, Quinton."

Chapter 9

A sign with script lettering hung from a wrought iron lamppost at the border between campus and the rest of the town. An arrow pointed down a road with large houses and trees that lined the sidewalks for Greek Row. It was the street where most of the fraternities and sororities had houses.

If the campus had been quiet, Greek Row was downright eerily silent.

"This is usually such a lively place," said Sage as they passed a white-pillared house. "Music's always spilling out of open windows. Kids are hanging out on the lawns and laughing." Shaking her head, she continued. "I guess everyone is upset about what happened to Josie."

"I'm sorry this happened to you," he said, rubbing his palm on her back.

Sure, it was a friendly gesture, but his touch stole

her breath. Her cheeks warmed with the remembered kiss. Or rather, her sad attempt at seduction.

Since her divorce a decade earlier, Sage hadn't dated much at all. She'd happily dedicated her life to the two things she loved the most, her daughter and her ranch. But as she walked down the street, she realized that having a life partner would be nice. Carrying the burden of the brutal attack alone was exhausting.

Sure, she'd decided to talk to Josie about her paternity before anyone else. But it was her decision to change. Right?

The perfect words came to her. *There's something I need to tell you about that summer we dated. I know this'll be a shock—but you are Josie's biological dad...*

A cloud passed over the sun, and the temperature dipped. She shivered and Michael draped his hand over her shoulder. It would be so easy to lean into him, to take some comfort from their physical contact. But they'd tried a romance and failed. What's more, their summer fling had changed every plan Sage had for her life. No, she couldn't get involved with Michael, especially since she was lying to him still. Veering to the right, she let his hand slip away.

"That's it," she pointed up the block. The brick home had three stories and at one time must've been a stately residence. But properties like this were expensive to maintain and Sage knew that years before, the owners had been more than happy to sell the house to the university. "That's the sorority house."

"I was in a fraternity during undergrad," Michael said. "As an incoming member, I hoped it would be all about the parties. Instead, I got brotherhood, study hours and community service projects."

"Must've been disappointing," she joked. At the same time, she was once again struck by the similarities between Josie and her father.

He gave her a wan smile and shook his head. "You wouldn't believe."

Large Greek letters in navy blue outlined with gold were affixed to the front of the house. A brick path led to the front door. Sage walked up the path, talking as she went. "She went through recruitment the second semester of her freshman year. She and her roommate, Corrin, joined together. She was so excited to move into the house. The busyness of the sorority appealed to her after growing up on a ranch in the middle of nowhere without any brothers or sisters."

Michael paused on the stoop. "You mentioned that before."

"Did I?" She sighed. "Well, the past twelve hours have been a bit of a blur. Hell, it feels like it's been days since Mooky stopped by with the news."

Michael knocked on the door, and in less than a minute it opened. A short girl—probably nineteen or twenty years old—stood on the threshold. She had long dark hair and wore a sweatshirt with her sorority's letters, shorts, and fuzzy flip-flops.

Sage said, "Hi, Abbey. Sorry that I didn't call before stopping by."

"Oh, Ms. Sauter. We heard. I am so, so, so sorry. Everyone is super miserable about what happened to Josie." Abbey gave Sage a big hug. On closer inspection, the girl's eyes were red. Her face was blotchy and tear stained, like she'd been crying. Was this outpouring of love and concern for her daughter?

Honestly, she hated to see the girl so upset. But the

fact that her daughter spent her life surrounded by those who loved her was a comfort.

Abbey stepped back, holding the door open wider. "I forgot my manners. Come in."

"Thanks, Abbey," said Sage. "Abbey, this is Michael O'Brien. He's a forensic doctor who's trying to help me figure out what happened to Josie."

The girl held out her hand to shake. "Nice to meet you, Doctor O'Brien. I'm Abbey Sanchez."

"Nice to meet you, too." They stood in a white-tiled foyer. To the left was a drawing room with floor-to-ceiling bookshelves and a set of Greek letters on the mantle. The walls were lined with composite photos that were taken each year of the girls in the chapter. To the right was a dining room with a long wooden table. At the table was an abandoned textbook and water bottle. A short hallway led to the back of the house and a set of stairs led to a second story.

"Ms. Sauter, we're real sorry about what happened. What can I do?" Abbey asked.

Sage realized Abbey might be able to help. "Is there anything at all you noticed that was out of the ordinary? Even if it seemed like nothing, it might be important."

Abbey pressed her lips together as she thought. "Right now, it's the end of the semester, so everyone's stressed. We all have papers and tests. That means all the sisters get a little bitchy. But nobody was fighting—and even if they were, Josie wasn't involved." She pressed her lips together again. "I know that when something bad happens, you're supposed to say, 'Everyone liked her. She was the best.' But in Josie's case, it's true."

"Even though it's for a lousy reason, that's nice to

hear." Sage's eyes burned and she blinked back her tears. "I want to get some of Josie's things. Is it okay if I go to her room?"

"Corrin's upstairs. She's super upset and doesn't want to be disturbed. But I think if you go up, it'll be okay."

"Thanks, Abbey." Sage walked toward the staircase. "I know the way."

Michael followed.

"Sorry, Doctor O'Brien. Men aren't allowed anywhere other than the foyer and the parlor—unless you're Josie's brother or dad."

Sage stiffened. Did Abbey see the family resemblance? "Excuse me?"

"Sorry, it was a little joke. Bad timing on my part."

Holding up his hands, Michael said, "I understand the rules. I'll just wait here."

"You can go into the parlor," Abbey said. "At least there's a place to sit."

Michael headed to the room with the framed composite photos.

"I won't be a minute," Sage said, as she climbed the stairs.

"I'll be fine. Take your time."

The steps ended at a long hallway that went both left and right. There were half a dozen doors in each direction.

Sage walked to the second door on the left and knocked.

From inside the room came a muffled voice. "I told you, I just want to be alone."

"Corrin, honey, it's Ms. Sauter. Josie's mom."

The door opened and a blonde girl in pajama bottoms and a large sweatshirt stood on the threshold. "Ms. Sauter." The girl covered her face and began to sob.

Sage wrapped her in a hug and made shushing noises. "It'll be okay."

"No," Corrin hiccupped and pulled away. "It won't be okay. I know we aren't supposed to talk about what happened because rumors make the police's job harder, but I heard she was kidnapped from campus. And there are no leads at all."

Sage said, "The police have some theories about what happened. Suspects. There's a lot of physical evidence to evaluate. The police are smart. There are lots of people working on this case. Soon, they'll figure out what happened."

Corrin stopped crying. "Do you really think so?"

Putting on a brave smile, she said, "I know so." And then, "Hey, even though she's going to get better, Josie's not coming back this semester. I want to pick up some of her stuff. Mind if I come in?"

Corrin stepped aside. "You're always welcome."

There were two beds, both lofted. Desks and a chest of drawers were tucked underneath. The walls were papered with snapshots. There were pictures of the entire sorority standing in front of the house. Giggling girls covered in shaving cream after a shaving cream balloon fight. The same girls in cocktail dresses at Spring Formal.

In the middle of it all was Josie. She was always smiling. Always hugging a friend. Until now, her daughter had been successful and happy. Still, she couldn't help but wonder, what would Josie's life have been like if Michael had been around? Would she have been happier?

A love seat and chair sat next to the window. Corrin moved slowly to the loveseat and sat down with a groan. “What do you think happened?”

Sage shook her head. “I have no idea.”

“Last night, Josie said she was going to meet with Ben. I think they’d been having some issues.”

The hairs at the nape of Sage’s neck stood on end. “What makes you think that?”

“Yesterday, I came into the room when she was on a video call with Ben. She was crying. And he was all like, ‘I’m sorry, babe.’”

True, Ben had already admitted as much to the police, but had Josie shared anything more? “That doesn’t mean Josie was upset with her boyfriend. She might’ve gotten a bad grade and he was being sympathetic. Isn’t that possible?”

“Possible? Yeah. Except when I asked her what’s the matter, she said, ‘Nothing.’ Then left the room. If it was something small—like a bad grade—she would’ve told me.” Corrin shrugged. “This seemed bigger.”

“What do you think of Ben? Do you like him?”

“Like him?” She drew out the words, considering them. “I don’t dislike him. I mean, he’s kinda like Josie. Perfect in almost every way.”

Honestly, she wasn’t sure what to make of that answer. “I better get Josie’s things. Do you know where she stores her duffel bags?”

“On the top shelf of the closet.”

There was a small closet near the door. Just like Corrin had said, Sage found both of Josie’s duffel bags. It only took a few minutes to fill the bags with clothes, a few personal items, and all of Josie’s toiletries. As she zipped the last bag closed, she said, "This isn't how it's supposed to work out. Josie should be safe and here, with you."

"I know." Corrin leaned forward on the loveseat. "Can I ask you a question?"

"Of course." Sage moved to the chair and dropped into it. She was suddenly aware of her bone-deep fatigue. "What do you need?"

"What do the doctors think will happen to Josie?"

Sage should've given Corrin an update as soon as they arrived. After all, the girls had been friends since the first day of their freshman year. "Right now, she's in a medically induced coma. There's swelling in her brain, and it needs time to heal."

"Did she say anything at all about what happened? I heard that she couldn't remember. Do you think she'll ever get her memories back?"

"At the moment, nobody knows." She repeated Lorraine's message, even if it wasn't word for word. "More than the physical trauma, there's the emotional stress as well. Even if she heals, she might not remember right away—or ever."

"But she might remember, right?"

"That's what we're hoping for, of course."

"Of course." Corrin stood and opened her arms to Sage. "You have my number. You'll keep me posted, right?"

"I will." Sage pulled the young woman in for a tight hug. She felt Corrin wince and she let go. "You take care of yourself and reach out if you need anything."

"I will."

There was nothing else to do or say. Yet, Sage stood in the doorway and looked around the room. It was almost as if she could hear the echoes of Josie's laughter. With a final wave, she stepped into the hallway and pulled the door closed.

Sunlight streamed through tall windows and reflected off the large pictures that lined the walls. Michael was so exhausted that his bones ached. A striped sofa sat under a window and for a moment, he contemplated taking a seat.

Then again, if he stopped moving, he'd be asleep in minutes.

Stifling a yawn, he walked to the first composite photo. There were twelve rows of twenty pictures. All the young women wore the same black velvet drape.

At the hospital, Josie's face had been swollen and covered in bruises. A breathing tube had been taped to her face and her head was in a bandage. In short, even though he'd examined her wounds, he hardly knew what she looked like.

He scanned the rows of pictures. Each girl was listed alphabetically by last name. Kaufman, Kramer, Kruger. Michael found Josie's photograph and his heart ceased to beat.

The woman in the picture was his youngest sister, Darla. But that was impossible.

He pulled the phone from his pocket and opened a social media app. He scrolled back through the posts until he found a post on his last birthday.

Happy birthday to the best big brother in the world, Darla had posted on his timeline. Along with her sentiments was a collage of family photos. There was one of Michael and Darla at his college graduation. If he was twenty-two years old in the picture, then his sister would have been seventeen.

Holding up his phone, he compared pictures of the two young women side by side. Sure, Josie had a rounder face and broader shoulders than Darla, but the coloring was the same. The eyes. The smile. The women definitely looked alike.

Tension pinched his shoulder blades together and Michael rubbed the back of his neck. He couldn't ignore his suspicions about Josie's paternity any longer.

"Hey." Sage stood at the bottom of the staircase, holding two duffel bags. "What're you looking at?"

"Come here," he said. "There's something I want you to see."

She drew her brows together and set the bags next to the door. "What is it?"

She stood next to him at the portraits. "I found Josie..." he began.

Sage looked at the wording at the bottom of the picture. "Looks like this is from her first year in school."

Was that all she was going to say? Michael tried another strategy. "Has she changed much since she was a freshman?"

Sage shook her head. "She's always looked like herself—even as a baby."

"I bet." Okay, being subtle wasn't working. He was going to have to be direct. "I think we need to talk, Sage."

"That sounds serious." She looked around the room. "I'm not sure this is the best place, though."

"Hi." Dark-haired Abbey stood on the threshold. "I heard voices and thought Doctor O'Brien was on the phone. But then I heard your voice, Ms. Sauter," she continued in her Texas lilt. "Do you need anything else?"

"No." Sage walked to the foyer and picked up the discarded duffel bags. "We're done for now. Once Josie gets settled, I'll get the rest of her things."

"Keep in touch and let us know how Josie's doing, okay?"

"Of course, I will. I have Corrin's number."

Abbey's expression changed, a cloud passing over the sun. She smiled again. "That'd be great."

Michael would've wondered about the look, but he had a bigger question in mind. He opened the door. As Sage approached, he reached for one of the duffel bags. "I got that."

"I can manage," she said, not letting go of the strap.

He knew enough not to fight with Sage. Almost two-dozen years earlier, she'd been proud and independent—or as independent as her controlling father allowed. Like the fact that her father knew when Sage took the car and where she was going, even though Sage had been in her early twenties.

They stepped outside and he pulled the door closed. The air was cooler and thin, gray clouds scattered in the sky. The breeze was filled with the scent of ozone. "Looks like a storm's coming."

She turned her face to the sky and nodded in agreement. "Looks like it."

Walking toward campus, neither spoke. The silence suited Michael; he was fine with his own thoughts. It was one of the things he liked best about Sage, she didn't need to talk all the time—even at twenty-two years old. With a few minutes to think, he knew this was the best opportunity to ask Sage about Josie's paternity.

"Can I ask you a sensitive question?" He didn't wait for her answer. "Why'd you marry Vance right after I left Mercy? Were you two an item while we were dating?"

Okay, he was still hedging his questions. For a moment, he wasn't sure why. But deep down, he knew. Michael wanted to give Sage every chance to be honest.

"We weren't an item before you left," she said after a moment. "But after you, I wanted love. Vance was in Mercy and available. He was a good friend. I hoped that friendship would turn into something more. The best we ever got was affection."

He listened as she spoke. Sure, it would be easy to believe her version of the truth. But what about what he knew to be true? Josie looked like his youngest sister. The birthdate was right for Michael to be the father. "Is that all?"

They'd made their way back to the parking lot and stood on opposite sides of his car. Sage watched him over the hood. "What else do you want me to say?" she asked, an edge to her voice.

The truth. "We still need to talk…"

"No," she said. The single word rang out like a shot. "I'm done talking about twenty-some-odd years ago. My daughter is lying in a hospital bed fighting for her life. Some psycho attacked her, and nobody knows who or why. That's what's important to me now."

Michael knew enough to back off, at least for now. "I didn't mean to upset you."

She worked her jaw back and forth. "I didn't mean to get so upset." Lifting the duffel bags, she asked. "Is there room in your trunk for these?"

He took the fob from the pocket of his pants and

found the correct button. The lock unlatched with a click. He opened the trunk. "There you go."

"Thanks." She smiled at him, but the expression was polite—not genuine. She dropped the bags into the cargo hold.

He watched her and realized one important thing—Sage would never freely admit to him that he was Josie's father—even if it was true.

It left him trying to figure out what to do—or say—next.

Sure, Josie's photograph looked just like his sister. That fact left him more rattled than he wanted to admit. The thing was, as doctor, he knew that genes were funny things. The resemblance might not mean everything. Or, it might mean nothing at all.

When he took it all into the total, he knew that inquiring about Josie's paternity was a singularly dangerous question—and one that Michael wasn't sure he'd ever ask.

Chapter 10

It had been months since he was shot, and still, Decker Newcombe's chest hurt. He couldn't lift his arm over his head and every time it rained, his shoulder ached. All the same, he knew he was lucky to be alive.

If it weren't for that old Mexican woman and her nephew, a doctor, he would've bled out in the desert. They didn't care who Decker was—only that he paid them in cash to take care of him. Then again, the cops thought he had actually died. For Decker, that was fine. There were advantages to being a ghost.

Like the fact that nobody was really looking for him.

Sitting in the front of a computer monitor at a small library branch in downtown San Antonio, Decker pulled the keyboard closer. As was his habit, he searched his own name twice a week. He typed his name into the search bar and hit enter. Leaning back, he folded his arms across his chest and waited.

The search ended and Decker went cold.

There was a new podcast about Decker—no surprise there. Although he'd never heard of Crimes with Quinton, by Quinton Yang. Still, the dude had over fifteen thousand listens and the episode had dropped only hours before.

"What the hell?"

An elderly man sat at the terminal next to Decker and glared. He glared back until the man looked away.

His pulse pounded, making the wound to his chest burn with each beat of his heart. He leaned toward the monitor and read the description of the episode that accompanied the search.

Is Decker Newcombe Back from the Grave?

On an abandoned road near Mercy, Texas, Josie Kruger was supposed to breathe her last breath. The college co-ed was strangled, beaten, cut, and thrown to the bottom of a cliff. There, she was left for dead. The injuries were like those inflicted on another victim of Decker Newcombe. As luck would have it, the local sheriff drove by as Kruger climbed out of the gulch. Forensic Pathologist Dr. Michael O'Brien was called onto the case to determine if Kruger was actually attacked by Decker Newcombe...

Decker closed the search tab and smothered a curse behind his hand.

Since his injury, Decker had denied his urges to hunt and kill. He knew he wasn't strong enough to evade police. And once he started killing again, the world would know his name and tremble.

But this?

He rose from his seat with a disgusted sigh.

This podcast ruined everything. Not only was Decker

back in the news, but it was for a crime he hadn't committed. Slowly, he walked through the library, the scar in his chest pulling with each step. He planned his next move. From the podcaster's bio, he'd noted that Yang lived in San Antonio. It was a happy coincidence for him that the podcaster was so close.

It meant that Decker could visit the guy and get answers to his questions. Because there was one thing that Yang needed to know—hell, the whole world needed to know. Decker never left witnesses and he sure as hell never left a victim alive.

Sage sat in the passenger seat of Michael's car as they drove back to San Antonio. She knew he was a smart man. More than being a physician and a forensic pathologist who worked on cases all over the country—hell, all over the world—he noticed everything. She supposed that was what made him successful at his job.

It didn't take an expert of any kind to figure out that he was Josie's father. So, she shouldn't have been surprised he'd brought up the fact that Josie looked like his sister.

And yet, she'd been shocked. Hell, she'd been living a lie for so long she'd forgotten what it was like to tell the truth.

Her heart hammered against her chest. It wasn't the same kind of exhilaration she got from a hard ride on the range. Sage imagined it was like standing at the door of an airplane and getting ready to jump. As she stepped into the void of the unknown, the fall could give her freedom that she never expected. Or her parachute might not open, and her leap would end in tragedy.

She had to tell him.

She began, "You know how you were analyzing Josie's clothing for hair and blood?"

"Well, we're looking for blood that's not her own. If there is a different type of blood, we should know by the end of today."

Michael had her attention now. "Then you'll know who attacked Josie?"

"It's not exactly that easy. If there's blood from a second person on her clothing, we need to get a DNA analysis. Then, if that person's DNA is registered with CODIS—the federal database—or the state of Texas, we'll know."

"If it's Decker Newcombe?" she asked, her confession about Josie's paternity almost forgotten.

"If it's him, we'll know."

"If it's not him?"

Michael rolled back his shoulders. "Then it all goes back to finding a DNA match in a criminal database."

"What if there's not a match?" Sage was desperate for answers.

"There are other options. Of course, the military has its own DNA database, but that's in place to identify remains from a combat situation. I've heard of cases where law enforcement was able to submit a sample to look for a match. The Golden State killer's identity was discovered from a genealogy testing service." He glanced in her direction. "Don't worry, we'll find out who attacked your daughter."

Our daughter.

"Listen, there's something I've been meaning to tell you." Sage looked out the window. Maybe if she didn't have to meet his eye, this would be easier. "It's about Josie."

Her phone pinged with an incoming message. Without hesitation, she grabbed her purse from the floorboard.

"There was something you wanted to tell me about Josie..." Michael coaxed. She could feel him watching her from the driver's seat.

She glanced at the screen and cursed.

"What is it?" Michael asked, his voice filled with concern. "Did something happen to Josie?"

The text was from Mooky Cafferty. Sage read the notification again before clearing her throat. "There's a new podcast that's gone viral. Serial killer Decker Newcombe is linked to attack on college co-ed."

Sage connected her phone to the car's Bluetooth system.

"You ready?" she asked Michael.

It wasn't a question of readiness. He had to listen to the podcast.

He gave a terse nod.

Sage began the episode.

We've all heard the name Decker Newcombe. For years, Newcombe committed murder for hire, and is suspected of killing over two-dozen people. The murder of a district attorney in northern Wyoming sent Newcombe into hiding for a year. When he re-emerged, the hitman was deadlier than before.

DNA testing proved that Decker Newcombe is a direct descendant of the man who science proved to be Jack the Ripper, the Victorian-era serial killer. Following a killing spree in and around Mercy, Texas, Newcombe was shot by a lawman. Newcombe escaped into the Mexican desert. To this day, his whereabouts is unknown.

That's a tale we all know well. But what if that's not the end of Decker Newcombe's story? What if Newcombe survived? What if he's still in Texas—and killing again?

There's a new chapter in the saga of the modern-day Jack the Ripper and this one is about Josie Kruger, a young woman who grew up near the town of Mercy, Texas...

The whole episode lasted twenty minutes. As the ending music played, Michael couldn't decide if he should laugh or scream. "There has to be a leak in the sheriff's department."

"What makes you say that?" Sage asked, her tone unfriendly.

"Somebody told this podcaster a lot. Hell, he basically knew everything about the case, including my involvement."

"But why the sheriff's department? Why accuse Mooky Cafferty and his deputies? It could be anyone, from anywhere. The campus police. The cops in San Antonio. The leak could've come from the hospital."

He kept his eyes on the road and his hands on the steering wheel. Lifting his fingertips, he surrendered. "Point taken." He glanced at Sage. "Is there a bio for the podcaster with the episode?"

"Let me see." For a moment, she scrolled in silence. "Says here, 'A graduate from the journalism school at the University of Texas in Austin, Quinton Yang has a passion for crimes, both solved and unsolved, in the Lone Star State. He lives in San Antonio.'" She paused.

"That helps a little. But San Antonio is a big city. How are we supposed to find him?"

"I have an idea." He switched from Sage's phone to his own before pulling up his contact list. Using the controls on the steering wheel, he scrolled until finding the name he wanted. Isaac Patton.

Isaac answered the call after the second ring. "Do you have a DNA match yet?"

"Not yet," said Michael. "But we're working on it. I have a favor to ask."

"Ask away."

"I need an address for Quinton Yang, he's a podcaster who lives in San Antonio."

Isaac asked, "Is this related to the Kruger case?"

"In a way," he said. "He just released a podcast about how Decker might've been the one who attacked Josie. I want to speak to Quinton and see how he got his information."

Isaac asked, "Why don't you turn this over to the San Antonio police?"

"What if they're the leak?" Michael countered. "Besides, everything he said is true. I doubt that publishing the truth is a crime."

"Good point. Give me a minute." And then, he said, "I've got him."

He read off an address.

Sage entered the address into a GPS app. "And I've got directions."

To Isaac, he said, "Thanks, man. I owe you."

"I'm still paying you back for everything that you've done for me."

He ended the call and switched to Sage's phone to get directions to Quinton's address.

"I get that you want to talk to the podcaster. But, Michael, what do you hope to find?"

There was only one thing he ever wanted. It was always the same. He glanced at Sage before turning back to the road. "I'm after the truth."

Quinton Yang stepped from the shower and reached for a towel. It was almost noon, and the past twenty-four hours had been like nothing he could have ever imagined. Beyond Gabrielle, representatives from two more podcasting networks had offered him staggering amounts of money.

He had to make a decision and fast.

What he wanted was advice, or at least someone with whom he could chat. Too bad Trevor wasn't answering his calls. Sure, Trev was sore that Quinton had called in the ultimate favor. But it had paid off, hadn't it?

He ran the towel through his short, black hair and paused.

What was it?

Had he heard something? Was someone in his apartment?

It'd be a hell of an irony if the landlord finally fixed that leaky faucet on the same day that Quinton was going to break his lease and move out.

Wrapping the towel around his middle, he opened the bathroom door. "Anybody here?" he called out. He hadn't anticipated a repairman showing up when he got in the shower. So, he hadn't thought to bring clean clothes into the bathroom with him. "I just gotta grab some pants."

He paused another beat. The apartment was still and silent, save for the drip-drip-drip of the faucet.

"Hello?" Quinton's hands turned clammy.

Nothing.

He peered into the single room. It was just as he left it.

Huh. What exactly had he heard? The creak of a floorboard? The click of the latch catching on the door? Honestly, he couldn't place the noise that caught his attention. Had it been in his imagination?

He shrugged but kept the towel around his waist as he walked quickly from the bathroom. Quinton's dresser was tucked into the closet. He opened the bottom drawer and removed a pair of chinos—the nicest pants he owned. He dropped the towel and stepped into the legs.

"Christ, man." He quickly removed the pants opened the top drawer of his dresser and found a pair of boxers. "Underwear first."

He dressed quickly—shorts, pants, button-down shirt. The noise had definitely gotten him shook. But it was time for Quinton to decide. He had to commit to a podcasting network. But which one?

His phone sat on the table. He'd entered the contact information for each person who'd called. On a pad of paper, Quinton had taken notes about the different offers. He reviewed his scrawled handwriting and at the bottom of the page, he stopped. His blood turned icy in his veins.

In neat block lettering was a single sentence that Quinton had not written. The message was chilling.

Do not make a sound or I will kill you.

He turned slowly. Where he hadn't been before stood a man.

Long, blond hair hung around his shoulders. A beard covered his cheeks and chin. The guy was thin, like a wire. And just like a wire, Quinton could sense the deadly power that surged through him.

"What the hell, man. You can't be here." Yet, Quinton could barely hear his own voice over the pulse that thundered in his ears.

"Shut up," the man growled. "I need information."

Of all the things Quinton expected the guy to say, that wasn't it.

"Information?" he echoed. "What kind of information?"

"About your podcast, stupid."

The guy looked familiar. "How do I know you?"

Moving slowly to the table, the man lowered himself into a seat. "You mean, you really don't know who I am? Really?"

Quinton ground his teeth together. He shouldn't have said anything—now, he looked like a fool. He thought fast. "You work at the Quickie-Mart next to the highway."

"No, dumbass, I don't work at no Quickie-Mart." He leaned back in the seat, draping his arm over the back. A small smile pulled up the corner of his lips. The man, whoever he was, was enjoying the moment.

Quinton looked at the door. It was across the room. If he wanted to escape, he'd have to get past the man. Sure, the guy was thin, but he wasn't exactly a wire. He was more of a predatory cat. No, that wasn't right either.

The man was a venomous snake. Quinton hated snakes.

The man rose from the seat and moved toward him. The stink of stale body odor crashed down on him like a wave. "I'll give you a little hint. I'm a ghost and your worst freaking nightmare."

There was little resemblance between the man who stood before him and the mugshot he'd posted with the link to his podcast this morning. But the eyes were the same.

Quinton's hands began to tremble. He tucked them into his armpits to stop the shaking. It only got worse, and his arms started to quiver.

"Decker," he whispered as a hard knot of panic dropped into his gut. "You're Decker Newcombe."

"Who told you about me? Who told you I was alive?"

With a shake of his head, he said. "I can't say. Journalistic integrity."

"I'm gonna give you a friendly piece of advice." Decker smiled. The expression was far from cordial. "I'd be less concerned about integrity and more worried about pain."

He drove his fist into Quinton's gut. For a moment, it was like falling. Suspended between surprise and agony. Then, the agony hit—radiating outward from his midsection. Bending, he retched on the floor. A string of vomit and spit hung from his lip. Quinton wiped it away and tried to draw a breath. "Help," he whispered.

Decker grabbed the back of Quinton's head and slammed it into his knee. For a moment, the world tilted sideways. He tried to stand. To take a step. He slipped in the puke and fell to his knees. Decker drew back his fist and punched Quinton in the face.

His nose shattered and blood flowed from his nostrils. His face throbbed with each beat of his heart. The colors in the room turned to gray. White spots erupted in his field of vision.

Decker grabbed the front of Quinton's shirt and drew

him close. "Now that I got your attention, I'm gonna ask you again. Who told you that I was alive?"

Quinton shook his head. "I'm not telling you a thing."

"You're a brave man," Decker sneered. "Most people would be pleading for mercy by now."

"I'm not brave. But I'm not going to reveal my source. Why would I? You'd only go after them."

Decker loosened his grip on Quinton's collar. He smoothed down the fabric with both hands. "You are brave and smart. I admire that, truly I do. Being a smart man, you gotta ask yourself—what are you willing to endure for your secrets? Because eventually, you're going to beg me to let you talk." Decker paused.

Quinton's mind filled with a hundred different ways to suffer. His bowels threatened to empty. He hated the idea of having barf on his hands and knees, and his boxers filled with crap. He blinked hard. "I…" He swallowed. "I can't."

Decker grabbed his arm and swung Quinton in an arc. The corner, where two walls met, came at him in slow motion. It was all a trick of the mind because he didn't have time to react. His face slammed into the wallboard and plaster. It left him dizzy.

If Decker hadn't been holding his arm, he would've fallen to the floor. He knew he needed to fight back. How?

Decker was obviously fast, mean and accustomed to violence—all things that he was not. His entire life, he'd been the kind of guy who made friends easily. It wasn't an act, either. He really was interested in people. So, okay, it wasn't exactly part of a plan when Quinton asked, "Why'd you do it?" It's just that he knew that to survive, he had to keep Decker talking.

"You say something?" Decker let go of his arm and he slumped to the floor.

Breathing hard, he leaned against the wall. "I asked, why'd you do it?" His lips were too thick for his mouth and every time he exhaled, droplets of fresh blood sprayed from his nose.

"Why'd I do what?" Decker asked. He sat down on the edge of Quinton's coffee table. "Break into your apartment? Slam your head against the wall? I need to know who told you I was alive. I need to know who else knows it, too. Christ, maybe you aren't so smart after all."

"Why'd you do it?" Quinton asked, again. One of his teeth was loose and he wiggled it with his tongue. He continued. "All of it. I've heard what other people have to say about your past, but I want to know from you. Why'd you become a hitman? Kill that woman in Mercy and cut her open? Attack that college student yesterday?"

"Let's get one thing straight." Decker poked his chest with a bony finger. "I didn't attack no college girl."

"You didn't?" That fact was a surprise. "The police think you did."

"Wasn't me," said Decker with a shake of his head. "You know how I can prove it?"

"How?"

"If I'd been the one who attacked that girl, she wouldn't be in the hospital. She'd be dead."

Chapter 11

In Quinton's estimation, Decker Newcombe really wasn't that bad of a guy—once he stopped beating the crap out him, at least. Sure, there was a twist in his personality. But the serial killer had sat for a short interview. The really good news was that Newcombe had allowed him to record every juicy second.

The killer's background had been sad, if predictable. A mother with a weak personality who was drawn to lousy men. At a young age, Newcombe learned that those who hit the hardest won.

"The first person I ever kilt was an old man who thought my buddy, Ryan Steele, had taken a radio from his place. It wasn't worth nothing, but the guy listened to it all the time." Newcombe continued, "Ryan and I were in middle school. One afternoon, we were hanging out near the edge of the trailer park and smoking cigarettes I'd stolen from my mom's latest douchebag boyfriend. The old man finds us and flips out. He just starts beating the crap outta Ryan. Calling him a punk-thief. Ryan was screaming, swearing he hadn't taken nothing. I remember my heart was beating so fast, I thought it was going to come right outta my chest because the coot was going to kill my friend." Quinton had made a cup of coffee for Newcombe. He paused to take a sip. "I tried to pull the guy off Ryan. But he was stuck on him, like a tick."

Quinton took a drink of his own coffee, impervious to the bitterness or the swelling in his mouth. "Then what happened?"

Decker set the cup on the table. "There was this board laying on the ground. I hit the old guy in the back of the head. Again and again and again. I kept hitting him, even though Ryan had gotten away."

"Do you think it was the adrenaline? After all, you were scared."

"Scared? Adrenaline?" Decker shook his head. "Once I started swinging the board, my heart rate slowed. And scared? Naw." Decker pushed his coffee cup aside and leaned toward Quinton. "The thing was—I liked it. The minute the life left his eyes, I became a man. I never had to be scared or hurt again. You know why?"

Quinton's word was a whisper. "Why?"

"Because I learned the secret to the whole damn universe. There is only one power. It's the one of life and death."

Damn. "That's profound." Sick. Perverse. But still profound. "Why'd you kill Trinity Jackson, the woman in Mercy? The killing is said to be linked to Jack the Ripper. But how?"

Decker sniffed. "You know how I said I liked killing

that old man?" He said, not bothering to answer Quinton's questions. He continued, "I knew that my reaction wasn't normal. Ryan was all worried about getting in trouble and such. Me, I didn't feel anything. But I knew I should. That's when I understood I was different from everyone else. It was only when I learned that I was a descendant of Jeremiah Newcombe—otherwise known as Jack the Ripper—that I understood why."

"What did you come to understand?"

"Bad blood runs in my family." He held out his arms to Quinton, the blue-green veins in his wrist were a roadmap under his flesh. "The need to kill is in my DNA. As a killer, Jack had one problem."

Quinton didn't interrupt with a question. He knew Decker would share whatever issue he'd taken with his ancestor.

Decker said, "It took over two hundred years for anyone to know his true identity—and by then, most people didn't care."

It was true. Quinton nodded.

"But for me, the world will know and fear my name." He sat back in the chair and folded his arms across his chest. "I'm done talking now."

He knew enough not to ask any more questions. Pressing a button, Quinton ended the recording. "Thanks, man. This'll make a great follow-up episode." He continued, almost speaking to himself, almost chatting with Decker. "First, I need to decide which sponsorship group to sign with…"

Newcombe took a sip of coffee and set the cup aside. "As a hired gun, you go with the weapon that gives you the maximum impact. Sign with whatever company will pay you the most now and give you the most exposure later."

"That's stellar advice." Quinton sent a text to Gabrielle, promising the podcast with Decker's interview once the money was received into his account. She texted back immediately with several questions, but he replied that he'd only speak to her once he had the money. The transfer took less than five minutes. So, sure, his face still hurt like hell from Decker's beating. But now, Quinton could afford to see a doctor. Maybe he'd even buy one of those insurance policies advertised on social media.

Holding up his phone, he showed Decker the bank balance.

The killer gave a low whistle. "Nice, man. Real nice. Since I done made you all that moola, you gotta be honest with me. Who told you I was still alive?"

Quinton gave a sheepish smile. "It wasn't real hard. I was at the hospital delivering food, my other gig. I went to sit on the patio and this couple bursts out the door and they're talking to each other about the woman's daughter, thinking they're alone. Turns out the man is a forensic pathologist—Doctor Michael O'Brien—and the woman is Josie Kruger's mom. Then, they started talking about you. I just sat in the shadows and listened."

"That's a lucky break, man."

"You know, I couldn't have done this without you." After setting his phone on the table, he pointed at Decker and smiled. "I get it. You're a stone-cold killer. But there's a part of you that's a good guy."

Decker returned the smile and shook his head. "No, there's not."

Quinton blinked, not quite understanding. "Not what?"

With a continual smile, Decker said, "There's no part of me that's nice at all. Now, here's what I need you to do. You need to send all that cash to the money exchange down the street in the name of Ryan Steele. Don't worry, he won't get a dime. I'll be the one picking up the money and using his name."

"No way." He covered his phone with his palm. "It's my podcast. My cash."

Decker grabbed Quinton's hand and peeled his fingers back toward his wrist. A lightning strike of pain shot up his arm.

Decker said, "I don't want to rough you up anymore."

Quinton cried out and dropped to his knees. He hit the cup of coffee and the dark liquid spread across the table.

The killer let go and reached for the pad of paper and a pen. As Quinton shook out his hand, Decker scribbled a note and ripped it off the sheet. He pointed with the pen as he spoke, "I will hurt you bad if you don't do what I say."

"Christ, man. I got bills to pay." Quinton looked around his tiny apartment and bile rose in the back of his throat. "I planned to move someplace better."

"Don't worry about your bills. Or your digs—although this place does suck. You can do more podcasts. Make more money." He paused, tucked the folded sheet of paper into his pants pocket. "That is, unless you don't do what I say."

Quinton's gut burned, but he knew he'd been outmaneuvered. Rising to his feet, he sat back in his chair. Using an app on his phone, he initiated the transfer. "It'll take a minute."

Decker rummaged through the kitchen. "Don't you have any grub? I'm starving."

"Grub?" Quinton snorted. "I was going to go to the grocery store, but now I'm flat-ass broke. Again." Or maybe it was still.

"Stop your whining. You'll be okay being poor a little while longer."

Quinton's banking app pinged when the transfer was complete. He held up the phone so Decker could see the screen. "It's done."

Decker said, "This isn't personal—just so you know."

"Funny, getting shaken down feels pretty personal."

"I'm not talking about the money."

There was a flash of silver as Decker shoved a steak knife through Quinton's gut. The killer twisted the handle as he withdrew the blade. His stomach felt as if it'd been set on fire. He looked down at his belly. Blood seeped from a hole in his shirt, turning the cloth crimson and then black.

Quinton's knees went soft, and he began to sink down. Decker held his shoulder and drove the knife in twice more.

His thoughts, caught in the fog of fear and shock, came into sharp focus. He should fight. Run. He tried to scream. His voice gurgled with his own blood. The killer lowered him to the ground.

"You stay here," said the killer. "It won't be long now before you're gone." From the pocket of his pants, Decker removed the note. He looked down at Quinton. "You still with me?"

He could only lift his eyes.

"Well, I imagine that it hurts like hell now and you're pretty scared," said Decker. "I'm gonna do you a favor and speed things up." He drove the knife through the paper and stabbed it into Quinton's chest.

Every nerve in his body screamed in pain. Yet, he could do nothing beyond suffer.

In a funny way, Decker had been right. It wasn't the slow leaking away of life as before. Now, he could feel death rushing toward him from all sides.

As Quinton lay dying on the floor, the killer stripped from his own blood-covered clothes and donned a new outfit—one of Quinton's favorites. The room started to waver, as if he was standing in the surf and watching the ocean's floor at his feet.

A cold hand pressed into his neck. "Not long now," said Decker. His words were muffled as if he spoke from underwater, too.

The door to Quinton's apartment opened and closed. He was alone, left to die. The room became the ocean. The floor became the warm waters of the Gulf. Quinton stretched out as the waves undulated beneath him and carried him away.

The cramped apartment building was in a part of San Antonio that Michael rarely visited. He found a spot on the street and parked his car. To the left, windows of a former laundromat were covered in grime on the outside and faded newspaper on the inside. A convenience store sat on the corner. An illuminated Open sign shone from a window covered with bars.

Thick clouds blocked out the sun, leaching the world of colors. Sage alone stood out. Her hair was gold. Her lips were pink. Her eyes were the same color as dark chocolate. His fingers itched with the need to touch her cheek. With an exhale, he ran his hand over the gearshift.

Looking out the window, she said, "I get that this is where the podcaster lives. But what are we doing here? What do you want to accomplish?"

"I need to find out where he got his information. If there's a leak at the hospital, or any place else, I need to know."

"You really think he's going to tell us?" Sage asked, her tone incredulous.

"He won't unless we ask him," said Michael. "You can stay here if you want."

She shook her head. "If he knows something about what happened to Josie, I want to go with you."

After pushing the ignition button, the electric engine whispered into stillness. Michael opened his car door as Sage opened hers. They stepped into the gray afternoon. "Smells like rain," said Michael as they approached the apartment building.

"Maybe," said Sage. "All I can smell is garbage."

He sniffed the air. Perhaps there was a little bit of a stench in the street. "Smells like the city to me."

"Exactly," said Sage. "Mercy's not a perfect place. At least it smells of earth and sky—just like God intended. Not like this."

An argument about city life versus living in the country would waste time he didn't have. So, he kept his comments to himself. Pointing to a brick apartment building, he said, "This is it." They climbed the set of four steps that led to the entrance.

At one time, the door leading to the apartment building had a lock. Now, there was only a large hole in the wood. He pulled on the handle and the door opened. Sage crossed the threshold and he followed.

A small foyer was made up of cracked tile. The ground floor had three units on each side of a narrow hallway and a set of stairs that led up. The apartments were organized alphanumerically. 1-A through 1-F.

"Which unit belongs to Quinton?"

Sage had the address on her phone. She glanced at the screen. "Three-E. Third floor." She started to climb the stairs. Michael followed. On the third-floor landing, she stopped. Mouth and nose covered by the back of her hand; Sage gagged. "What the hell is that stench? It's worse than an unmucked stall in the middle of July."

Michael could smell it too. It was a familiar and unpleasant scent that made his skin crawl. "It's blood and bile." He paused. "And coffee."

Stepping around Sage, he scanned the doors for apartment 3-E. It was the middle of the three and on the left. Using the side of his fist, he knocked on the door. Silently, it opened an inch.

"Hello," he called out. "Is anyone home? I'm looking for Quinton Yang."

There was no answer.

Looking over his shoulder, he met Sage's eye. She shrugged. Turning back, he yelled into the opening between door and jamb. "This is Michael O'Brien—the doctor you mentioned in your podcast. Quinton, I'd like to talk to you."

Still, no answer. This time, Michael didn't expect one. The smell was coming from the apartment. Using his toe, he nudged the door open farther and crossed the threshold. Sage followed. Inside the apartment the stench was stronger.

He scanned the apartment. It was only a single room. In front of him was a kitchen table, complete with a laptop and two microphones. Two mugs lay on their sides. Twin puddles of coffee had run across the table and joined in the middle. The murky liquid dripped to the floor, staining the carpet.

"Michael. Look." Sage pointed a shaking hand. Blood was splattered across the walls. "What happened here?"

"Nothing good," he said taking another step into the apartment.

Sage reached for his hand and pulled him to a stop. "You said yourself that nothing good happened in here. We should call nine-one-one. The police will know what to do."

Michael had been in enough crime scenes to know one when he saw it. The overturned dishes. The blood on the wall. "Someone's been attacked in here. But it's more than finding out what happened. I need to know if anyone needs medical care."

She kept her hand in his and gave a quick nod.

Michael walked farther into the room. At the edge of the sofa, he could see a foot. For Michael, time slowed as his eyes followed the foot to the cuff of a pair of chinos. A leg. There, lying on the floor, was a body of a young man. His lifeless eyes stared at the ceiling and a knife protruded from his chest.

At San Antonio Medical Center, autopsies were conducted by the medical examiner. On rare occasions, Michael filled in. This was one of those occasions. The victim from the apartment had been identified as Quinton Yang. Beyond having his Texas state driver's license recovered from the apartment, Yang had a longtime friend from the SAPD, Trevor Kane, who also gave a positive ID.

A stainless-steel table stood in the middle of the morgue. Upon the table was the body. Quinton looked exactly as he had when discovered. He was still fully dressed. The knife still protruded from his chest.

For this procedure, Michael wore surgical scrubs, gloves, eye protection, and a surgical cap. His assistant, Dustin, was dressed the same.

"Our investigation starts now," said Michael. Typically, the medical examiner determined the cause of death. Then, if it was a homicide, forensic pathology was called in to start the inquiry. This time, Michael and his tech would be able to collect their samples in real time while determining the cause of death.

A microphone hung from a wire in the ceiling. As was done in all autopsies, Michael planned to make a verbal record of his findings. He nodded to Dustin, and the tech turned on the device.

"This is Doctor Michael O'Brien, conducting an autopsy of Quinton E. Yang, a twenty-six-year-old male who was found dead in his apartment approximately two hours ago." Michael glanced at a clock hanging on the wall. "The time is three o'clock in the afternoon."

"Mr. Yang is approximately five feet, nine inches tall. He weighs one hundred and seventy-two pounds. His clothes are covered in a black substance, which appears to be blood and a knife is impaled in his chest."

The next step was to get Quinton out of his clothing, while also searching for evidence as to who stabbed him—and why. For the record, he said, "I'm going to remove the knife. It appears to be a kitchen knife with a metal blade and plastic handle. Dustin, do you have an evidence bag ready?"

If they were lucky, the killer left their fingerprints on the knife. Dustin held open the bag and Michael carefully removed the knife. A piece of cloth stuck to the blade.

"Is that a part of the victim's clothing?" Dustin asked.

Michael examined Quinton's shirt. The fabric was intact. "I don't think so." He held the knife closer to the light. The material on the blade was white with blue lines and had rough edges. "In fact, I don't think this is cloth at all." He moved to a stainless-steel counter and slid the blade under a magnifying glass. "I think this is paper."

He looked up at Dustin. The tech's shocked expression must've mirrored Michael's own.

Knowing that a criminal investigation—and possibly a trial—was sure to follow, Michael said, "Make sure you get pictures of each stage," Michael said, although Dustin knew his job well enough.

"Will do, boss." A camera sat on the counter. Dustin took several photographs.

With tweezers, Michael carefully removed the sheet from the blade. The paper had been folded before being stabbed into Quinton's chest. He unfolded the page and laid it flat on the table. The fibers were dark with blood, but the ink was still visible.

"Holy crap," Dustin breathed. He held up the camera and snapped several pictures. "Does that say what I think it says?"

"It does." Michael stared at the bloody paper. He read the cryptic warning again and his hands went cold.

My victims never survive.

Chapter 12

Michael sat on the sofa in his office. Sage was to his left. Isaac Patton was also in the room, sitting in a chair that had been moved to the front of the desk. He'd concluded the autopsy of Quinton Yang less than an hour before. That was when he called both Sage and Isaac for a meeting. They needed to know what he'd learned.

Isaac, because Texas Law was still involved in the hunt for Decker Newcombe.

And Sage?

Well, his feelings for her were complex. Yet, he respected her enough to keep her appraised of the situation—because what happened to Quinton had to do with Josie.

"It was death by homicide," he said, speaking of Quinton. "The victim was stabbed five times and the knife was left in his chest with this." He handed a picture to Sage.

She looked down at the photo of the bloody note and shivered. "What does it mean?" she asked, handing the picture to Isaac.

"'My victims never survive,'" Isaac said repeating the words. "Is it some kind of warning?"

"I think it's that, along with a bit of pride in his work—if you want to call it that," he said.

Isaac handed him back the picture.

"Any idea who did this?" Sage asked.

"The killer wasn't careful about concealing evidence at all. The police found fingerprints and hair everywhere. My tech was able to pull a set of prints off the murder weapon. It was Decker Newcombe." He paused to let them absorb the truth—especially since the re-emergence of the serial killer wasn't the most shocking evidence. "In fact, the killer allowed Quinton to interview him for a podcast. The whole thing is on the victim's computer."

Isaac cursed.

"So, you think that Decker attacked Josie?" Sage asked.

"Actually," he said. "I don't."

Isaac gave a barking laugh. "You're kidding, right? A female is attacked and her body is dumped in the same area of Decker's killing spree. The next day, the man whose podcast was about Newcombe as the potential attacker of Josie Kruger is murdered. Then, Decker's prints happen to be on the murder weapon. You think it's all just a coincidence?"

Michael knew his theory was unorthodox. In fact, his outlandish idea was another reason he had Isaac and Sage with him now. The police weren't going to believe him, so Michael needed allies. "Just hear me

"One Minute" Survey

GET YOUR FREE BOOKS AND A FREE GIFT!

✓ Complete this Survey ✓ Return this survey

▼ DETACH AND MAIL CARD TODAY! ▼

1 Do you try to find time to read every day?
☐ YES ☐ NO

2 Do you prefer stories with suspenseful storylines?
☐ YES ☐ NO

3 Do you enjoy having books delivered to your home?
☐ YES ☐ NO

4 Do you find a Larger Print size easier on your eyes?
☐ YES ☐ NO

YES! I have completed the above "One Minute" Survey. Please send me my Free Books and a Free Mystery Gift (worth over $20 retail). I understand that I am under no obligation to buy anything, as explained on the back of this card.

☐ **Harlequin® Romantic Suspense** 240/340 CTI GRSD

☐ **Harlequin Intrigue® Larger-Print** 199/399 CTI GRSD

☐ **BOTH** 240/340 & 199/399 CTI GRSZ

FIRST NAME | LAST NAME

ADDRESS

APT.# | CITY

STATE/PROV. | ZIP/POSTAL CODE

EMAIL ❑ Please check this box if you would like to receive newsletters and promotional emails from Harlequin Enterprises ULC and its affiliates. You can unsubscribe anytime.

Your Privacy—Your information is being collected by Harlequin Enterprises ULC, operating as Harlequin Reader Service. For a complete summary of the information we collect, how we use this information and to whom it is disclosed, please visit our privacy notice located at https://corporate.harlequin.com/privacy-notice. From time to time we may also exchange your personal information with reputable third parties. If you wish to opt out of this sharing of your personal information, please visit www.readerservice.com/consumerschoice or call 1-800-873-8635. Notice to California Residents—Under California law, you have specific rights to control and access your data. For more information on these rights and how to exercise them, visit https:// corporate.harlequin.com/california-privacy.

HI/HRS-1123-OM_123ST

out. For a minute, let's forget about Quinton and only focus on Josie."

"It's a waste of time when we should be looking for Newcombe," Isaac grumbled. Folding his arms across his chest, he leaned back in his seat. The body language was easy to read. The security operative didn't like what Michael had to say.

Sage was a different story. "Go on," she urged.

"There're several things that bother me in assuming that Decker was the one who attacked Josie. First, the location is all wrong. Serial killers often have hunting grounds." He hooked the last two words with air quotes. "Places where they feel comfortable finding their victims or dumping them. It would make sense that the desert around Mercy was where he felt comfortable dumping the bodies." Now that Michael was verbalizing his thoughts, his mind was working overtime. "But why Josie? Why drive hours to a college campus to kidnap her and then hours back?"

"A college campus seems like a reasonable place to find victims," said Isaac. "Lots of parties. Students staying in different rooms. Could be a while before someone was considered missing."

It made sense to Michael, except… "There are a lot of other populations that are easier to lure into a car." Which brought up another puzzle piece that didn't quite fit. To Sage, he said, "You indicated that Josie's a responsible girl."

She replied, "She is."

"Then, she's not the type to get into a car with a man she doesn't know."

Sage shook her head. "No, she's not." She paused a beat. "What're you getting at?"

"We've all seen the campus video. Josie was walking to the library. A bus blocks the view and in ninety seconds, she's gone."

"What if Newcombe had a gun and threatened to shoot?" Isaac asked. "That'd compel her to get into the car."

"But on a busy street?" Michael asked. "It doesn't make sense for Decker to try to abduct someone when there are witnesses around."

Sage added, "I don't think Josie would meekly get into a car—even if someone pointed a firearm at her. The first thing she'd do is run and scream for help."

"That's what you'd like to think she'd do," said Isaac. He held up his hands. "I mean no disrespect to you or your daughter. Nobody actually knows how they'll react until they're in the situation."

"Isaac's right," said Michael. "But from Decker's point of view, kidnapping a random victim from a crowded place doesn't make sense. Which means two things to me. First, Josie wasn't a random victim, and second, she willingly got into the car with whoever assaulted her."

For a moment, nobody spoke.

Isaac cleared his throat. "Your thinking is solid. But we have to circle back to Quinton Yang and the fact that Decker's fingerprints were found on the murder weapon. The only link between Decker and Yang is the podcast about Josie. I hate to tell you this, but that link is pretty damn strong."

"I can't disagree with that, either," Michael said.

Sage reached for the photograph of the bloody note. "But what about this?" She held up the picture so they could all see the words.

My victims don't survive.

"Well, Quinton certainly didn't survive." Isaac glanced at Sage. "Sorry if I'm too blunt. I know the unvarnished truth makes people uncomfortable."

"I appreciate complete honesty. So, if we're being honest, Quinton might not have survived an attack by Decker, but Josie is still alive." With a sigh, she tossed the picture back to the sofa. "It's all a damned knot, isn't it? By pulling on one part of the thread, you snarl up another."

Michael leaned forward as adrenaline surged through his system. "What if that's what Decker's saying in this note? Josie's alive, because he wasn't the one who attacked her."

Before anyone could answer, the trilling of an incoming call filled the silent office.

Isaac said, "That's me," as he pulled a phone from his pants pocket. He glanced at the screen and continued. "It's Jason Jones with the FBI. I think he'd be interested in what you have to say, Michael."

Was he ready to share his thoughts with the FBI agent? Then again, maybe he was asking the wrong question. Could he keep his theory to himself when lives were at stake? The ringing continued.

"Go ahead," he said to Isaac. "I'll talk to him."

"Jason," Isaac said, answering the call. "I'm putting you on speaker phone. I'm with Michael O'Brien and Sage Sauter—she's Josie Kruger's mom."

Isaac pressed the speaker button and Jason's voice filled the room. "It's good that you're all together. I've got some news that concerns you both about where the podcaster got some of his information." Jason had Michael's attention. He looked at Sage and she lifted her brow. It seemed that the federal agent had her attention as well. Jason began. "Quinton made a call at three in the morning to his friend on the police force."

"Trevor Kane," said Michael. "He was able to identify the body." He paused. "Why's a late-night phone call remarkable? After all, both men were in their twenties and kept odd hours."

"It's more than the timing," said Jason. "It's also the place the call was made. Quinton Yang's phone was connected to the hospital's cell phone tower."

"Has anyone questioned Trevor to see what he knows?" Isaac asked.

"I brought him down to my office and he gave us a complete story. It seems that Quinton worked for a delivery service and had brought some food to the hospital. According to Officer Kane, his friend had a habit of listening in on other people's conversations—especially when they never thought they'd be overheard."

"Sneaky," said Sage, "but probably harmless."

"Most of the time, I'd agree with you. But Quinton was always looking for a story that he could turn into an episode of a podcast."

It all made sense to Michael and his gut filled with acid. He cursed. He'd been completely candid with Sage, but only because he assumed they were alone on the patio. "Last night, he overheard what I said about Decker being involved in Josie's attack."

"Not entirely," said Sage. "I'm almost positive you never mentioned her last name."

"That's where Officer Kane comes into the tale. It seems that Trevor asked around in the PD to get facts for his friend."

"What's going to happen to the police officer?" Isaac

asked. Michael knew that Isaac used to work for the SAPD. He imagined the security operative still cared what happened in his old department.

"There'll be some sort of investigation and then disciplinary action taken," said Jason. "But I don't know what kind."

His answer seemed to appease Isaac. He nodded slowly, though the agent was on the phone. "Good to hear."

Jason continued. "But there's more to worry about than just the fate of Officer Kane. If Decker went after Quinton Yang, we have to consider he might come after others associated with the case, including Michael and Sage."

Sage heard what the FBI agent had said. She might be a serial killer's next target. Truly, that thought chilled her soul. But if Decker went after either her or Michael, it meant only one thing. "He might come after Josie, too."

She bolted from the sofa. In two steps she was at the door. She pulled the handle open. The lab beyond was dark as a cave. She rushed forward and motion lights clicked on.

"Sage, wait." Michael reached for her arm and pulled her to a stop. "Where are you going?"

It was a stupid question and they both knew it. "I'm not leaving my daughter unprotected. Even the FBI thinks the killer might come after her."

"Come back to my office and see what Jason has to say. If I know him—and I do—he has a plan." He laced his fingers through hers and tugged. Sure, he was trying to draw her back into the office and the meeting, but Sage wanted Michael to pull her into his embrace.

Yet, she remained rooted to the floor. "No."

"Five minutes," he said. "Then, I'll take you up to recovery."

Sage knew she should be grateful for Michael's help but, she couldn't muster thankfulness for much of anything. "Two minutes," she said, "and you have yourself a deal."

They returned to the office.

Isaac stood, but he still held the phone. "Yeah," he said, speaking to the FBI agent. "That's them. Sage and Michael are back."

"You have two minutes." Sage knew full well that she was being contrary. The thing was, she didn't care a bit. "I need to see Josie and make sure she's safe."

"Security is our top priority. I'm going to assign a detail to watch over all three of you. There will be a police presence in the hospital for Josie. Michael will get a week off because he'll have to stay home. Which leaves us with where to place you, Sage."

"Me? I'll stay right here with Josie."

"That's not going to be possible," said Jason. "The hospital will be placed on lockdown until Decker's been arrested."

"Then, I don't know where I'm supposed to go. Because I sure as hell am not leaving here without my child."

"We can place you in a local hotel," said Isaac.

"Does that work?" Michael asked, holding out his hand.

She wanted to reach for him, but to what end? They

weren't kids anymore and they weren't in love. Keeping her arms by her side, she stepped toward the door.

"A hotel?" she echoed. It was the last place she wanted to wait, but she didn't have any choice. "That'll work."

"I'll be in touch with more details." Jason ended the call.

Isaac followed Michael and Sage from the office. Without speaking, they walked through the lab and out the door. In the hallway, Isaac said, "I'm going to contact Ryan Steele and let him know Decker's on the loose." Ryan used to manage all the money from Decker's murder-for-hire business. The two grew up together and Steele was as close to a friend as Newcombe ever had. All that changed when Ryan was given the chance to come clean. He'd spent a year undercover with Isaac to catch the killer. In return for his hard work, the FBI expunged his criminal record.

In a showdown with each other, Newcombe stabbed Ryan.

"If Newcombe has a hit list, Ryan's at the top," Michael said. "Best that he be warned."

For over a year, Ryan Steele and Isaac Patton lived and worked in Mercy. Yet, the whole time they'd only been laying a trap to catch the killer. It was all part of the Decker Newcombe lore that circulated through Mercy and all the towns nearby.

During the year that Ryan lived and worked in Mercy, Sage had seen him more than once. But the ploy to get Decker out of hiding had drawn a killer to her town. It was hard to like the guy who'd brought destruction to the place she lived.

"I liked Ryan," said Sage, "when I thought I knew who he was."

"What's that supposed to mean?" Isaac asked. Sage suspected he already knew what she meant.

She paused, not sure if he she wanted to answer Isaac's question. Then again, if she didn't speak up, who would? And if she didn't say anything now, when would she?

"Ryan turned that abandoned building next to the post office into a thriving business." As part of the trap to catch Decker, Ryan had been set up with two businesses to run—a bar and a tattoo parlor. The bar had been the local hangout and from all accounts, he was a good boss. "I understand that your ploy worked. But at what cost? You know that people died."

There was also the dead podcaster—another life, wasted. His young face flashed in her mind. Even in death, he grimaced in pain.

Then there was Josie.

Sage had to admit that if her daughter was attacked by the serial killer, luck alone was what kept her alive. But what of her future? Was it still as bright as before? Emotion caught in Sage's throat. Yet, when she spoke, her voice was clear. She glared at Isaac. "You were the one who brought this maniac into our lives."

Isaac had enough grace to look Sage in the eyes. "I am sorry for what happened in and around Mercy. Aside from apologizing, there's nothing else I can do."

"Yes," she said, her word the crack of a whip. "There is."

"Yeah? What's that?"

"The same thing I've told my daughter her whole life. You make a mess. You clean it up."

"This time, Decker won't get away." Isaac spoke with such conviction that Sage believed him.

"How many more people will he kill before he's caught?" Sage asked.

"It depends," said Isaac, answering her question with one of his own. "Are you willing to follow Jason's plan?"

"Point taken."

"I'm going to call Ryan now and will be in touch with you later. You both be careful," Isaac said before walking to the end of the hallway. The sound of his footfalls ricocheted off the walls. After turning a corner, he was lost from sight. Finally, even the sound of his steps faded to nothing.

Michael still stood at her side. Now that she'd opened the valve on her anger and let off some of her steam, Sage wasn't sure how she felt. "I let my temper get the better of me with your friend."

"Don't feel like you owe me an explanation. I doubt that Isaac or Jason realized how much collateral damage Decker would cause." He pointed down the hallway. "The stairs to the main floor are this way."

They walked down the corridor. Up one flight on a set of metal stairs. Down another hallway that ended at a bank of elevators. Michael pushed the call button.

"Seriously," she said with a sigh. "This place is a maze. It's a surprise that anybody finds their way around here."

"Eventually, you figure your way." The elevator doors slid open. Michael waited as Sage entered the car. He followed her in and pushed the button for the seventh floor.

The walkway on the seventh floor was a wall of windows that overlooked the parking lot below. It looked familiar. She'd been in this corridor before but couldn't recall how to get to surgical recovery. It didn't matter. Michael knew the way.

A plastic sign was affixed to the door.

Surgical Recovery. Employees Only.

An electronic pad was mounted to the wall. Michael swiped his ID over the sensor and the lock opened with a click. He pushed open the door and waited as she crossed the threshold. The area was the same as last night. The nurse's station sat in the middle and the patient's rooms radiated out in a circle, like the rays of a sun.

Michael's friend Lorraine looked up as they entered. She gave them a tired smile. "I heard there was some excitement earlier today. Something about the body of a podcaster being found." Lorraine held a tablet computer and set it on the desk. "I also heard that police officers are going to be stationed in my unit."

"Rumors travel fast in the hospital."

"Rumor, hell. The story was on the news."

Sage fretted that her daughter would become part of the media coverage. No. She wouldn't add another concern to her long list of worries. She asked, "How's Josie?"

Lorraine began, "We still have her in a medically induced coma. She's still intubated. It's going to take time for the swelling in her brain to go down. I've ordered another MRI in the morning. By then, we'll have a better idea of what we're dealing with."

"Can I see her again?"

"Go ahead. She's still in Room Eight," said Lorraine. Then to Michael, "I need a favor from you. A friend dropped off a copy of your book. Apparently, her brother is a big fan of your book, and his birthday is next week…"

Sage walked toward Room Eight. Michael's conversation with his friend faded with each step. She stopped at the doorway to Josie's room. A large bandage was still wrapped around her head. Her face was still covered with scrapes and bruises. Sage's heart both squeezed like a tight fist and filled with so much love that it hurt.

"Oh, honey," she said, moving closer.

That's when she noticed the silence. There was no whir from the breathing machine. The constant beep-beep-beep of her heart monitor was silent.

Josie lay on the bed without moving. Her chest neither rose nor fell.

Sage looked at the line of machines meant to keep her daughter alive. All the screens were dark. For the span of a heartbeat, Sage felt weightless. Then, her stomach dropped to her shoes. Sprinting from her daughter's bedside, she yelled, "Someone come quick! There's an emergency!"

Chapter 13

Michael rushed toward Sage. "What's going on?"

"Josie's not breathing." Her memories were fractured, and she could only examine one sliver at a time. "Her chest isn't rising and falling."

Lorraine stepped forward. "Your daughter's intubated, so a machine is doing all the breathing for her."

Sage pictured the medical equipment and their darkened screens. "All of the machines are off."

Lorraine's eyes went wide. "That's impossible."

Michael ran to Josie's room. The hospitalist followed. Sage stood at the door, her pulse racing.

"What in the hell happened?" Lorraine asked. "Why is every piece of equipment turned off? Why didn't an alarm sound at the nurses' station?"

"Right now, it doesn't matter." Michael pulled the tubing from Josie's throat. "Help me with CPR." He then shouted. "I need a trauma team in here. Stat."

Several nurses ran to Josie's bedside. The tiny room filled with people, jostling Sage from every direction. She felt as if she were caught in a riptide and being carried out to sea. She stepped out of the room. She wanted to hold her daughter's hand. But she also wanted to let the medical professionals do their job.

Behind her, she heard a hollow thud. Sage turned at the sound. A figure slipped behind the door leading to the stairwell.

She knew sabotage was possible for what happened to Josie's life support. Had the saboteur just snuck out through the back door?

Sage had only an instant to come up with a plan. Did she find someone to help? Or did she chase after the person on her own?

She glanced into Josie's room. Everyone in the unit was crowded around her bed. A handheld respirator covered Josie's nose and mouth. One nurse squeezed the bellows and counted. "One and two and three and four."

Another nurse pressed a stethoscope to Josie's arm. "I have a pulse."

Lorraine shone a penlight into Josie's eyes. "I have equal brain reflexes from both eyes. But she's got to get back on the breathing machine. How's it going, Doctor O'Brien?"

Michael knelt before a piece of medical equipment and pressed series of buttons. "It's not rebooting. I need a tech up here right away."

Sage hesitated a second before sprinting across the tile floor and pulling open the door. The walls of the stairwell were concrete. The stairs and the railing were metal. Steps headed both up and down. Holding her breath, she listened for the telltale sound of feet on the steps.

The stairwell was silent.

Had Sage mistaken what she'd seen? After all, she hadn't slept more than a few hours in two days. Was she so tired that she hallucinated?

No. She'd watched someone slip out of this door.

What did she know about the person? Not much.

They'd had on dark blue scrub pants, a white lab coat and a light blue surgical cap. She hadn't seen anything beyond their back as the door closed behind them.

The person could be any gender and any race. Sage could see them again and never know.

She wanted to curse, but she needed to think.

Did she go up or down?

If someone was trying to escape unnoticed, they'd go downstairs to the patio.

She followed, her footsteps clanging.

She passed the landing for the sixth floor. The fifth floor. On the fourth-floor landing, Sage stopped. Sweat snaked down her back and she wiped a sleeve across her brow. Maybe the person hadn't gone down at all. Maybe they went up to the next level. From there, they could blend in. They'd be just another medical employee out of thousands who worked at the hospital.

Now she needed to decide what to do next.

Well, that was an easy decision.

Sage had to go down—because she certainly wasn't climbing up all those steps. She moved slower this time. The rubber soles of her sneakers barely made a sound. She passed the third-floor landing and that's when she heard it. A door on the ground floor slammed.

Gripping the railing, Sage froze. Then, she began to

sprint down, down, down. She pushed the door open. The clouds from the afternoon had amassed into a storm.

It was early evening, not much past 6:00 p.m., if Sage had to guess. Yet, the storm turned the outside dark as night. The concrete patio was wet. Lights on tall poles shimmered in the puddles. Rain dripped from sun umbrellas that did little to keep the tables underneath dry.

Aside from the rain and the tables, the patio was empty. There had to be something she missed. Someone had to be out here and nearby. Lights from the cafeteria shone through the windows and cut wedges of light out of the gloom. She peered in one of the windows. The room was empty.

She had seen someone leaving the recovery unit. She had heard the stairwell door slam. She hadn't imagined it all. Then again, that's exactly what hospital security would say. Sage was a woman past forty, under extreme stress, who was functioning on almost no sleep. Of course, they'd think she was losing it a bit.

But she wasn't.

Water soaked her clothes. It filled her shoes. It dripped from her hair, her nose, her chin. She turned in a slow circle. A garbage can sat near the corner of the building. A flash of white caught her eye.

She moved to the bin. Caught in the receptacle's push door was a piece of cloth. Sage pulled the fabric loose. It was a lab coat.

The staccato of footfalls mixed with the patter of the rain. Sage didn't realize what she'd heard until it was too late. She started to turn at the same moment that someone gave a feral scream. The pole from an umbrella connected with her back and the air rushed from her lungs. She bent over and the umbrella pole slammed into the back of her skull. She dropped like a sack of bricks. Her head hit the concrete pad, and she saw a flash of white. Then her vision started to fade as blackness crept in from the edges. She could feel herself slipping down, down, down, until she was swallowed by the darkness.

Michael inhaled deeply, trying to slow his elevated pulse.

Lorraine raked her fingers through her hair. "It wasn't supposed to happen," she said. "There are safeguards in place to stop a complete system shutdown."

He knew she wasn't ready to see the obvious. "It wasn't a random act. It was deliberate. What's worse, whoever turned off Josie's breathing machine knew what they were doing." To keep Josie stable, a complete life support system had to be brought in from other parts of the hospital. He continued. "The interruption hadn't been meant to disrupt, but to kill."

Hospital security had been notified. A guard stood near the wall. A Taser hung from his utility belt and a mic head was attached to an epaulette on his shoulder. It was a start, but more needed to be done to keep Josie—and the rest of the hospital—safe.

"I need to grab Sage and make some calls." His words trailed off as he scanned the unit. The techs who'd restarted all of Josie's life support were leaving the area. The nurses had dispersed to other rooms to check on other patients.

He knew she couldn't stay in Josie's room. Maybe she'd been told to leave the unit entirely.

He checked his cell phone for messages. There were none. Sage wouldn't just wander off when there was a cadre of medical professionals trying to save her daughter's life. But where had she gone?

Michael stopped a nurse who was walking past. "Josie Kruger's mother was just here. Do you know where she went?"

The nurse said, "Sorry, Doctor O'Brien. I don't recall seeing her at all."

Dammit.

Michael turned to Lorraine. "I'm going to make some calls. If Sage comes back, tell her to reach out." While walking across the floor, Michael wasn't sure how to feel about Sage's disappearance. Concerned? Disappointed?

His stomach grumbled as he shouldered the door open. It was then that he realized he hadn't eaten since breakfast. It was after 6:00 p.m.

He turned at the next corner and the short hallway led to the corridor of windows. Leaning against the railing, he pulled up his contact app and found Sage's information. With the press of his thumb, he placed the call. The phone rang three times before being answered by voicemail. "You've reached Sage Sauter of the Double S Ranch. Leave a message and I'll call you back."

"It's Michael," he said. "Not sure where you went. We need to talk. Call me." He ended the call and stared at the screen. The back of his neck itched, like someone was watching him from behind. He turned. There was nobody there, except his reflection in the rain-streaked glass.

He placed another call. Isaac answered after the second ring. "Hey, you miss me?"

Michael ignored the joke. "Josie Kruger's breathing machine, along with her heart monitor, was disabled.

It's not an easy feat to override all the safety features in place, so it didn't happen by accident. Someone took her off life support. What's more, they knew what they were doing."

Isaac asked, "Do you think it's Decker?"

He had to admit, at least to himself, that it was a possibility. "How would he know how to override the system?"

"He's intelligent," said Isaac, "and adaptive. He could have taught himself what he'd need to know. C'mon, man, everything's out on the internet now."

Suddenly, Michael was exhausted. He was going on forty-eight hours without any sleep and almost eleven hours since he last ate. Now there was no telling when he'd get either some shuteye or a meal. "But why would he come here and try to kill Josie?"

"You were the one who discovered the note that had been stabbed into the podcaster's chest. *My victims don't survive.* It was a warning that he was going to finish the job he hadn't completed."

Michael had seen the meaning differently. "Or maybe he was pointing out that if he'd attacked Josie, he wouldn't have pitched her down a ravine in hopes that she would die."

He bit off his last word. The hallway in which he stood was empty. Who was to say that another podcaster wasn't listening at the corner? He exhaled. "When are the officers from SAPD expected?"

"I'd tell you that coordinating between agencies takes time. But I don't think you want to hear any excuses."

Michael worked at a hospital. He understood bureaucracy as well as anybody. "Just get the cops here and I'll be happy." He checked his phone for messages. There was nothing new. Where in the hell was Sage?

Leaning his elbows onto the rail. He looked out the windows. In the distance, the parking garage rose four stories high. Lights shone from tall lampposts. The rain was captured in the glow and made it look like the world was melting.

Isaac continued. "I'm going to tell Jason about what happened to Josie. If there's even a chance that Decker's involved, the FBI needs to know."

Closing his eyes, he pinched the bridge of his nose. It was in his mind's eye that the scene replayed itself. A hard ball of dread dropped into his middle, and he looked again. A person lay on the empty patio. Even from seven stories up, he could tell it was Sage. There was one thing he didn't know. Was she alive—or not?

His blood chilled in his veins and his breath caught in his throat. He started to run. The phone was still pressed to his ear. "Call the police. Tell them there's been another attack. The victim's on the patio by the cafeteria."

"A what? Who?"

Michael pushed open a door that led to a stairwell. "Just call," he said, running down the stairs. "It's Sage."

His phone beeped as the connection failed. He had to hope that Isaac heard him—and that he wasn't too late to save Sage.

Michael sat in a chair and watched Sage as she slept. The room was like most of the other patient rooms in the hospital. The bed, surrounded by a plastic and metal railing, sat in the middle of the small room. Light shone from behind a plastic grate in the ceiling. Another light shone down from the head of the bed. A single window looked out onto the parking garage.

In the hour since he'd spied Sage from the walkway, several things had happened. First, she'd been treated for her multiple injuries. She had seven contusions to her face, arms, and shoulders. One of her ribs was bruised, but not broken. She'd been knocked unconscious, but she didn't have a concussion. Despite her injuries, Sage was expected to recover fully.

Law enforcement had been notified about the sabotage to Josie's breathing machine and the attack on Sage. All parties—including Michael—assumed that the same person committed both crimes.

A lab coat was found at the scene. It had been left in the rain. He knew all too well that the elements could destroy evidence. Still, there might be something—a hair, a carpet fiber—to be found. The discovery of the lab coat meant that Michael had a job to do. It's just that he refused to leave Sage's bedside.

Dustin was at work and the lab tech was more than capable.

He brushed his thumb over the back of Sage's hand. "You'll be okay," he whispered. "Everything will turn out fine, you'll see."

But would it? Someone had tried to kill Josie twice. It was simply luck that Sage survived her attack. Michael didn't know who tried to kill Josie. But he did know that they wouldn't stop until she was dead.

Sage moaned softly. Her eyelids fluttered.

"Hey," he said. "How are you feeling?"

She swallowed. "My head hurts like hell. Can you turn down the lights?"

A long light shone above the bed. He flipped a switch turning it off. "Better?"

"Better," she echoed, before opening her eyes. "How'd I end up here?"

"I was on the phone with Isaac and saw you on the patio. You'd been knocked out. I told Isaac to call hospital security—which he did. I ran down to you. By the time I got there, whoever had attacked you was gone." He added quickly, "Hospital security is working with the San Antonio Police. They're scouring video from the hospital and searching for any evidence." Leaning forward, he rested his chin on the bed's railing. "We'll figure out who attacked you—and why."

She brushed her knuckles over his cheek. "I guess I need to thank you again."

He wanted to kiss the inside of her wrist. Instead, he leaned back in the chair. "I should get the doctor and have them check you out first. Then we can talk."

She reached for his hand. "You're a doctor."

His arm warmed at her touch. "Yeah, but I practice the wrong kind of medicine."

She tightened her grip. "Don't go. The last thing I remember was…" She paused and let her eyelids close. "There was a person in the recovery unit. I saw them sneaking into the back stairwell. Everyone was so busy with Josie, so I followed."

"And then?" he urged.

She opened her eyes, "I ended up in the hospital."

"To be fair, you started off in the hospital. It's just that now, you're a patient."

She chuckled at his small joke. "Ow," she winced, tucking an arm across her ribs. "Damn. Laughing hurts."

"I'll try not to be funny." He paused. "I need to get the doctor to come in here and give you a more thorough examination."

"What happened upstairs with Josie wasn't an accident."

Michael wasn't sure if she'd asked him a question or made a statement. Then again, it didn't matter. He shook his head. "It wasn't."

"Was it Decker Newcombe? Did he come after my baby again?"

That was the question everyone was asking. "What do you remember about the person who attacked you? Any kind of description can be helpful."

Sage squeezed her eyes shut. "I'm not sure. I mean, they jumped me from behind. I did see that the person wore scrubs." She paused. "They were taller than me. Maybe." Another pause. Opening her eyes, she met his gaze. "I know it's not a lot."

It wasn't. "I'm going to call Agent Jones and let him know what you told me. But first, I'm going to tell the doctor that you're awake." He rose to his feet and stepped toward the door. "I'll be right back."

"Michael, wait." Sage grimaced and pushed to sitting. "There's something else I remember."

He paused. "What?"

She said, "They screamed."

Michael drew his brows together and repeated her words. "They screamed."

"The person screamed before they attacked. They didn't grunt or curse or yell. It was a scream—and whoever made it sounded like a woman."

Chapter 14

At 1:00 a.m., Sage was released from the hospital. She couldn't have stayed any longer if she wanted. The entire complex was on lockdown. Nobody was allowed inside, unless they were a patient, the parent of a minor or a staff person who was scheduled to work. Security was increased throughout the whole facility. But thankfully, a police officer was assigned to guard Josie 24/7.

Despite offers from the San Antonio Police Department, the FBI, and Texas Law to provide her with a motel room and a guard outside, she'd decided to stay with Michael. In many ways, being at Michael's place made sense. If they were together, the police didn't have to bother with officers guarding them at different locations. But the real reason she went home with Michael was that she loathed the idea of being alone.

They arrived back at his apartment only minutes after leaving the hospital. A police cruiser was parked in front of his building. Another uniformed officer sat in the lobby. She knew that the building was well-guarded, but was it enough to keep them safe?

"I'm starving and I'm exhausted." Michael said once they were in his apartment. He dropped onto the sofa with a weary sigh. "I don't know if I want to eat or sleep first."

She was simply starving. "What kind of food do you have on hand?"

"I just got off the book tour, so I'm going to guess I've got a whole lot of nothing in the pantry and even less in the fridge."

She sat on the recliner. "Can I rummage through your kitchen?" she asked. "And see what I can come up with to fix?"

"I should be the one offering to make you something to eat," he said. "I can order something to be delivered. There's a good Thai restaurant that's open all night."

"There has to be something other than waiting for a delivery." She wandered into the kitchen. "A can of soup. Sandwich fixings."

"Right now, I'd be thrilled with a bowl of cereal and milk."

Sage opened the refrigerator. A meal that simple would certainly work. "Do you have either milk or cereal?" She scanned the shelves—they were empty save for a few items. Three different varieties of mustard. A large container of ketchup. Pickles in a jar. A six-pack of beer. It was like a parody of a bachelor's grocery list.

Oddly enough, he had a bag of baby carrots and a stalk of celery, held tight with a red band. The vegetables looked fresh. She grabbed both and held them up. "What's up with these?"

Michael shook his head. "It's Lorraine's idea of a joke. She thinks I need to eat healthier."

Sage returned the carrots and celery to the shelf in the refrigerator. Next, she opened the cupboard. There were two cans of tuna fish—no, make that one can of tuna and one can of chicken. There was also a bag of egg noodles and a box of crackers. Tapping her bottom lip, she knew she might be able to make this work. "Do you have any herbs or seasonings?"

"Seasonings?" He repeated the word like she'd spoken a brand-new language. "The cabinet to the left of the sink."

There, she found everything she needed. Sage assembled the ingredients on the counter. "Where do you keep your pots and pans?"

Michael rose from the sofa and came into the kitchen. He picked up the can of chicken. "What are you making?"

Sage couldn't help but smile. "Soup."

From a cabinet next to the stove, he found a soup pot. "Soup sounds great. What can I do to help?"

For a moment, she considered telling Michael to sit back and let her make him a meal. Instead, she said, "Grab a knife and cutting board. You can chop the vegetables for me."

She spent some time mixing bouillion, herbs, and spices, with water. She then set the pot on the stove and waited for the broth to steam. She added the can of chicken. Michael stood next to her. After everything that happened over the past day, Sage couldn't feel happy. But she had to admit that in this moment, she was at least content.

"How're you doing with the vegetables?"

He held up the cutting board. The ribs of celery were sliced, and the carrots were cubed. "How's this?"

"Looks perfect. Put those in the pot. We'll let everything boil for a bit. Then once the vegetables are tender, I'll add the noodles. After those are cooked, we'll have soup."

Using the knife's blade, he scraped the vegetables into the broth. "You make it sound so easy. I always thought that homemade chicken noodle soup took forever to cook."

Sage stirred the vegetables into the chicken broth. "Of course, soup is better if you make your own stock and let everything simmer all day. But sometimes you need something hot, healthy and quick." She fit the lid on the pot and set the burner at *simmer*. "When Josie was younger, this was one of her favorite meals." The memories of Josie at the kitchen table came at her fast, like a flip-book in her mind. Finally, she recalled the first time a twenty-year-old Josie set a bowl of soup in front of Sage. *How'd I do, Mom?* "I guess it still is..."

Was now the time to tell Michael the truth about Josie? Good God, she'd asked herself that question a hundred times in the past twenty-four hours. The indecision was starting to make her head hurt. Or maybe the headache came from being hit in the back of the skull with a pole.

Michael interrupted her thoughts. "I'd offer you a glass of wine or a beer. But after your attack, I don't know that alcohol is best."

"Water is fine," she said.

From one of his gleaming wooden cabinets, he found a glass. "Ice or no ice?"

"No ice," said Sage.

He filled her glass with water from a dispenser on the refrigerator's door. "Here you go."

She took the glass and sipped. Her legs ached. Her arms were sore. Her head throbbed with each beat of her heart, reminding her that she'd taken quite a beating. "We still need to let the soup cook. Mind if we sit down?"

Michael filled his own glass with water. "Just so long as you promise to wake me if I fall asleep."

She gave him an exaggerated eye roll before walking to the sofa. Sinking into the cushions, she admitted that over the years she'd convinced herself that she recalled everything about Michael. She knew how he smelled. The taste of his lips. She remembered the timbre of his voice and the way his hands looked on her thighs.

But there was so much more about him that she didn't know. "When did you get the corny sense of humor?"

Michael sat on the opposite side of the sofa. "It's always been there, but the exhaustion is making it worse."

"Ha-ha," she gave a fake laugh, before tossing a pillow in his direction. "Maybe you do need a nap."

He grabbed the pillow and tucked it behind his head. "The soup smells good. I bet you're a good mom."

"Now is the exhaustion making you sentimental?"

He shrugged. "Honest."

The one word hung in the air. Could Sage continue to lie about Josie's paternity? It was more than just telling Michael the truth. It was the daily struggle of living a lie. But she'd lied to more than the man who sat next to her. She'd lied to her daughter. Josie was her priority. She had to tell her daughter the truth first. Or maybe not...

"I'd like it if we could be honest with each other," she began, her mouth dry.

"Me, too." He took a sip of water and set the glass on the coffee table. "I need to ask you a question about that summer I worked in Mercy."

This is it. Placing her glass on the table, she turned to face Michael. She refused to fear the truth anymore. This was her chance to put down the burden she'd been carrying for twenty-three years—every year of Josie's life plus the time she was pregnant. "Go ahead," she said, "ask."

"When we were together, did you… Did we… The feelings we had for each other—those were real. Right?"

"Of course, my feelings for you were real." Her heartbeat thundered until her pulse echoed in her skull. "There's something I need to tell you about what happened that summer."

"You really don't need to say anything else." Guilt, a hard fist, slammed into her stomach and left her breathless. He seemed not to notice her wheezing and continued. "I wondered what I got wrong about us all those years ago. But there's something else I need to tell you…"

Now that was a twist. "What is it?"

He reached for her hand. She let him slip his fingers between hers.

"Your father came to see me at the clinic about a week before I left. He told me that you and Vance had always been a couple."

Had she heard him right? "Wait. Say that again?"

"You and Vance had always been a couple," he repeated.

"No, the other part."

"Your father came to see me..."

"And he told you that Vance and I were...?" Her father had always been controlling, but what he'd told Michael was a lie. She and Vance had always been friends, but there was never a romance. Her gut burned with indignation. "What else did he tell you?"

"That your ranch and the Kruger ranch shared a property line. To keep both businesses afloat, they needed to merge."

It all made complete sense. "You, being a gentleman, stepped aside so my family could keep the ranch."

"It was more than being a gentleman. I thought you loved Vance. I thought it was best to leave and not look back. That's the thing, Sage, I've never been able to see a future."

How different would her life be now if her father hadn't meddled?

"I'm here, now," she said.

"You are." He moved closer to her.

A thousand butterflies were let loose in her middle. It was a sensation she imagined she'd outgrown, along with everything else from her adolescence. Like braces. And acne. And writing bad poems.

But she was wrong.

"What are you thinking about right now?" he asked.

"About how much we've changed over the years."

"Oh yeah? I feel like the same guy."

"Your voice is deeper. Your shoulders are broader. You have some gray in your hair. You aren't as excitable. You're wiser and kinder. It works well on you."

"You haven't changed one bit," he said, tracing the back of her hand. "You were perfect twenty-three years ago. You're perfect today."

Leaning forward, he placed his lips on hers. The fluttering in her belly turned frantic and Sage knew she was at a crossroads. She wanted more of Michael—more of his kisses and his touch. At the same time, anything beyond their amicable partnership was a distraction that could be dangerous—or even deadly.

He wrapped his arm around her waist, and she didn't move away. She let him draw her to him, closer still, until their bodies were pressed together. He slipped his tongue into her mouth and Sage couldn't recall the last time she was properly kissed.

For a moment, she worried that she'd forgotten how. As Michael explored and tasted and savored her with his tongue, she remembered what it felt like to be loved and to have someone to love in return. She lay back on the sofa. Michael moved with her until his body covered hers.

She opened her thighs and he slid between them. It didn't matter that they were both fully dressed, she could tell that he was hard. That suited her just fine. Sage was already wet. He moved his mouth to her cheek, her neck, the lobe of her ear. "Oh, Sage," he whispered. "I've missed you. I've missed this. I've missed us."

"Michael," she said. "Touch me."

He traced her arm with his fingertips. Then, he moved to her stomach and reached inside her shirt. His touch scalded her flesh, but she didn't care about being burned. She wanted more. She kissed him again, deeper this time. Hungrier.

His touch moved higher, and he slipped his hand inside the cup of her bra. He rolled her nipple between finger and thumb. She cried out with pleasure and pain.

"Do you like that?" he asked, placing kisses on her shoulder.

"Yes," she gasped.

"What else do you like?"

After Vance left, she mostly ignored the part of herself that was sexual. The need to be held and to hold had weakened over the years, until it finally stopped altogether. Now she knew that her sexual nature hadn't exactly died—only hibernated.

With Michael, her libido was fully awake.

He kissed her again. "Sage, what else do you want?"

She met his gaze. What did she need from Michael? Then again, she knew. "Everything."

Michael pressed his mouth to Sage's palm. His kisses traveled from her hand to her wrist to her arm. At the nape of her neck, he nipped her with his teeth. She sucked in a deep breath.

Tell him, a voice inside her head whispered.

"Michael," she began.

He smothered her word with a kiss. As his tongue slipped into her mouth, she almost forgot what she needed to say.

Running her hand down his chest, she explored the muscles of his chest and abs. They were hard. A sprinkling of hair covered his pecs.

He lifted her shirt, exposing her abdomen.

"Oh, Sage." Placing a kiss on her side, he murmured. "Who did this to you?"

A bruise, already purple and blue wrapped around her middle. It was a reminder of what she wanted to forget. A killer was after her child. "I don't know," she said. "I wish I did."

Her pulse still raced, and she still craved more of

his touch. But the moment for passion had passed. She moved out from beneath Michael and sat up. Smoothing the hair back from her face, she tried to smile. After a lifetime of lying, she was proficient at pretending. "I better check on the soup."

After rising from the sofa, she walked to the kitchen. Her legs were weak with unmet desire, but she kept herself upright. At the stove, she removed the lid and a cloud of fragrant steam rolled out of the pot. Using the side of a spoon, she caught a carrot and sliced it on the metal rim. The flesh was tender. "Looks like the vegetables are cooked." Michael's kisses lingered on her lips with every word spoken.

The bag of egg noodles sat on the counter. She opened a corner and poured them into the pot. After giving the soup another quick stir, she replaced the lid. "Not much longer now."

Michael sat at the breakfast bar that separated the kitchen from the living room. "Should we talk about..." He hooked his thumb over his shoulder, pointing to the living room. "You know, the kiss?"

She shrugged. Pain shot up her side. "What do you want me to say? It was better than this morning. Still, we should ignore that it ever happened," she said, although Sage knew that she never would forget. "I don't expect anything from you. I can't promise you anything, either."

"Your life is complicated, I get it."

Did he?

Michael watched her, a smile on his face. "You look good at the stove."

She instinctively bristled. "Why? Because I'm a woman?" Even now, most ranches were still run by men. It had taken a lifetime of hard work and shrewd business dealings to be treated like an equal. "Isn't that sexist of you?"

He shook his head. "It's not a gender thing. You just look like you belong here, is all. In this place. That's all I meant."

Earlier, Sage had wondered about the type of people who lived in an apartment like this one. Hadn't she even tried to imagine herself in the kitchen. In the end, she'd cast a different woman in the role of mother and wife.

"Me?" she gave a short laugh. "I'm a Texas rancher through and through." She deepened her drawl with each word. "I need to see the horizon stretch out for miles and feel the dirt under my boots. Being in the city feels like being trapped in a box."

"Seems like a bleak assessment."

"It's not all bad. In Mercy, Josie wouldn't get the medical care she needs." Sage chewed on her bottom lip, not sure what else to say. "City life isn't for me, is all I'm saying." She turned to the stove and lifted the lid from the pot. "Soup's ready. Where do you keep the bowls?"

Michael rose from his seat and came into the kitchen. "You cooked. I can serve and clean up."

"Sounds fair." Turning off the burner, she leaned on the counter.

Michael ladled soup into two bowls. He set the bowls on plates and added a spoon to each. "Can you grab the crackers? We'll sit on the sofa to eat and watch some TV."

The moment felt completely normal. Guilt, a knife to the chest, stole her breath. She pressed her fingertips against the countertop. How could she be eating soup and watching a show while her child lay in a hospital bed fighting for her life? What's worse, a killer was on the loose and Josie was in their crosshairs. Her appetite was gone.

Michael placed his hand on hers. "You won't help anyone—especially Josie—by making yourself sick. You need to eat, and you need to rest."

She scoffed. "How'd you know what I was thinking?"

"I've spent my career working on murder cases. We all say we're looking for justice for the victims. Don't get me wrong, we are. But we're also looking for the truth so the families can find peace. At moments like this, it's hard to accept any peace that life offers."

She laced her fingers through his. "I'm not sure that I can."

He squeezed her hand. "It's okay if you try."

Sage wasn't sure if she believed him. Still, she reached for the box of crackers. "C'mon, let's eat before the food gets cold."

He lifted the soup from the counter. "This really does smell terrific."

She walked to the living room and sat on the end of the sofa. Michael set a plate, along with the bowl and spoon, in front of Sage before sitting at the opposite end. She ate a spoonful of soup and swallowed.

Honestly, it wasn't her best effort. At least, it was edible.

"This is great," said Michael. He'd already emptied half of his bowl.

Sage wasn't sure if he really was hungry or if he actually liked her cooking. Then again, she got the impression much of what he ate came from a delivery container. "Everything tastes better when it's made with love."

He looked up from his bowl. Their gazes met and held. So help her God, that fluttering started in her middle again.

"Love?" he echoed.

"When the cook cares about the recipe and the people they're feeding. That's what I meant." She took another spoonful of soup.

"I know what we can watch." Michael lifted a set of remote controls from the coffee table.

"Not the news." Although, there was a part of her that was interested in what the media was reporting.

"Not the news." He pressed several buttons and brought up a streaming service.

"What is it?" she asked, bringing another spoonful of soup to her lips.

"You'll see..." The prow of a large sailing ship cut through the waves.

"Is that the pirate movie we saw at the drive-in?"

"It's still one of my favorites." After shoving his plate and empty bowl to the middle of the table, Michael propped up his feet.

"Mine, too." Sure, the movie was funny, and exciting, and had a hell of a twist. But that wasn't why she liked the flick so much. Going to the drive-in was Sage's first date with Michael. At the time, he drove a sedan with faded blue paint. They shared popcorn and when he kissed her, he tasted of salt and butter.

"When Josie was about eight or nine years old, I bought the DVD. We watched the movie at least once a week for months. She dressed up like a pirate that year for Halloween." Each time mother and daughter watched the movie, Sage wanted to talk about her first date with Michael.

She never did.

How different would their lives be right now if Sage had told the truth?

Chapter 15

Michael woke to the sound of music. Before he opened his eyes, he knew that he'd fallen asleep in front of the TV. But this time was different from all the others. A set of feet rested on his lap. So help him, he was already hard. Sage stretched in her sleep. Her feet and ankles slid over his lap. Michael stifled a groan. Sure, his hard-on was just a natural response. But if he stayed, well, then he'd be a creep.

He lifted her feet and slipped off the sofa. Reaching for the remotes, he turned off the TV.

"Hey." Sage's voice was a husky whisper. If possible, his erection got harder.

He untucked his shirt and let the hem hang down. "Sorry. I didn't mean to wake you."

"What time is it?"

From where he stood, he could see the clock on the microwave. "Almost four-thirty."

She sat up. Giving a soft groan, she held her side.

"How're you feeling? Do you need something for the pain?" The doctors at the hospital had given Sage prescription meds for the discomfort.

She shook her head. "I'll be alright. I just need some rest."

He held out his hands to her. "Let me help you up."

She placed her palms in his. He pulled her to standing. Then, they were face to face. Sage's breasts, firm and round, were pressed against his chest. Adrenaline surged through his veins and his heart started to race. There was a connection between them that went beyond the merely physical.

Did she feel it, too?

His gaze met hers. Sage's eyes were wide. Her pulse fluttered at the base of her neck.

So, it wasn't just him. What did that mean for now? And in the future?

"God, you're beautiful," he whispered.

She dropped her gaze but gave a small smile. "I can't be much to look at right now. Although I don't think I'm much to look at on my best days."

Placing a finger under her chin, his titled her face to his. "You are always beautiful. You are strong and fierce. You are the Texas sun and the earth and the sky. I don't know what else to say…"

"You don't have to say anything. Just kiss me."

He placed his lips on hers. She sighed and he slipped his tongue into her mouth. She pressed her palms against his chest and his pulse began to race. He pulled her closer and she moaned.

"Is that painful?" he asked, his breath ragged. He needed to be careful with Sage.

She reached into his shirt. Her touch electrified his skin. "There's only one way you're going to hurt me and that's if you don't kiss me again."

He pressed his forehead into hers. Michael knew what he needed from Sage. Even after all these years, he wanted to take her again as his lover. The question was—what did she want?

He said, "You were attacked. Your daughter's in the hospital. I get that you've had an emotional upheaval. I don't want you to feel pressured now, or regret anything that happens later."

"Can you do me a favor?" She didn't wait for an answer. "Stop talking and take me."

It was all the invitation he needed. Michael wanted to be inside of Sage so badly that he could taste it. Sure, he wanted to take his time to savor and explore her body. But it had been years—hell, decades—since he'd wanted someone this much. He'd have better luck stopping the tide than curbing his lusts.

He reached into her jeans and into her panties. He slipped a finger inside of her. She was tight and already wet with want. He slid his finger over the top of her sex, and she mewed. The sound was too much. He laid her back on the sofa and knelt on the floor.

She slipped one leg out of her jeans. He unbuttoned his fly and spread Sage's thighs.

"Michael," she panted, "do you have protection? I'm not on the pill…"

He was almost inside of her and stopping now was a special kind of hell. But she was right. Thankfully, he did have a condom. He pulled his wallet from his back pocket and removed the foil packet. He tore it open and took out the translucent disk.

"You always keep one of those with you?" Sage asked, although he understood her real question. *How often are you getting laid?*

"Isaac gave me a box of condoms as a joke when I went on my book tour. He figured I'd meet someone I wanted to sleep with."

"Did you?"

He rolled the prophylactic down his length. "Not until now."

He entered Sage in one stroke. He knew that it wouldn't be long before he came. But he had to take care of Sage first. He slipped his hand between their bodies and found her clit again. She was swollen with a need that he was determined to satisfy.

"Oh, Michael." Her eyes were closed. Her mouth was open. She shuddered beneath his touch. He drove into her hard and continued to rub. "Oh, Michael," she cried out again.

He placed his lips on hers and she sighed into the kiss. Sage draped one leg over his shoulder. He dove into her deeper. Harder. Faster.

He knew he wouldn't be able to hold on much longer.

She squeezed his shoulder between her calf and thigh. Throwing her head back, she cried out with her orgasm. Michael kissed her neck and surrendered to the tide of pleasure. He came, his pulse throbbing through his whole body.

She held his face between her hands and kissed him once more. "That was great," she said.

"Yeah, great," he repeated. Being with Sage was more than great. In her arms, Michael discovered something he thought he'd lost a long time ago.

His ability to care for someone else.

* * *

Decker sat in a stolen car and stared at the apartment building from half a block away. The lights had been on in Dr. Michael O'Brien's unit just a minute earlier. What had kept the forensic pathologist up until after 3:45 in the morning?

A police cruiser was parked on the street. The front door was guarded by a doorman on the outside and another cop on the inside. It meant that the note he left with the podcaster had been found. It also meant that everyone was scared.

That was fine with him. The thing Decker wanted most of all was to be feared.

At a fast food restaurant, he'd walked away with a smart phone belonging to an old man who was there with his nagging adult son. The way he figured it, the old man would think he misplaced the phone and would say nothing to his son yet. It meant Decker could use the device without worry of being tracked for a day or two.

He used the phone to google online videos of Michael O'Brien speaking to crowds all over the country. At each of his stops, someone asked a question about Decker. For the most part, the doctor's answers were vague. *He couldn't really discuss an open investigation in detail,* blah, blah, blah.

But in Chicago, Michael was asked about Decker's childhood. Turns out, the doctor had a lot to say. Turning up the volume on the phone, he watched the video.

Michael stood in front of a lectern. "The case of Decker Newcombe is one of the most interesting in my career. It brings up the age-old question of nature versus nurture. Is a behavior inherited, like eye color? Or is it a product of an environment and family habits?

Just as children of smokers are twice as likely to start smoking by the age of twenty-one than the children of nonsmokers.

"Decker suffered from multiple childhood traumas that made him a prime candidate for a life of violent crime. Before he was born, Decker's father was sentenced to two consecutive life sentences for killing a bank teller during an armed robbery. It left Decker to be raised by his mother, a high-school dropout who spent much of her life working as a restaurant server. Often, his mother worked twelve to sixteen hours a day, leaving young Decker alone or in the care of others. As a boy, his mother had multiple romantic partners who were abusive to both mother and son.

"In school, Decker was disruptive in class and received poor grades. He was a bed-wetter until nine years old. At the age of seven, he was diagnosed with attention deficit disorder. According to his mother, he was never compliant with his treatment, even at such a young age.

"Hundreds of thousands of people have similarly difficult upbringings to Newcombe and very few of them become serial killers.

"What makes Decker Newcombe different?"

Tossing the phone onto the passenger seat, Decker glared out the window. He couldn't believe the doctor's audacity to find his mother. He also couldn't believe that she spoke about Decker's childhood. Then again, she wasn't much for loyalty.

Besides, he knew his mom would like Dr. Michael O'Brien. The guy was handsome, smart, charming. Decker could imagine his mother flirting and eager to impress—even if it meant the world would know that he used to piss the bed.

His face burned with something beyond rage.

It was an emotion he swore he'd never feel but now it was back.

Humiliation.

It was time to make the doctor pay.

The single lamp still illuminated the living room. Michael had gone to the bathroom—presumably to take care of the condom. Sage redressed and then sat on the sofa—languid, like a cat in the sun. She'd been divorced for a decade and had little romance in her life. She'd found Michael again but wasn't sure what their love-making meant. He was more than an itch that needed scratching.

On a very elemental level, reconnecting with Michael was a door into Sage's past. It brought up regrets, sure. In being with him, she couldn't help but wonder about her future as well.

Future? What kind of a mother was she to be worried about her future while her daughter was in the hospital? What's worse, she still hadn't told him about being Josie's father. She had to confess everything. Rising quickly to her feet, her vision exploded with white spots. The dots danced in front of her eyes and the floor seemed to tilt underfoot.

"Whoa." Michael stood on the other side of the room. He moved to her and gripped her elbow with his strong hand. "Are you okay?"

She started to sweat. "I stood up too quick and got a little lightheaded, I guess."

"It's okay now. I'm here to help."

She wanted to believe his words. It was going to turn out okay. Despite everything, Michael would stay around to help. Still, she knew it was too much to expect after one passionate session on the sofa.

Her vision cleared. Her legs were steady. She drew in a long breath. "I'm good now. Thanks."

"You sure? I'm letting go."

Sage gave a nod. "I'm fine, honestly."

He picked up her glass, half full of water, and handed it to her. "Drink this. You might be dehydrated, which isn't good."

She finished the water in a single swallow. "Better."

He took the glass and set it on the table. "Let's get you to bed. After you get some rest, you'll feel more like yourself."

"Maybe I should call the hospital and check in on Josie."

"If there are any changes to your daughter's condition, they'll call. Trust me, no news is a good thing. I also promise that she's getting the best medical care in the world. If anything happens, the doctors know what to do." He paused. "Let's get you ready for bed."

She knew he was right. But now, she had another interesting question to answer. Where was Sage supposed to sleep? In the spare room, like a guest? Or should she go to bed with Michael? After all, they'd just had sex. Yet, she could feel the lie between them. It was a wall that kept her from truly connecting emotionally with Michael.

She'd been silent for too long. "I can sleep on the sofa."

"I'm not going to lie, it's a great place for a nap. But

after everything you've been through, you need a comfortable mattress."

A comfortable mattress? Sage didn't even have one of those in her own bedroom. "Lead the way."

Michael led her to a short stretch of hallway that separated the master bedroom from the guest suite. "Take your pick. You can have the guest bed all to yourself or..." He nodded toward his room.

Michael slept in a king-size bed with a dark blue comforter. A large TV was affixed to the wall opposite the bed. A table sat beneath the TV and a dresser filled the adjacent wall. There were several pictures above the bed. Even in the dark, she could see enough to know they were photos of mountains and sky. Was Michael the photographer? Had he visited those locations?

There were so many questions she wanted to ask.

She knew that spending the night with Michael wasn't the best idea. Right now, she could walk away from the past twenty-four hours with only a little bit of heartache. But if she slept in his arms, well, that would be a different story.

Then again, there was more to risk than a few weeks of being sad or lonely. If she didn't take her chance with Michael now, there was a lot she would regret later. "Tonight." She slid her palm over his chest as she crossed the threshold. "I could use a little company."

He followed her into the room and closed the door. Sage was plunged into darkness, save for a seam of light around the jamb.

Without being able to see anything, her other senses became keener. The slow exhale of Michael's breath danced along her flesh. The pressure of his fingertips on her wrist sent a shiver of desire down her spine. His lips on her neck left her trembling.

"Michael," she whispered, her voice loud in the silent room. "Make love to me."

He held her hand and led her to the bed. "There's so much I want to do to you."

She lay back on the mattress, her knees resting on the edge and her feet dangling toward the floor. Michael hovered over her and placed his lips on hers. She slipped her tongue inside his mouth, hungry for the pleasure that only he could bring.

He found the waistband of her jeans. After unfastening the button, he pulled down the zipper. "Lift your hips." His words mingled with the kiss.

She pressed her back into the mattress and lifted her pelvis. He pulled down her jeans and her panties. After working them both over her feet, he dropped her clothes to the floor. Sliding between her naked thighs, he pressed his lips to her ear. "Scoot back and open your knees."

She did what he asked. Her eyes had adjusted to the dim room. She could see Michael's form kneeling between her legs. But she didn't want to watch. Sight dulled all her other senses. Relaxing into the mattress, she let her eyelids close.

He kissed her calf, her knee, her thigh. Then, he kissed her sex. It was a slow and sultry kiss. She was still sensitive from their earlier lovemaking and a jolt of pleasure shot through her body. "Oh, Michael," she moaned.

He slid a finger inside of her, Sage feared she might shatter into a million pieces. Then again, she was already broken. Was it through Michael that she could repair all the damage to her life? To her soul?

He continued to kiss her sex and explore her body. A spark of passion grew into a flame. He continued to touch her and taste her. The flame became an inferno, consuming her with white-hot ecstasy.

Holding tight to Michael's shoulders, she cried out with her orgasm.

As her breath settled back in her chest, the only thing left of Sage was ash and dust. "You are magnificent," Michael said, kissing her stomach. He pulled down the cup of her bra and rolled his tongue over her nipple.

Right now, Sage felt pretty damn magnificent. But she couldn't just lay on the bed and let Michael take complete control. Reaching for the front of his jeans she worked open the button at the fly. She slipped her hands inside his boxers. He was hard and smooth; steel wrapped in silk. After catching a bead of moisture from the head, she worked her hand up and down his length.

He hissed. "Damn, that feels good. But you have to stop, baby. Or I'm going to lose it."

She wanted to give him pleasure, like somehow it would make up for the years of keeping her secret. Kissing him deeply, she whispered, "That's the whole point."

"Oh, Sage." He kissed her back.

"Now you need to take off your pants."

He stood and kicked off his shoes. After, he pulled down his pants and removed his underwear. Next, he stripped out of his shirt. Michael stood naked in front of her.

True, the lights were off, but she could tell that he was well-built. His pecs were defined and covered with a sprinkling of hair that led down the middle of tight abs and then lower. She slipped her hand up and down his length. Then, she took him in her mouth.

He gripped her shoulders and she winced.

"Oh, Sage. I'm so sorry. I didn't mean to… I forgot… We don't have to do this."

She lay back on the mattress. The small voice in her mind whispered, *You have to tell him the truth.* She shoved it aside, desperately, needing him. "Come here," she said, "and take me."

This time, she didn't have to ask him to wear a condom. Michael kept a box of condoms in his nightstand. He opened the rubber and rolled it down his length. Without another word, he knelt between her knees and slid inside of Sage. She closed her eyes and let the sensations fill her.

Wrapping her legs around his waist, she hooked her ankles across his back. "Harder, Michael. Deeper."

Maybe he could drive all the thoughts from her mind.

He kissed her and complied.

She gripped the covers, as she rose out of her body and exploded among the stars. Her heartbeat raced as she sank back to the earth. A sheen of sweat covered Michael's brow and with a low growl, he came.

She kissed him again. Slowly. Deliberately.

He draped an arm over Sage and pulled her to him, "That was phenomenal." His words washed over her hair.

"It was," she agreed.

It'd been too long since she'd been held by a man. But Michael wasn't just a random guy—he was the father of her child. He was the one she dreamt of at night and thought of during the day. She'd never forgotten him. The truth was, she never would.

After kissing the back of his hand, she said, "You're phenomenal."

"Not to argue," he said, his voice slow. "But I think that you're the fantastic one."

She smiled but said nothing. Sage liked the idea of being fantastic—at least for Michael.

Laying in his arms, she tried let her breathing match his. A long inhale followed by a slow exhale. But her mind kept moving. Had she made a mistake in making Michael her lover again? Certainly, there was more to their intimacy than simply sex.

Yet, she hadn't been able to give herself to him fully. *It was the damned lie.* Now was the time to tell him the truth. To do anything less would truly be wrong.

Rolling to her stomach, she gazed at him. His eyes were closed. His breath was slow and steady.

Asleep? Already?

They'd only finished making love a few minutes earlier.

Then again, he hadn't slept for more than a few hours in almost two days. She imagined that he was exhausted. Laying her head on his chest, the soft cadence of his heart lulled her toward sleep.

Snuggling into his arms, Sage knew that couldn't change her past. But she did have control of what happened next in her life. If she told Michael the truth would that make a place for him in her future?

Chapter 16

Michael woke in the same bed he'd used for years—in the same room he'd slept in for nearly a decade. Yet, everything was different. Sage was asleep on the pillow next to his. It didn't take much thinking for Michael to figure out why he'd never married.

Sure, he had his standard line that he'd fallen in love once and it didn't take. It was also true that he wanted to avoid the soul-crushing heartbreak that came when a great love unraveled. But there was more. Sage really was the only woman for him. He'd spent a lifetime thinking that she'd betrayed him with Vance.

While in reality, she'd married a friend to ease her own broken heart.

It wasn't exactly a fairy tale, but he hoped he'd get another chance at happily ever after.

Her phone sat on a charging stand on his bedside table. The screen lit up a moment before it began to ring. He recognized the number. Chest tight, he reached for the device.

Blinking, Sage sat up "Is that my phone? What time is it?"

It was 5:47 a.m. He handed her the cell phone. "It's Lorraine. She's calling from her personal phone." He wasn't sure what his friend was going to tell Sage, but he knew it wasn't going to be good.

Sage swiped the call open before turning on the speaker function. "Hello?" Her voice came out as a croak.

"This is Lorraine Espinoza. I'm sorry to call you so early, but we have an issue. Josie's not able to process all the meds she's been on. I just got her most recent set of labs." She paused. "Her kidneys are shutting down."

"What does that mean?" Sage asked. Michael reached for Sage's hand, and she gripped his fingers. "Can you do dialysis or something?"

"I think it's best if you come down to the hospital and we can talk about Josie's options in person."

"I'll be there in a minute," she said before ending the call. She turned to him, her eyes wide with fear and concern. "What's all this mean?"

As a physician, Michael knew there were thousands of different scenarios—some would be more serious than others. "Right now, I don't want to give you a guess."

Rising slowly from the bed, she picked up her discarded jeans from the floor. "I'll go to the hospital and see what's happening. Once I know, I'll call you."

Michael was also on his feet. "I'm coming with you, Sage. That is, unless you don't want me to."

"Are you sure? You've done so much to help already..."

"I want to help now. Always." He knew this wasn't the time to tell her how he felt about her. About how he'd always felt. He dressed quickly. "As long as you want me, I'll be at your side."

"I appreciate that." She tried to smile, but her eyes watered. "What am I going to do if Josie doesn't make it? Michael, she's the center of my life. Everything I do—everything I've done—it's all for Josie."

During his career, he'd met with grieving families more times than he cared to remember. But this was different. Whatever happened to Josie would affect him profoundly and personally. True, he didn't know Sage's daughter at all. But he knew Sage. What was important to her was important to him. "Your daughter knows that you love her. You've been strong for her for years. She's going to need your strength now more than ever."

"I do try to be strong, but it's exhausting to do this all on my own."

He reached for her hand. "You aren't alone. Not anymore."

"Michael, I..." She shook her head. "Never mind, let's go. Your friend is waiting for me. For us."

Us. He liked the sound of that.

They finished getting ready and left his apartment without saying a word. His car was parked in front of the building. The police cruiser was still at the curb and when he pulled onto the road, it followed. His place was only minutes from the hospital and at this time of the morning, he was able to find a physician's spot near the front doors.

As they walked toward the employee entrance, he sent Lorraine a quick text.

With Josie's mom. Where are you?

She sent an instant reply.

Meet me at my office.

They had to take two elevators and walk down several corridors before making it to the office wing of the hospital. A nameplate was affixed to the door. Lorrain Espinoza, MD.

Michael gave a sharp knock.

Lorraine's voice came from inside the room. "Come in."

Michael turned the handle and pulled the door open. He let Sage cross the threshold and he followed.

Lorraine sat behind her desk. She stood as they entered. "Thanks for coming so early," she said, as if she hadn't sent an emergency summons. There were two blue chairs on the opposite side of the desk. She gestured to them. "Please, make yourselves comfortable."

Sage clutched her purse to her chest and dropped into a chair. "You said there was a problem with Josie's kidneys. Aside from dialysis, what are our options?"

Michael stood behind Sage and placed his hands on her shoulders. He wanted to offer her support. To show her that he had her back—literally. But he also knew that none of Josie's options were going to be good or easy. What's more, he couldn't afford to have Sage read the concern on his face.

"For starters, dialysis isn't really an option. The damage to her kidneys happened quickly and is severe."

Lorraine pulled out a sheet of paper from a file. "There's only one option. A transplant."

"A transplant?" Sage echoed.

Lorraine continued, "There's another complication. It looks like Josie's blood type is AB negative, which makes finding a donor difficult." She continued. "A relative is the best choice."

Sage looked over her shoulder at Michael. Her complexion was ashen. He knew she needed time to process the information. He also knew that Josie's condition was dire, and time wasn't a luxury they had. "What's your blood type?" Lorraine asked.

She swallowed. "I'm O positive."

"Does Josie have any siblings?" Lorraine asked. "They might be a match to donate their kidney."

Sage shook her head. "She's an only child."

There was only one option. Michael dropped into the chair next to Sage and reached for her hand. "Her father's out of the country. Most likely he's a blood type match for a transplant." He turned to Sage. "Can you get in touch with Vance?"

She stared at him, a tear leaked from the corner of her eye. Wiping it away with the heel of her hand, she shook her head. "Getting in touch with Vance won't help. I'm so sorry…"

"Don't apologize," he said. "It doesn't matter what happened between you and your ex-husband. He needs to get here now. As her father, he's the most likely candidate for a transplant."

"That's just it." She reached for his hand and held tight. His fingertips throbbed with the loss of circulation. "Vance isn't Josie's biological father, Michael. You are."

* * *

Michael stared at Sage. For a moment, he thought he'd misunderstood her words.

That's just it. Vance isn't Josie's biological father, Michael. You are.

But he'd heard her right and what she said filled with cold fury. "You had over twenty years to tell me about my child—and you didn't. Hell, you *lied*."

She still held his hand. Her touch burned his flesh, and he shook off her palm.

She said, "I wanted to tell you the minute I saw you. But Josie's my daughter and she's an adult. I needed to tell her first. I owed her."

"What about me? You didn't think you owed me anything?"

"I wanted to tell you. I tried, but the time was never right."

He definitely wasn't going to accept that excuse. "In more than twenty years, you've never found a moment to tell me I have a child." His voice shook with rage. Sure, he was furious with Sage, but he was angry with himself, too. Michael should have asked her—point blank—about Josie's paternity. Instead, he was too damned busy falling in love with her all over again.

Like he'd been sucker punched, the muscles in his gut clenched.

She said, "I tried to get in touch with you when I found out. But the people with the Peace Corps said nobody was able to get a message in those first few months unless it was an emergency. If I waited to get in touch with you, my father would've found out about the baby and disowned me. Besides, we'd broken up before you left. I wasn't even sure if you'd want to hear from me again. And if you did, I didn't know what you'd think about the baby. What was I supposed to do? Then Vance offered a solution of marriage." She seemed to run out of steam. "I wasn't even sure that you'd want the baby, anyway."

"But you never thought to let me know…"

"I thought about it, sure."

He glanced at Lorraine. For her part, his friend looked as if she wanted to be anywhere other than her own office. "Maybe I should give you two a minute alone." She rose to her feet.

"Don't worry about it." He stood as well. "Call the operating room and get Josie ready. I'll do it."

"You'll do what?" Sage asked, her voice was a sad mixture of confusion and hope. The tone would've caught him in the feels—that was, if he had any feelings at all.

"My blood type is AB negative. I'm Josie's father. The risk of her rejecting my kidney is low. I'll donate for the transplant."

"Oh, Michael. Thank you." Sage stood and tears filled her eyes.

"I'm going to make some calls," said Lorraine, moving to the door. "A nurse will get you prepped for surgery, Michael."

Once they were alone, neither of them spoke. There was so much he wanted to say, but the words didn't come.

"I am sorry," she began. "I was young and dumb and scared. I knew I wanted to give my daughter a good life and Vance offered us that opportunity."

In a way, he understood her predicament. What's

worse, he knew why she made her choices. He didn't blame her. But at the same time, he did.

"Say something," she urged.

"You said that you'd do anything to give your daughter a good life. She's *our* daughter. Don't forget."

"I've never forgotten." Her voice was a whisper. She looked up at him. Their gazes met and held. In that moment, his heart began to race and betrayed Michael and his hurt. "Michael, thank you for doing this for Josie. After the surgery we can talk..."

He shook his head, cutting off her words. He recalled when Sage had refused his help on the case. In that moment, he thought about walking away. Despite his better judgment, he had stayed. It did no good to curse his bad choice now. Still, it didn't mean that he had to keep making the same bad decisions. "After the surgery." His words tasted like flint. "You and I are done."

The surgery took four hours. With Decker Newcombe at-large, the hospital was still on lockdown, which meant no visitors. An exception was made for Sage, and she sat in an empty waiting room.

A coffeemaker sat on a counter. Aside from a variety of single-serve coffees, there were juices in a small fridge and individual crackers in a basket. Over the hours, Sage had helped herself to two cups of coffee, a juice and several packages of crackers. A TV hung on the wall. The channel was set to home improvement shows. She watched the programming without seeing anything.

There was so much to think about—to worry about. First and foremost was Josie. Kidney failure was not something she'd expected. What other issues might arise? Once she was released, how long would it take for Josie to recover? Sage didn't care about her own life, but what kind of future could her daughter expect?

What about Michael? How was he? Was their newfound love really over before it began?

"Sage?"

She startled at the mention of her name and looked up. Lorraine stood in the doorway. "I wanted to let you know that Josie's out of surgery. It'll take a few hours—or maybe a day—for the new kidney to start functioning. But it looks like everything was successful."

She slumped in her seat, exhausted and grateful. Still, she wasn't ready to let go of her concern. "What about all her other injuries? The head wound. Her cuts and the bruising around her neck."

"To be honest, if Josie had tolerated the medications better, I'd have kept her in a coma for another day or so. But she didn't, so when she comes out of anesthesia, she'll be awake. The other injuries are healing on their own."

"Awake." Sage was on her feet. "Can I see her?"

"I'll let you wait in recovery with Josie. It shouldn't be long now."

Sage's chest filled with so much gratitude that it hurt. "Thank you." But she had more questions. "And Michael? How is he?"

"He did well in surgery. It takes about two months to fully recover from being a kidney donor. He'll be in the hospital for a week before going home. After another week or so, he'll feel up to getting around. You should expect the same time frame with Josie."

"How is he now? Is he awake? Can I see him?"

Lorraine looked at the floor for a moment, before

leveling her gaze at Sage. "It's obvious that you and he have a past. I'm not passing judgment on anyone. Nor am I taking sides. But Michael left specific instructions that you aren't allowed to see him or know anything about his recovery." His words were a slap in the face. It was a shock and left her ears buzzing. Lorraine continued, "I'm sorry."

"I'm sorry, too." Sorry didn't begin to cover the despair that filled her. She knew he was mad and hurt. Maybe she'd get a chance to speak to him once he calmed down…

Who in the hell was Sage kidding? Nobody, other than herself. It had been foolish to hope for a future, especially since their past was based on a lie. "If he changes his mind…"

Lorraine finished her sentence. "I'll let you know the minute he does."

Sage sat at Josie's bedside and held her daughter's hand as she slept. It was only a matter of time before she woke from the anesthesia since the surgery had ended nearly an hour ago.

She'd used the time to update Mooky Cafferty on Josie's prognosis and check in with the foreman on her ranch. There was no news from the local investigation and still no results from the DNA samples taken at the crime scene. The wait was excruciating. But not all the news was bad. The ranch was being run well, even without her help.

It left her with time to focus on Josie. Watching her daughter's chest rise and fall with each breath, Sage was thankful for the person who'd made her a mother. All the same, she couldn't keep her thoughts from wandering to Michael. She lied to him about an important truth. With that lie, she'd destroyed any chance they had of a life together.

Now all she could hope for was a chance to apologize.

Josie stirred in her sleep. Sage rubbed the back of her daughter's hand with her thumb.

"Mom?" Josie croaked without opening her eyes. "Is that you?"

Sage kissed Josie's palm. She let her tears fall onto the hospital blanket. "It's me, honey. I'm here."

Josie swallowed. "My throat hurts badly. My head hurts worse. Where am I? What happened?"

"You're in the hospital. You were injured." A call button was attached to the bed by a thick wire. Sage pressed the outline of a nurse's cap. "What do you remember?"

Blinking, Josie opened her eyes. She stared at Sage. "Remember?" she echoed. "Nothing."

Sage was certain the police would need to talk to her daughter. "It's okay if you don't remember anything right now." She stood as a nurse in green scrubs entered the room. Two doctors and another nurse followed. The small room was crowded. "I'm going to let you get an examination and I'll be right outside." She paused. "I love you."

"I love you, too." And then, she said. "Corrin."

Sage stopped. "What about her?"

Josie's eyes were closed again.

"Honey, what did you want to say about Corrin?"

Eyes still shut, Josie said, "I don't remember."

"Do you want me to call her?" Sage asked. "She's worried about you. All the girls in the sorority are."

"Yeah, call her."

One of the doctors said, "Excuse me, ma'am. I need to get your daughter's heart rate."

Sage moved through the crowd of people who surrounded Josie. Standing outside the room, she couldn't help but smile. True, Josie had a long road to travel, but she'd made the most important climb of all. Her phone was in her pocket. She took it out and pulled up the contact for Josie's roommate, Corrin.

The call was answered after the third ring. "Hello?" Corrin was breathless. "Ms. Sauter, is that you?"

"Hi, Corrin. I wanted to share the good news. Josie's awake."

"Oh, really? She is? That is good news. What has she said? Does she remember anything?"

"She just woke up a minute ago. Right now, she doesn't even remember why she's in the hospital. She did ask me to call you, though."

"Oh, she did? That's sweet."

Sage wasn't sure what kind of reaction she expected from Corrin. But she at least thought the young woman would be enthusiastic. "Honey, are you okay?"

"I am. You woke me from a nap and everything just seems so surreal. It's like I'm still dreaming or something." She exhaled. "I'm so, so, so happy that Josie's awake. Can she have visitors? Everyone in the sorority will want to see her."

"Right now, the hospital is on lockdown."

"That's okay, we'll send flowers." Corrin continued. "Thanks for letting me know that Josie's awake. That's really good news. Will you keep me updated?"

"I will," said Sage, finally happy to hear a friendly

voice. "We might get to go home in a couple of weeks. It all depends on how she heals."

"Two weeks. That's amazing. Thanks for the update."

Sage ended the call as a nurse exited the room. "Are you Josie's mom?" the young man asked. "You can come back in and sit with your daughter. We've been ordered to let the FBI know when she wakes up. An Agent Jones is on the way."

Sage hurried back to the room. Josie looked up as she entered. "Mom. You have to tell me what happened. The doctor just said the FBI wants to speak with me. How was I hurt?"

Honestly, she wasn't sure what to do or say next. Since Josie remembered nothing of the attack, learning what happened would be a shock. All the same, she couldn't lie to her child—not about this, at least.

Chapter 17

Sage settled into the chair and took Josie's hand in her own. It seemed like yesterday that Josie's hand was so small. Now, her fingers were longer than Sage's. What was she supposed to say about the terrifying night when a maniac attacked Josie and left her for dead?

She tried to swallow but her mouth was dry. "You were more than just hurt, honey." She rubbed her thumb across the back of Josie's hand. "You were taken from campus and attacked. Whoever attacked you dumped your body near Mercy. It was luck that Sheriff Cafferty found you when he did."

Tears welled in Josie's eyes. "I don't remember any of that..."

"What's the last thing you do recall?" she asked.

"I remember eating lunch on campus." Josie screwed her eyes shut as if searching for the memories was painful. "I had a group project and we all met at the student union."

"What day was that?" Sage asked.

Josie's eyes sprung open. "What day is it now?"

The sound of shoe leather slapping against the tiled hallway stopped their conversation. Sage turned as three people—two males and one female—entered the room. They all wore dark suits and crisp white shirts. Without being told, she knew the FBI had arrived.

Lorraine was also with them.

The man in the front was clean-shaven and had short blond hair. He held up a small leather wallet, which contained the FBI badge and his picture on an ID card. "Ms. Sauter, my name is Jason Jones, I'm the Supervisory Special Agent from the San Antonio office. We'd like to speak to your daughter."

Sage recognized his voice from the phone call in Michael's office. She stood. "It's nice to finally meet you in person."

"You as well." Jason continued, "These are my colleagues, Special Agents Ramirez and Castaldo."

Sage wasn't sure who was who, but she nodded at both.

Turning to Josie, Jason continued. "I know you've had a heck of a few days, but I'd like to talk to you a bit about what you remember."

"I was just telling my mom that I don't remember anything after lunch on Tuesday. And what *is* today?"

"It's Thursday. Late evening," said Sage.

"That can't be…" Josie slurred her words. Her eyes drifted closed. Within seconds, she was breathing deeply.

Lorraine said, "It's not uncommon when a patient has

a head trauma to lose memories. Most of the time they come back within days. Occasionally, it takes weeks."

"What happens if the memories don't resurface?" Jason asked.

Exhaling, Lorraine said, "There are a few things we can try. First, there are some medications we can use…"

"If there are meds Josie can take, why wait days or even weeks? She's the best witness to her own attack. We need to know what happened and we need to know now." Jason poked the air with his finger as he spoke.

"The patient just had a kidney transplant because her body wasn't processing medications and she went into renal failure. I'm not pumping her full of different meds just to help you with a case," said Lorraine.

"When will we know if her kidneys are functioning properly?"

"Six months." Lorraine rocked her hand from side to side. "Give or take a few weeks."

"Six months?" Jason's face started to turn red. "That's unacceptable."

Sage had dealt with men who bullied their way through life. It started with her father. So, she definitely wasn't going to let Supervisory Special Agent Jones push her around. "I know you want to find out who attacked Josie and why," said Sage. "I do, too. I'm not going to risk my daughter's health. I'll call you when she's stronger and can stay awake long enough to answer a few questions. Until then…"

Jason seemed to know he was beat. He removed two business cards from the inside pocket of his suit jacket. He handed one to Sage. He gave the other to Lorraine. "We're still waiting on the results of the DNA tests. Hopefully, we'll have something soon. When that happens, I'll reach out. Until then, call me if anything changes or if Josie says something important."

Sage looked at the card before tucking it into the back pocket of her jeans. "Will do."

"I'd like to keep security tight while Josie recovers in the hospital. We'll have to address security at your ranch, too."

The Double S was home. Sage always felt safe there—but she knew the truth. They were isolated on their plot of land. "I'll contact Isaac with Texas Law and see what he recommends."

"Sounds like a good plan." Jason gave a nod and walked out of the room.

The other agents left as well, but Lorraine stayed. "How're you holding up?"

"I'm relieved that Josie's conscious. She seems okay—tired. But she's definitely the same old Josie."

"Fatigue is to be expected, but it's good to know that her personality seems to be unchanged. Over the next few days, we'll run some tests and that will give us a baseline." Lorraine continued. "If you need anything else, tell the nurses. They'll get in touch."

Sage wanted to ask about Michael. But the doctor had already been clear that she couldn't share any information. Still, Lorraine was Michael's friend. "All of my stuff is at Michael's place." Now there was the question of where Sage could stay. After all, there was still a killer on the loose.

Lorraine must've realized the predicament, too. "I'll make arrangements for you to stay here with Josie. Michael gave me his apartment key when he went on the book tour. I'll grab your belongings."

"Thanks," said Sage. Now, there really wasn't anything else to say. "Truly, thanks for everything."

The doctor left. Sage returned to the chair at her daughter's bedside. While watching her daughter sleep, she couldn't help but wonder about Michael. Where was he? Was he thinking about her, too?

Michael woke in a small hospital bed. An IV was taped to the inside of his arm. The tube tethered him to a bag that hung from a pole and dripped clear liquid into his veins. He looked around the room. A nurse stood at the end of the bed and scanned his chart.

"Water," he croaked.

"Doctor O'Brien," she said. "You're awake." She lifted a large plastic cup. Placing a straw to his lips, she let him take a sip.

Just getting a drink left him exhausted and he sank into the pillows. "Thanks."

"Doctor Espinoza wanted to know when you woke up." The nurse pressed her fingers onto the inside of his wrist, checking his pulse. "I'll call her now, if that's okay with you."

Michael felt as if he were floating on a cloud—a side effect from the anesthesia, no doubt. Still, the sensation was fairly pleasant. "Sure," he said. "Why not?"

The nurse left the room, and Lorraine seemed to appear from out of nowhere.

"How're you feeling?" she asked. "Looks like you're still a little groggy."

Had Michael fallen back asleep? He supposed that he had. "How'd the surgery go? Did the kidney take?"

"Josie's doing fine so far. She's awake. Her labs look good."

"Did you say she's awake? What does she remember from the attack?"

She chuckled. "After a major surgery, you're allowed some time off from forensic pathology."

The fatigue melted away and Michael's mind was clear. "You know what they say—doctors make the worst patients. You have to tell me what she's said."

"Right now, Josie doesn't remember anything about her attack." Lorraine slipped the earbuds of her stethoscope in place and pressed the chest piece to his sternum. She listened for a moment before hooking the tube around her neck. "Like I told the FBI agents, it's not uncommon to suffer from short-term amnesia with head trauma. Before you go asking, I'm not giving her any meds to clear up her memory."

"I should hope not. That's my kidney in there." He tried to laugh but it hurt too damn much. "So, what's Josie like?"

Lorraine shrugged. "She seems like a nice kid. You could meet her, you know."

Michael shook his head. "Not now."

"I can tell that you and Sage have quite the history and I don't want to get involved..."

"Then don't," he snapped, cutting her off. He inhaled. Exhaled. "Sorry for being short with you, but there's nothing between me and Sage—not anymore." He paused. "I think some of her stuff is still at my place..."

Lorraine said, "She mentioned that to me. I'm going use your spare key to get her things, unless that's going to be a problem."

So, Sage wanted her things out of Michael's apartment as much as he wanted her gone. Hell, after what he said, he didn't blame her for wanting to be rid of him again. "Not a problem," he said.

"I'm going to let you rest."

"Thanks for stopping by to check on me."

Lorraine left and the room was quiet. The silence gave him enough room to think. Had he been wrong to cut Sage out of his life completely—especially when he'd just started caring about her again?

Or maybe that was the problem. If he didn't allow himself to care, then he never would've gotten hurt. It had worked for Michael for forty-six years. He never should have let his feelings get involved.

Decker had driven for hours to find the right place and the right person. In Central Texas, he found a small town. A park and the county courthouse stood in the middle of the business district. Then like arteries off a heart, quiet streets ran out in all directions. The police station was located in a brick building that was five miles to the south.

He parked under a large tree at the end of a dead-end road and sank down in the driver's seat. If anyone glanced at the car, they'd assume it was empty.

She was the perfect victim—a woman who lived alone. She resided in a one-level house with two cats. A large window faced the street and allowed him a perfect view of the living room. He watched as she moved back and forth from the living room to an adjacent room at the back of the house. She had short, dark hair, glasses, and wore a floral t-shirt. Decker guessed she was in her late forties or early fifties. Never married, divorced or widowed? He couldn't tell.

On the wall of her living room were school portraits

of a boy and a girl. Framed pictures showed the two children year by year from kindergarten to high school graduation. The smiling faces were illuminated by three lamps that sat on side tables. A TV stood on a stand. At 6:00 p.m., the woman watched the news while she ate dinner. Then, she watched a string of police procedural shows and played with her cats. During that time, she talked on the phone twice. At 10:15 p.m., after watching the local weather forecast, she turned off the TV and left the living room.

A light came on at the back of the house. Five minutes later, even that was turned off. The house was dark. The woman was presumably in bed. It was time for Decker to go to work.

He slipped from the car, careful not to make any sound. Running quietly and quickly across the street, he slipped into the shadows that surrounded the house. He rounded the corner to the back of the property, where he couldn't be spotted from the street. The backyard was large, and a line of trees separated the woman's property from that of her rear neighbor and gave her privacy. Decker smiled to himself. He really had found the perfect location.

Keeping low next to the exterior wall, Decker moved to the first window. He peered inside. A shade was drawn, covering the glass completely. He assumed it was the woman's bedroom and made a mental note. There were two more windows along the back of the house and a single door.

He peered into the next window. It was an office. He pushed on the pane. It didn't budge. He moved to the next window and looked inside. It was a small bathroom—toilet, tub/shower, sink and vanity. He pushed on the glass, and the frame moved.

Bingo.

Honestly, it amazed him that the woman had survived this long. Like many people, she opened the window to vent out the steam when showering. Also like many, she closed the window but never bothered to engage the latch.

Then again, a locked window wouldn't have deterred Decker. Yet, to simply open the window made his job so easy he almost felt bad for what he was about to do next.

Using a steak knife he'd stolen from a restaurant, he sliced through the screen and peeled it back from the glass. Holding the knife between his teeth, he pushed the window open and hefted himself inside. He landed on the balls of his feet, not making a sound.

The house smelled of lavender and something else. It was an earthy scent. Patchouli, maybe?

A set of shades was pulled up at the top of the window. Using his knife, he cut off a length of cord. He held onto the shade as it unraveled to the floor. Decker wrapped the loose ends of cord around each palm. In his left hand, he also held the knife. He crept down the hallway, careful not to make a sound. The last thing he wanted was for the woman to know he was in the house and have time to react.

Using the toe of his shoe, he opened the bedroom door slowly.

There was a single window on the back wall. Enough light filtered around the shades that he could clearly make out everything in the room. The dresser. The chest of drawers with a mirror. A treadmill, with clothes hanging off the handrail, stood in a corner. The bed sat in the middle of the room. The woman was curled under the covers, completely still.

He glanced in the mirror on the chest of drawers and saw her reflection. Her eyes were open and full of terror. Her fear was his power. He smiled.

"I know you're awake. This isn't a nightmare and the only way for you to survive is if you do exactly as I say." Sure, the last bit was a lie. But it always worked to keep people calm. It shocked him that folks actually thought they could reason with someone who'd broken into their house and meant to do them harm. "Nod your head if you understand what I said to you."

The woman's head moved on the pillow. "I understand." Her voice was small and timid. Then, she asked, "What do you want? I don't have much money, but you can have it all, if you leave."

Throwing back his head, Decker laughed. "I'm the one in control. Who are you to think you can negotiate with me?" He didn't wait for her to respond. Decker launched himself across the room. He knelt on the bed and looped the cord around her soft neck, pulling the frayed ends together. She bucked and heaved on the mattress, clawing at the garotte at her throat. He pulled tighter and the stench of piss filled the small room. Somewhere in the house, one of the cats howled, but they weren't loud enough to alert the neighbors.

Then, the woman stopped struggling. Her eyes were wide, and tears streamed down her face. Yet, she made no noise, not even a wheezing for air. The end was near. He pulled harder on the cord. "After this," he said, whispering in her ear. "Everyone in the world will know your name. People will come from miles around to lay flowers at your door. Too bad you won't be around to enjoy it."

The woman gave one final gasp. Then she died.

All her weight rested on the rope. He loosened his grip, the pressure from the strands were imprinted on his flesh. The woman slumped to the bed and Decker shook feeling back into his hands.

He reached for her wrist and felt for a pulse. Her skin was still warm, but blood no longer pumped in her veins. He wrapped the corpse in a blanket that smelled of urine.

Now he had everything he needed to bring terror to this town.

Chapter 18

Two weeks later

Sage held a pile of papers in her hand. Standing next to her daughter's hospital bed, she read the instructions for Josie's home care. Lorraine used a pen to point as she explained the rules for discharge from the hospital.

She said, "We've made arrangements for a home health nurse to come by every day to see Josie and change her dressings as needed. A physical therapist will visit three times a week. After a month, we'll assess progress and adjust the frequency of visits. It can be trying to have people in and out of your house all the time, but you understand why we need to keep up a level of care."

"I don't care if someone else lives with us. I'm just excited that Josie's recovered enough to go home. You've been a great doctor and everyone on the staff is so nice, but I'm ready to get out of here." Her daughter sat on the edge of the bed and Sage glanced down. "What about you? You ready to get home?"

"Everyone here is the best, but I just want to sleep in my own bed."

Lorraine slipped the pen into the breast pocket of her lab coat. "So, I heard you're a biology major with plans for med school," she said to Josie. "After all this time in the hospital, you still want to be a doctor?"

"To be honest, I want to be a doctor now more than ever." Josie was dressed in a Texas Midland State University sweatshirt and gray sweatpants. Her hair had been completely shaved and now her scalp was covered with reddish-gold stubble. A large pink scar was still visible. As soon as her hair grew back, even that would be hidden. Would it be like that for her emotional scars as well? Hidden but always present? Josie continued. "If it weren't for you and all the other people at San Antonio Medical Center, I wouldn't have survived. I feel like I've been given a second chance at life. I need to make that count for something."

Lorraine nodded her head, "Then, I wish you all the best of luck. Do you have any questions before I sign these discharge papers?" She looked at Josie and Sage both.

Sage had about a million things she wanted to know. Starting with, would Josie fully recover? When could she go back to school? Finally, she wanted to know if Michael had even asked about her at all.

No. She swore she wouldn't worry about him—not when Josie needed her undivided attention. "I'm sure we'll have lots of questions once we get home. I promise not to bother you too much."

"I have a question," said Josie. "What about my memories?" Even after two weeks of therapy, the night of the attack is still a blank page.

"Be gentle with yourself," said Lorraine. "The memories will come back, possibly when you aren't prepared. What you recall will be traumatic, so make sure you ask for help."

Sage stroked her daughter's cheek. "I'm always here for you and we'll get through this together." True, she understood that her daughter wanted to know what happened—to fill in that missing piece of the puzzle. As a mom, Sage was just as happy to have Josie free of the trauma of her attack.

It didn't seem like much of a mystery what happened. Since that fateful night, Decker Newcombe had been linked to several murders in Central Texas. The police were searching for him. For now, he seemed to be done with Mercy and Josie was forgotten.

It didn't mean that Sage wasn't worried about the killer. She was. Arrangements had been made at the ranch. Texas Law had put in new security cameras. The ranch hands were armed and taught how to correctly use firearms—even though they knew already. Mooky had promised increased police patrols.

Lorraine asked, "Have you talked to Agent Jones recently?"

She'd spoken to the FBI agent several times in the past two weeks. "We're supposed to contact him as soon as we get home."

"Alright, then. We have everything we need." An orderly pushing a wheelchair entered the room. "Looks like you're ready. I'll say goodbye now." The doctor stepped from the room.

Sage watched her go. Sure, she'd promised herself not to ask about Michael. Yet, the need to know was strong. "Hold on, honey. I want to ask Lorraine one last thing." She jogged after the physician. "Hi."

Lorraine turned. "Did you forget something?"

She hesitated. "How is he?"

The doctor gave her a small smile. "I can't tell you anything about his condition, you know that."

"I know you can't tell me anything about Michael medically. But that's not what I'm asking. How is he? Has he said anything to you? Is he still mad?" She had several other questions but stopped there.

"More than being a patient at the hospital, he's also my friend. I won't betray his confidence."

"I get it," she said. "You're a loyal person." Sage couldn't help it. Her eyes started to burn with tears she refused to cry.

Lorraine pointed behind Sage. She looked over her shoulder. Josie was settled into a wheelchair and the orderly had pushed her out into the hallway. "Looks like you really are ready to go. I hope you take care of yourself, Sage."

"Sincerely, thanks for everything." There was nothing left for her to say or do. She turned back to her daughter. Her chest ached. It was filled with both hope and regret. Wiping her eyes with her sleeve, she asked, "Are you ready?"

Josie sighed. "Did you call Corrin and let her know I'm on my way home?"

"There's been so much going on." She dug through her purse, looking for her phone. "I forgot."

"That's okay. I'll call her once we get on the road."

"The truck's parked outside. Let's go."

Within minutes, Josie was settled into the passenger seat and Sage was behind the wheel. She pulled out of the parking lot, glancing once in the rearview mirror at the hospital. For the past two weeks, the massive building had been Sage's home and refuge. Within those walls, Josie's life had been saved. There was more. Sage had rekindled an old love and lost it again.

At some point, she'd have to tell Josie about her real father. She glanced at her daughter, who already snored quietly in her seat. She had a long drive ahead of her and could use a momentary distraction—especially if it meant keeping her word to Josie. Using the controls on her steering wheel, she brought up Corrin's number and placed the call.

"Hello?" Corrin answered before the first ring stopped.

"Hi. It's Ms. Sauter. I just wanted to let you know, Josie's been released from the hospital and we're on our way home."

"I thought you were going to call me before you left," said Corrin, her tone sharp.

Sage wasn't in the mood to take crap from a college kid. "There's a lot happening right now. Josie asked that I call beforehand, but honestly, I forgot. You know now."

"You're right. I'm sorry for being rude. It's just that Josie and I have been so close for so long that it's hard to hear things after the fact. Ya know?"

Sage wasn't sure that she did know, but she was willing to forgive Corrin. After all, everyone had been under a lot of stress. "Don't worry. Besides, you're the first person I'm calling." Sage realized that she should also contact Mooky and the ranch's foreman to let them know she was on her way home.

"Thanks for thinking of me first. Can I talk to Josie?"

Sage glanced at the passenger seat. "Sorry, she's asleep. If she wakes up, we'll call back."

"Okay. Thanks." Corrin paused. "How is she?"

"Tired, obviously. She won't be back this semester. Fingers crossed she'll be able to attend classes after the break."

"I've got my fingers crossed, too. Hey, what about her memory? Can she remember anything at all? When we chatted last, she said it still hadn't come back."

"Still nothing," said Sage. On the road ahead, taillights glowed red. A traffic jam. Just one more thing to dislike about being in a city. "There's some kind of snarl on the highway. I've got to get back to driving. I'm sure Josie will call you in the next few days."

"Okay, thanks for reaching out." Corrin ended the call.

Sage gently slowed the car as the traffic in front of her came to a stop. She realized that life really was a strange journey and she didn't know what would come next.

Since coming home from the hospital several days earlier, Michael had done next to nothing.

No, that wasn't true.

He'd spent hours thinking of Sage. He dreamt of her when he slept. Lying in bed, he stared at the pillow she used the one night they'd spent together.

Now their time together seemed like a forgotten dream.

His incision had healed, and he hadn't needed prescription pain meds for almost a week. He needed something to keep his mind occupied and wanted to go back to work. The hospital had placed him on leave for a full six weeks, so that wasn't an option. Even if he couldn't go back to the hospital, he could still make a few calls. Rolling to his side, he grabbed his phone from the nightstand and opened the contact app. He scrolled through the names. Lorraine. Isaac. Sage.

Just seeing her name brought it all back, the passion and the deceit. Or maybe deceit was too strong a word. True, she had lied to him. In a way, he understood why she'd kept everything a secret.

Had he been too harsh?

Eventually, he'd reach out to Sage—maybe in a week, or a month, or a year. He wanted to get to know Josie. Heck, he had money set aside. He could pay for med school. It wouldn't make up for all the years he missed, but he could at least help with her future.

So, yeah, he'd call Sage. Just not right now.

He called Lorraine instead. She answered the call after the second ring. "Hey," she said, brightly. "How's my favorite patient?"

"Tired. Bored," he said. "And tired of being bored."

"You're resting. Recuperating. Give your body time to heal now and you'll be back at work sooner."

She was right, he knew. Still, he hadn't called for any medical advice. "How's Sage? How's Josie?"

"You know I can't discuss a patient with you, unless there's a medical reason." After he donated his kidney, Josie's case had been assigned to another forensic pathologist.

"Sage isn't your patient," he said.

Lorraine exhaled loudly. "She asked about you before she left. She wanted to know how you were doing."

Shock slammed into his middle. Pain radiated outward. Maybe he wasn't as healed as he thought. "She left?"

"Josie was discharged about an hour ago."

"Where'd they go?"

"Home."

"Home?" he echoed. Decker was still at-large. "How can that be? They won't be safe…"

"If it makes you feel better, I overheard her chatting with your friend, Isaac. It seems like she hired him to set up a security protocol for the ranch."

So, Sage left and everyone knew—except him, that is. The bed seemed to spin, and he sat up. Raking his fingers through his hair, he sighed. His gut churned with anger, frustration and emotions he refused to feel. She'd left town without saying goodbye. Then again, he hadn't given Sage many options to contact him. Maybe her leaving was all for the best. Finally, he could truly move on with his life.

"Thanks for everything, Lorraine." Even his throat was sore, and it hurt to talk. "I'll let you go."

"I feel like I should say something. Have words of comfort for you."

The thing was, Michael was beyond comforting. "Really, I'm okay. Or I will be."

"Do you want me to stop by on my way home? I can bring you dinner."

He wasn't hungry before. Now the thought of food turned his stomach. "You get home to your kids. I'll order delivery later."

"I'll call you soon," she said. "And don't forget to eat."

He ended the call and stared at his phone. Did he call Sage now? Lorraine said she left the hospital an hour earlier. That meant she was somewhere between San Antonio and the ranch near Mercy. Sure, there was a lot he wouldn't say while she was driving—and presumably with Josie in the car. He could make a quick call. Then he'd say what? Honestly, he wasn't sure.

Until he knew, he wouldn't call. Rising from the bed, he moved slowly to the living room. There, he powered up his laptop and opened his email. The first message in his inbox was automatically generated. Test results/ Kruger, Josie.

So, the analysis on the hair and fibers had finally come back. The case was no longer his. Still, he wanted—no, make that—needed to know what happened and who attacked his child.

The truth was, no matter how angry he might be at Sage for keeping them apart, for hiding the truth, he cared about her safety. *Their safety.* Maybe…maybe they did need to talk. About the past. About how to handle things in the moment. About the future…if they even had one.

Huffing out a frustrated breath, he opened the email. There were three files attached to the message.

He opened the first document.

The dark red fibers that were found on Josie's clothes were consistent with carpeting often used in automobile manufacturing. The analysis was accompanied by a list of more than fifty cars that used the same type and color of rugs.

The evidence wasn't helpful on its own. If one of the many cars listed could be connected to Decker, it would be another link in the chain of evidence.

The second document outlined the DNA analysis of

cells taken from under Josie's nails. He read the findings once. Then he read them again.

The DNA was that of an unknown female.

Unknown female?

It made no sense.

But there was something else—something from the night that Josie's life support had been disconnected. Hadn't Sage mentioned that the person who attacked her on the patio sounded female?

Could they be the same person?

He returned his attention to the last document. Over eighty hairs had been found on Josie's clothing. At the time, it'd seemed like an inordinately high number to find. He recalled that moment in his lab when he'd shown Sage the two separate hairs.

The red one belonged to Josie. The blond hair, she had said, presumably came from her roommate, Corrin. *They're always wearing each other's clothes.*

In the moment, the fact that Josie had red hair—just like everyone else in his family—had piqued his interest. Because of that, he hadn't questioned the rest of the evidence. Now he wondered if he'd missed a clue.

He read the report. Just like he expected, several of the hairs found belonged to the victim. The rest were from an unknown person. Which meant there was no evidence linking Decker to Josie's attack.

But Michael did have a suspect.

His phone sat on the coffee table. He reached for it and placed a call. Isaac answered after the second ring. "Michael." His tone was jovial. "Good to hear from you, man. How're you feeling?"

He ignored all geniality and asked, "What do you know about Josie Kruger's roommate? Her name is Corrin Akers." He recalled the smiling picture of the young woman from the composite photo. "I think she might be involved in the attack."

"I don't know much of anything, but give me a minute to open the case file." Isaac was now all business. "I've got information on her here. Corrin Akers is a twenty-one-year-old college student, majoring in nursing. But I gotta ask, what's her motivation for hurting Josie?"

All this time, it'd been like staring into the fog. Sure, they could see elements. But the truth had been obscured and now, the haze was lifting. A third-year nursing student would know how to disable a breathing machine. Josie was kidnapped next to campus, and she'd certainly get in her roommate's car. He answered Isaac's question. "Could be that she was jealous of Josie and her boyfriend's relationship. Or maybe she was simply jealous of Josie." He paused a beat. "Can you find out if she owns a car? Then again, as a college student, any vehicle she drives might not be registered in her name."

For a moment, Isaac said nothing. In the background, he could hear the clicking of a keyboard. "It looks like she's got a car registered with the school."

"Can you tell me the make and model?" His pulse began to climb.

Isaac cursed. "It's not listed on the file. You still haven't told me why you think Corrin is involved."

"I just saw the analysis report from Josie's crime scene. None of Decker's DNA was found. Skin cells from an unknown female were found under Josie's fingernails. Out of the eighty-plus hairs found at the scene, none belonged to Decker either."

"Let me guess," said Isaac. "The hairs that were

found are going to belong to Josie or the same unknown female."

Michael knew that the hairs and tissue from the unknown female would be compared to make sure they came from the same person, but it would be days before they had the results. "One thing we do know is that Decker wasn't at the crime scene. He never interacted with the victim." With Josie. With his daughter.

From the beginning, he hadn't liked the theory that Decker Newcombe was involved. Now he knew why. "There are two different criminals at work. One is Decker—and the other one wants us to think he's involved."

Isaac cursed. "Do you have any idea who attacked Josie?"

"Call it a gut feeling with enough circumstantial evidence to order more testing. But until we have proof..." He paused a beat. "Keep your phone close. I'll be back in touch." He ended the call.

Michael found the business card for Bernadette Hayes, the campus police chief at TMSU, and placed a call. As the phone began to ring, he checked the time. It was 6:02 p.m. He hoped the chief was still at work.

She answered after the third ring. "This is Chief Hayes."

"Chief, it's Michael O'Brien, forensic pathologist with San Antonio Medical Center. I need you to speak to one of your students." It was then that he noticed road noise in the background. "Corrin Akers."

"You caught me on my way home," said the police chief. "I can reach out to her in the morning."

"The morning will be too late," said Michael. "You need to bring her in to your office now." Unless Corrin gave her DNA willingly, he'd need a subpoena. That would take time. Since Sage and Josie were on their way home, Corrin needed to be in custody—at least until she was ruled out as a suspect.

The police chief gave a weary sigh. "Well, Doctor. It seems like you're in luck. I'm right by the sorority house." The road noise stopped, leaving only the purr of an idling engine. "Before I bring in one of my students, I need to know why you're asking me to have her detained."

"I need her DNA to rule her out as a suspect in the attempted murder of Josie Kruger."

For a moment, Chief Hayes said nothing. "You think she had something to do with what happened? I thought the FBI was searching for that serial killer, Decker Newcombe."

"Right now, there's no evidence connecting Decker to the crime scene. There is evidence that an unknown female was Josie's attacker. I have reason to believe it was Corrin…"

"Hold up," said the Chief. "I'm walking to the house now." In the background Michael could hear the ringing of a doorbell.

"Police Chief Hayes." The voice was that of a female. Since Michael had visited the sorority house before, he imagined that it was one of the students who was assigned to watch the door. "What can we do for you this evening?"

"I need to speak to Corrin Akers."

"Sure. I'll go get her. Come inside."

After a moment, the chief was back on the phone. "Doctor O'Brien, did you hear that?"

"I did. Thanks." He looked at his phone and watched

the time slip by for a minute. And then, a minute more. "You still there?"

"I am," said Bernadette. "And I'm still waiting."

"Chief Hayes." It was the same young woman from before. "I'm sorry. She was here earlier but she's not in her room now."

The police chief's voice was filled with alarm. "What do you mean she's not in her room?"

The student answered, "Just what I said. She's not here, which is strange because she said she was going upstairs to study for some big test and that we wouldn't see her."

"Thanks for your time," said the police chief, speaking to the girl at the door. Then, she spoke to Michael. "I need to get off this call and figure out where Corrin went."

"Hold up a minute." He paused. "Do you know what kind of car Corrin drives? She registered a vehicle on campus."

"Give me one minute. I can access that through my phone." It took only a few seconds before she was back on the line. Corrin registered an eight-year-old sedan with campus police. She gave him a make and model.

It was one of the vehicles on his list with matching carpet fibers. Corrin wasn't simply missing—she was gone. Michael bet he knew where she was going. "Call the FBI office in San Antonio and speak to SSA Jones. Tell him to put out an all-points bulletin for Corrin and her car. She's wanted in connection with the attack on Josie Kruger. Got it?"

"If I'm calling the FBI, what are you going to do?"

"I'm going to warn Josie and her mother, Sage."

He ended the call and pulled up his contact list. He found Sage's name and called.

The phone was answered with an automated message. *The caller you are trying to reach does not have service at this time. Please leave a message or try your call again.*

He bit back a curse. "Sage, it's me. Call me as soon as you get this message. And don't trust Corrin Akers. If she contacts you, call the police. I think she had something to do with the attack on Josie… Call me as soon as you can."

He ended the call and pulled the personal number for the sheriff in Mercy. He placed the call. It was answered by the same automated message.

Dammit. "Mooky, it's Michael O'Brien. We need to talk. Call me."

After ending the call, he rose to his feet. A dull ache radiated from his side. If he couldn't reach Sage by phone, then he'd have to warn her in person.

Chapter 19

It was dark by the time Sage got home. Even then, she could tell that her employees had done a good job during her absence. The horses were in the barn. Chickens were in the coop. The porch lights were on, giving the front of the farmhouse a warm glow. Sage parked her car near the front door and gave a contented sigh.

Josie stirred and opened her eyes. “Home,” she said, her voice was still hoarse with sleep. “I’m so happy to be back.”

“Let’s get you settled inside.” After turning off the engine, she slipped out of the driver’s side and rounded to the passenger door. There, she helped her daughter out of the truck. Holding her around the waist, Sage took on Josie’s weight. “You can lean on me as much as you need, honey. I’ve got you.”

“I’ve known that my whole life, Mom.” Josie kissed Sage’s head.

Slowly, they made their way to the front porch. Sage unlocked the door and pulled it open with one hand and guided Josie across the threshold with the other. The shoes that had cluttered the foyer were gone. The floor had also been swept and mopped. The scent of beef, broth and potatoes filled the air.

Josie inhaled. “Smells like someone left us dinner.”

“Looks like our neighbors came by to take care of us.” As she spoke, her chest filled with appreciation. “You want dinner in the living room or in your bedroom?”

“Living room,” said Josie. “I want to watch a TV without a beeping heart monitor in the background.”

Sage led her daughter into the living room and helped her onto the sofa. She handed her three remotes—one for the TV, another for cable and a final device for the streaming services. “I’ll see what’s in the kitchen and be back in a minute.”

Josie turned on the TV and started scrolling through the romantic comedy recommendations. “Thanks, Mom.”

The kitchen was as neat and tidy as the entryway. A sheet of paper sat on the table. The ranch foreman, Bruce, had cramped handwriting. Sage recognized his scrawl the minute she picked up the note. “Glad that you’re home and Josie’s out of the hospital. We all pitched in and spruced up your house a bit. We figured you’d be busy for the next few days. I made you my shepherd’s pie. It’s in the oven. There’s a cake in the fridge. I’ll stop by in the morning, but don’t worry about a thing. We’ve got you covered.”

She set the note on the table and then opened the oven. The shepherd’s pie was in a glass dish. The potato topping was golden brown, and gravy bubbled around the edges. She found a set of potholders and pulled the casserole dish out. After scooping large helpings onto two plates, she poured two glasses of water. Napkins were in a basket on the table and the forks were in the silverware drawer. Everything for the meal was collected and Sage picked up the plates.

She stopped and set the plates on the counter.

Before they ate, she should call Bruce and tell him they were back. She pulled her phone from her jacket pocket and hit the power button. The screen remained dark.

Damn. She'd let the phone lose its power. With an exhale, she found the power cord in another basket on the counter and plugged it in. Thunder rolled across the plains. She didn't know there was a storm headed their way. As a rancher, she was always careful about the weather. But she'd been too busy with Josie to worry about the forecast.

Was this a passing rumble of thunder or a major gale? She picked up her phone to check for any severe storm warnings. She snorted with a laugh at her own behavior. "No power to the phone, no app for the weather."

Setting the phone down, she grabbed the plates of food, silverware, and napkins, and turned for the living room.

Decker returned to San Antonio. After killing the woman in Central Texas, there were searches for him all over the state—and that's exactly what he wanted. If they were looking for him from Austin to Dallas to Texarkana, they wouldn't worry about him being back where it all started.

He'd sat in front of Michael O'Brien's apartment for less than an hour when the doctor appeared. He watched him drive away, but this time, no police cruiser followed.

It left Decker with a choice to make.

Did he follow the car? Or did he wait for the doctor to come home?

The sleek blue car drove silently down the street. Without another thought, he followed. Decker kept several car lengths between his auto and that of Michael O'Brien.

When the car pulled off the highway and onto a lonely stretch of road, it was easy for Decker to guess where the doctor was headed. He'd made it a point to know everything about the college student who was attacked. She lived outside of Mercy at the Double S Ranch. If he had to bet, he'd put money on the doctor heading to her home. Since he spent a year living off the grid, he knew all roads in the area. He'd take a shortcut, giving himself time to wait for the doctor's arrival.

Michael should've taken a painkiller before he left San Antonio. The drive to Mercy was several hours and it was the longest amount of time he'd been out of bed since the kidney surgery. His side and back ached. His head throbbed. As sick as he was of staying in bed, he could use another nap.

Rain turned the nighttime sky to an inky and wet black. The pavement was slick. His wipers worked double-time, their constant *swish-swish-swish* was almost hypnotic.

Still, he refused to give up or give in. While driving, Michael had alerted law enforcement about his newest findings. Currently, he was on the phone with Isaac. The other man's voice came through the car's speakers.

Isaac said, "I've spoken to Jason, Mooky Cafferty, and Bernadette Hayes. An APB went out for Corrin Akers and her car. So far, we haven't found anything."

Michael inhaled and exhaled deeply, trying to release some of the pain with his breath. "Can't the local sheriff stop by the Double S Ranch and warn Sage? Or at least send a deputy?" He spoke through gritted teeth. Just talking left him breathless. "She has to know what's going on."

"No offense, man. You don't sound too good. Are you sure you should be driving all the way to Mercy?"

"If you tell me that the Sheriff will stop by Sage's ranch and warn her about Corrin, then I'll turn around right now." His words were a lie. He was less than an hour from her home.

"You're driving into a hell of a storm. There's flooding all over the area. The sheriff and all his deputies are dealing with that. Cafferty promised to get someone to the Double S Ranch soon."

"Then Sage and Josie have nobody to count on but me." Michael shifted in his seat, easing away some of his pain. "And I'm not going to let them down."

Decker arrived at the Double S Ranch. The ranch sat behind a set of ornamental gates that never closed. Beyond the gates was a mile-long driveway lined with trees. A stream, dry most of the year, bisected the lane. A wooden bridge spanned the creek bed. A heavy rain fell, and dark water rushed under the boards of the bridge.

Decker couldn't drive right up to the house, not without warning everyone on the ranch of his arrival. With a quarter mile to go, he pulled off the narrow road and parked behind a large tree. After collecting branches that had been blown down by the wind, he covered his car.

Satisfied that his vehicle was suitably camouflaged, he headed toward the main house. By the time he arrived, Decker was soaked. His hands were numb from the cold. His boots were filled with water. A barn stood near the house. A single pickup truck sat in the driveway.

With time to plan, Decker knew there were a million ways to dispatch the physician. An ambush as he walked from his car to the front door. A single bullet through the window. A knife between his ribs as he slept.

First, he needed a layout of the house. He wanted to know who was inside and what kind of resistance he would face. Lights from several rooms spilled into the night. He approached one window and peered inside. It was a kitchen, complete with a round table in the middle of the room and a long wooden counter. Aside from the appliances, the room was empty.

He moved silently to the next window. A TV hung on a wall. The credits from a movie rolled across the screen. There was a person, covered with a blanket, on the sofa. A blond woman slept in a recliner. He recognized the woman as Sage Sauter. She was the mother of Josie Kruger—the college student he didn't attack.

He moved closer to the window, his breath fogging the glass.

Sage opened her eyes. Sat up. Decker stepped back, blending with the darkness. He watched as she rose from the chair and turned off the TV with a remote control. She moved to the sofa. "Josie, honey, the movie's over. You should probably get in bed. If you sleep on the sofa, you're going to be sore in the morning."

Josie sat up. "I'll head to my room."

"You need help? What can I get you?"

"Can you bring me a glass of water so I can take something for the pain?"

Sage left the room but returned moments later with a glass and prescription bottle. She handed the glass to Josie first and then two pills. "Take this now and we'll get you upstairs."

The college student placed the pills on her tongue before drinking a swallow of water. She handed the glass to her mother.

Sage set both the glass and the prescription on the table. Holding out her hand, she said, "Let me help get you to bed."

Josie rose slowly from the sofa. Leaning on her mom, she shuffled out of the room and a few moments later, a light shone from behind the curtains of an upstairs window.

Wind whipped around the house, and an old tree creaked. In the distance lightning cracked, a whip of fire splitting the sky in two. Thunder rumbled, the percussion resonating in his chest.

A set of headlights cut through the storm. Decker raced to the barn and watched through a chink in the boards. The car lights turned off. He heard the distant slamming of the car's door. A moment later, a figure crept out of the rain. Even in the dark, he could tell by the figure that it was a woman. So not the doctor. But who?

Hair, lank and wet, hung around her shoulders. She stood by the rear of the truck, watching the house.

Lightning struck again. This time it hit the old tree. Sparks flew as the trunk split down the middle. The uppermost branches caught the power lines as they fell, plunging the house into darkness.

Standing in the barn, Decker was oblivious to the wet and the cold. The woman approached the house. Even in gloom, even with the rain, Decker could see the knife in her hand. She stared at the blade before slipping it into her pocket.

He murmured under his breath, "Now this is getting interesting."

Sage was halfway down the stairs when the power went out. "Dammit," she cursed. "Hey, Josie. You okay?" she called out.

"I'm fine, Mom."

"I'm going to start the generator. You stay put."

She'd lived in the house her entire life. She didn't need a light to find her way down the staircase and to the entryway. From the closet, she got her rain jacket and opened the door. The spray of the cold shower hit her in the face, and she stepped into the night. A small stream ran through the middle of her driveway. She slogged through the mud to the corner of the house, where the generator was stored under a tarp.

Pulling off the tarp, she grabbed the handle of the recoil rope and pulled. The engine coughed, spluttered, but didn't catch. She pulled the starter cord again. And again. Nothing.

Then she remembered. The generator was out of gas.

Did she call one of her employees in the middle of the night? Or did she and Josie ride out the storm in the dark?

* * *

Corrin was filled with fury. How was it that Josie had everything? Looks. A nice mom. A boyfriend who still loved her even though they'd broken up.

What did Corrin have?

Nothing but an attack to hide before Josie's memories came back.

The power was out in the house. She'd raced to the back of the property as Josie's mom came out the front door. Now she stood next to the kitchen door and looked through an inset pane of glass. She pushed down on the handle. It didn't give.

Well, she'd come too far to turn back now.

A terra-cotta pot filled with the gangly skeleton of a long-dead plant sat on the patio. Picking it up, she smashed it against the small window. The pane shattered. She reached through the hole for the handle and unlocked the latch. She pulled the door open and stepped inside, then took the knife from her pocket.

Sage was standing on her porch when she heard breaking glass. The sound sent a chill up her spine. She opened the front door and stepped inside. Somehow, her home felt different. The air rested heavily on her bones. Water dripped from her rain jacket, forming a puddle on the ground. "Josie, you okay?" Her words were swallowed by the darkness.

Her daughter didn't answer.

Of course, there might be a reasonable explanation for everything. The crack of breaking glass could have been Josie dropping a cup on the floor. She might not answer her mother's call because she was asleep.

No. Josie couldn't be both sleeping and breaking a glass.

Sage moved slowly toward the stairwell. She could see the bottom two steps before the rest was swallowed by shadows. "Josie?" she called out again.

Nothing. The metallic taste of panic filled her mouth.

She put her hand on the newel post and that's when she noticed the breeze, along with the scent of rain. Maybe another branch fell and that's what broke a window. Still, she kicked off her shoes before soundlessly creeping toward the kitchen.

Glass covered the floor and a pane in the back door was broken. A shard of broken pottery lay on the floor as well. So it wasn't an accident. Sage's phone still sat on the counter and she reached for the device at the same moment that she heard footsteps on the stairs.

Whoever had broken the window was in the house. Calling the police and waiting for them to arrive would waste time that Sage didn't have. In the study, where she managed all the business of the ranch, was a gun cabinet—along with three firearms. One handgun and two shotguns. But she didn't have time to grab a gun either. After reaching for a knife from the wooden block that sat on the counter, she raced up the stairs.

Compared to the downstairs, where there were windows in every room, the hallway was dark. Pressing her back to the wall, she hustled to Josie's room. The door was open a crack and she peered inside. The bed was empty. The room was silent.

Where was Josie?

Michael turned off the county road and passed through the gates to the Double S Ranch. Funny, he'd only visited Sage at home a handful of times during that fateful summer. Yet, all these years later, he still remembered the way.

Rain thrummed on the roof of his car, matching the pounding in his head. He couldn't decide if he was freezing or feverish. He did know one thing. He couldn't get out of the car soon enough.

The lane narrowed as it crossed over a stream. The car jostled as the tires rolled over the abutment. Below, the water was black and licked at the sides of the bridge. As the car eased onto the muddy track, Michael let his foot off the gas. A sedan was parked on the lane. It was an exact match to the vehicle driven by Corrin Akers. Sure, he could stop and check the license plate, but he wasn't going to waste his time. Slowing, he maneuvered onto the soggy ground, and peered through the windows. The car looked to be abandoned.

Was Corrin already at the house?

Had Michael arrived too late to save Sage and Josie?

All his ailments were forgotten, and he dropped his foot onto the accelerator. The car shot down the road.

Using the steering wheel controls, he placed a call.

Isaac answered after the second ring. "Hey, man."

"She's here," said Michael. Even he could hear the fury and fear in his own voice. "Her car is on the private road that leads to Sage's house. Get the sheriff here pronto. Hell, call in the FBI."

"I'll do both. But what are you going to do?"

Michael didn't have to think before answering. "I'm going to protect Sage and Josie—even if it means my life."

Decker saw the headlights long before he heard the car. As the vehicle pulled in front of the house, he realized it had an electric motor. From his hiding place in the barn, he knew that his patience had finally paid off.

Michael O'Brien had arrived.

He stepped closer to the door and watched the doctor stumble from the car and run through the rain. He was soaked by the time he reached the porch. He beat his fist on the door, the thud sounded like the house had a heartbeat.

He stepped back and waited. Nothing.

True, Decker was curious about what was happening inside the house. So far, it was quiet and dark. It was easy to think that inside a family slept safely in their beds. But he knew better.

Had the intruder already killed Sage and her daughter?

Was now the time for Dr. O'Brien to die as well?

Chapter 20

The knocking seemed to shake the house, and Sage froze where she stood in the hallway. She wanted to call out, but she dared not make a sound.

From outside came a voice. “Sage. It’s me. Michael. Are you home? Let me in.”

Thank goodness. Michael had come. She still didn’t know what had happened to Josie, but at least she was no longer alone. With an exhale, she stepped from the shadows. Moving back down the hallway, she took the steps two at a time to the ground level. At the bottom of the stairs, she rounded a corner.

“Don’t move.” The cold tip of a knife pressed into the back of her neck. Sage let the long sleeve of her raincoat fall over the blade that she carried. “Or I will run you through.”

She recognized the voice, but nothing made sense. “Corrin?”

"Don't turn around and don't look at me."

Corrin pushed the blade until the tip pierced the first layer of Sage's skin. Blood trickled down the back of her neck.

"What do you want?" Sage asked.

"Where's Josie?"

"You mean you don't know?" Sage almost sobbed with relief that the person with a knife didn't have her daughter.

"Don't play games with me," Corrin snarled.

Sage inched away from the knife at the back of her neck. "I'm completely honest. I don't know where Josie's gone. The last I knew, she was in her room. But…" She took another step forward, creating more space between her and the knife. "Why are you here?"

"You haven't figured it out?"

Corrin being in the house with a knife could mean only one thing. She was the one who attacked Josie.

In an instant, Sage connected all the clues. Josie would get into the car with her roommate. On the day after Josie's attack, Corrin had moved slowly around the room. At the time, Sage assumed that was because of fear and worry. But now, she knew. Josie fought her attacker and most likely, Corrin was bruised. She'd flinched when Sage had given her a hug. It must've been from physical, and not emotional, pain. The long-sleeve shirt and sweats she had worn were hiding her bruises and scrapes.

Now, there was one thing Sage didn't know. "Why?" she asked. "You two were friends. Why try to kill Josie and make it look like the work of a serial killer?"

"I was the one Ben slept with after Josie broke up

with him. Then the next day, they got back together. Do you know how used that made me feel?"

Sage had been young once. "Of course, I'm sure you felt awful. That was all the guy's doing—not Josie's. Sure, you two might not have been friends anymore. Still, that's no reason to try to kill her." It was more than the first attack. Corrin had been at the hospital and now here, at the ranch. The why of it all really didn't matter. She had to stop Corrin before she completed her grisly and murderous goal. She held the knife in the loose sleeves of her jacket. She let the blade slip out of the fabric as she turned to look at Corrin. "There's more to your story. What is it?"

"I'm pregnant," she sobbed. "Ben doesn't want me. What he wants is to marry Josie and have the two of them raise the baby. He planned to tell her everything and propose that night." Corrin howled as if wounded. And Sage supposed that she was. "I couldn't let that happen. I didn't mean to hurt her, but when I did, I knew that I'd be in trouble. So, I tried to copy what Decker Newcombe had done so he'd get the blame. When she survived…well… I couldn't let her remember what happened—"

Sage didn't wait for Corrin to finish her confession. She swung out with the knife. The blade caught the back of the younger woman's hand. She screamed as blood flowed down her wrist.

"If you think a little scratch is enough to make me give up," said Corrin, "you are dead wrong."

Michael slammed the side of his fist against the door once more. The frame shook. "Sage? Can you hear me?"

Her truck was in the driveway. It was an awful night

to be out. Was she even home? He tried to open the front door. The handle was locked, and the door didn't budge. There had to be another way inside.

All those years ago, Michael recalled standing in Sage's kitchen. The back door had been open and the breeze blew through the room. He sprinted around the house and found the door, just like he remembered. Part of a broken pot lay on the ground. That's when he noticed the shattered pane of glass. He pushed the door open and stepped into the kitchen.

His foot crunched on broken glass and he heard voices. He followed the sound. Pressing his back into the wall, he glanced around the corner. Enough light filtered in through the windows that he could see and his blood went cold. Sage and Corrin each held a knife. Blood dripped from Corrin's arm. She lunged for Sage. The blade connected with her chest but only ripped the fabric of her jacket.

He couldn't stay hidden any longer. Launching himself at Corrin, he tackled the younger woman around the middle. They felt to the floor. He pinned her wrist to the ground. Corrin wrenched her hand free and stabbed at his face. He dodged the blade and Corrin scooted out from beneath him. She lunged at him again.

Michael kept his eyes trained on the knife in her hand. He reached for her wrist, and she pulled back. He fell on top of her, shoving her back to the floor. Corrin went limp. His hands were covered in hot blood. Had he been cut?

Michael rolled Corrin to her side. A knife protruded from her chest. Blood leaked from the corner of her mouth. She gasped for air. An arc of blood sprayed out from her chest wound.

"Get me towels." He no longer saw Corrin Akers as a threat—but a patient who needed medical care. His training as a physician came to him with the same ease as breathing. After stripping out of his own jacket, he used it to apply pressure to the wound. Blood soaked the fabric. It leaked through his fingers. "I need a first-aid kit. If you don't have sutures in your kit, bring a regular needle and thread."

"Josie's missing," she said, breathless.

"Missing?" Could this night get any worse? "Did Corrin do something to her?"

"I don't think so," said Sage.

It looked like there was another mystery to solve. First, he needed to save Corrin. Too bad he couldn't see much of anything. "I need some light."

"The house lost power." She paused, breathing hard. "I'll grab a flashlight."

He watched as she ran toward the kitchen. Sure, Sage was rattled. Who wouldn't be? But she was keeping her emotions in check and doing what needed to be done in a crisis. He admired that about her. He pressed the jacket harder into Corrin's chest wound. The fibers didn't absorb much blood. That meant she was bleeding out. "C'mon," he said to Corrin. "I need you to listen to my voice. Focus on what I'm saying and don't give up."

Her eyes were closed but her lips moved, as if in a silent prayer.

Leaning closer, he said, "Corrin, can you hear me?"

A pool of blood spread out around the young woman.

If he wanted to save her, he had to remove the knife. Then, the wound needed to be stitched close. But he couldn't perform surgery in the dark. Where in the hell was Sage? She'd been gone for too damn long.

Corrin let out a single breath and her head lolled to the side. He felt under her chin for a pulse. There was none.

Decker entered the house through the open back door. A butcher block sat on the counter. A single knife was missing. He selected another with a steel handle and a sharp blade.

Moving into the shadows, he waited.

Sage rushed into the kitchen. Her phone sat on the counter. She reached for the device, and he stepped forward. He held the knife like it was an extension of his arm. "Put that down," he said.

She set the cell phone back on the counter and held up her hands. "Wh-who are you?"

"Are you sure you don't know?" He moved closer to her.

Her eyes got wide, and she sucked in a sharp breath. "Decker Newcombe. You aren't the one who attacked my daughter. I know that. Why are you here?"

It was a complicated question with a simple answer. "I'm going to kill the doctor. Then, you'll have to die."

"Michael," she gasped. "Why him? What has he done to you?"

"Did you know that in 1888, during the Autumn of Terror, the London police worked with a renowned surgeon? During the killings, the doctor became a media darling. He was the first person to use the term *serial killer*. His name was Thomas Bond, and he was more famous than Jack in 1888."

Sage drew her brows together. "That's why you want to kill Michael—because he's more famous than you?"

He hated her incredulous tone. He should kill her

now. He struck, grabbing Sage by the wrist. She twisted in his grip and slipped free. Decker, like a fool, only held her coat. He was never a fool. Now he'd have to kill her slowly.

She ran from the room, screaming. "Michael, he's here."

Decker wanted to kill them one at a time. After all, a single victim was easier to control than multiple people. That didn't matter. He'd kill Sage first and make Michael watch. Decker would get a certain level of satisfaction in the doctor's sorrow and terror.

He followed Sage down a narrow hallway and toward the front of the house. There, at the foot of the stairs was the body of a young woman—but no Michael.

Sage looked up at him, confusion and horror were in her eyes. She must've been expecting to see the doctor as well. It didn't matter, he'd find the doctor soon enough.

He approached Sage slowly, forcing her to back up one step at a time. Only when it was too late did she realize that he had literally forced her into a corner. What's more, there was no way for her to escape.

Sage screamed and the sound pierced Michael's heart.

He'd heard Decker in the kitchen with Sage and knew he couldn't fight the killer one on one. What he needed to do was outwit him. Thank goodness he remembered every moment of his visits to the ranch decades earlier. Each second was an indelible mark on his brain.

That's how he knew the gun cabinet was in the office off the den. He also remembered where Sage's father had kept the key. He was lucky she hadn't moved the hiding place. There was one handgun and two shotguns. In such a small space, a shotgun wouldn't work. Once fired, it would send pellets flying in all directions. It left him with his only option—the handgun.

With his back pressed against the wall, he held the firearm. He didn't like the idea of trying to shoot if Decker was close to Sage. In truth, he wasn't a good shot. But with her scream, he could wait no more.

He stepped around the corner and lifted the gun, aiming at the back of Decker's head.

"Get away from her, you bastard."

Decker stopped and turned to look at Michael. "You really think I'm afraid of you? You must be stupid."

"At least I'm smart enough to not bring a knife to a gun fight."

Decker shook his head and laughed. "I can see why she likes you. Charming. Funny. *A doctor.*" He said the last word like it was a curse. Sage moved out of the corner. Decker spit on the floor. "Tell me this, how'd you get her to talk?"

The *she* wasn't Sage. "Who are you talking about?"

"Who's the stupid one now? My mother, you idiot. How'd you get my own mom to betray me?"

As a medical professional, he had empathy for Decker. He was a person the world had mistreated from the beginning. But Michael was more than a doctor, he was also a man. A man protecting the woman he loved—and their child. He did love Sage. The realization left him winded.

"Aren't you going to say anything?" Decker sneered. "After all, you're about to die."

"If I'm going to die," he said, "then I'll see you in hell."

Michael pulled the trigger. Fire erupted from the

barrel. A clap of thunder exploded in the small space. The landing filled with the stench of gunpowder. Plaster and smoke mixed as the bullet punched a hole in the wall next to the killer.

Decker looked at Michael and sneered. "You missed."

"Yeah, but I've got a full magazine left to fire." He pulled the trigger again. Decker dove to the side and sprinted down the hallway. Michael tracked him with the gun. Fire. Fire. Fire. The bullets peppered the wall as the killer ran. Michael followed, shooting as he went.

Decker wrenched the back door open and sprinted into the night.

Outside, cold rain pelted his face. Michael ran but he could hardly draw a breath. His head buzzed. His side ached. He wanted to retch. He feared that he'd pass out. At least Sage was inside the house and safe. For that, none of his ailments mattered. Decker dashed across an open field and stopped short. He turned around and glared at Michael.

As Michael approached, he realized the killer was trapped. To his front was Michael and his gun. At Decker's back was the raging water of the creek. "Gotcha."

He pulled the trigger. *Click.*

Decker smiled. "Looks like you're outta bullets, Doc. And here I am." He lifted the knife. "Still with my blade." With a roar, he launched himself at Michael.

He turned the gun in his hand, holding it like a cudgel. When Decker was in range, Michael swung out. The butt-end of the gun caught the killer in the jaw. His head snapped back. The impact wasn't enough. Decker drove his blade into Michael's side.

The pain came in a flash of white and red. Holding onto his middle, he staggered backward. He had to think, but it hurt too damn much.

"What do you think about dying slow, as I cut you up piece by piece?" Decker asked.

Michael opened his mouth, but he couldn't make a sound.

"I think that's a lousy idea." Someone else answered the question. Michael turned to the sound of the voice.

Sage came out of the rain, a shotgun propped up against her shoulder. It was as if the storm's fury had created a vengeful goddess. "I'd say my prayers if I were you, Decker. Because if you don't drop that knife, you're going to meet your maker."

He held up the blade. "You mean this one?" He threw the knife. It somersaulted through the air, heading straight for Michael.

At the same instant, a blast of fire exploded from the barrel of the shotgun. Michael ducked as the knife's tip caught his shoulder. A bullet slammed into Decker, knocking him off his feet. He landed next to the creek. Blood frothed at his lips. "You can't think that you've won."

Soaked by hours of rain, the bank crumbled beneath him. He gave a surprised curse as the earth gave way and the creek swallowed him whole.

Michael stumbled to the bank as Decker slipped under the dark water. He dropped to the ground. Every part of his body hurt. He reached for his feet and slipped off a shoe. Sage dropped down at his side. "What're you doing?"

"What does it look like? I'm going after Decker. Someone's gotta save him."

The distant sound of sirens cut through the night.

Sage asked, "The police?"

"I called Isaac when I saw Corrin's car. He called the sheriff."

"You stay put." She placed her hand on his shoulder. "I'll let Mooky know that Josie's missing, and Decker went into the water. He's got the equipment for a search and rescue and people to look for my daughter." She paused. "Our daughter."

Waving her arms, Sage ran toward the narrow lane. The police cruiser stopped. The lights shone, red and blue, atop the car. The siren went quiet. From a distance, he couldn't tell what she said. Since she pointed to the creek, he could guess she was telling the sheriff about Decker.

Cafferty got out of the car and rushed to the bank. Using a high-powered flashlight, he searched the water. Sage came back to Michael. She slipped her arm under his shoulder and helped him to stand.

"Can you make it back to the house? EMTs are on their way." She paused a beat. "Plus, I want to look for Josie."

Having her next to him felt better than good—it felt right. They walked slowly toward the house. "About what I said the other day…" he began.

"Save your strength, especially if you're going to apologize. I was wrong to hide the truth from you. It's something I've always known I needed to make right. It's just… I never knew how."

Together, they climbed the porch steps. "What're you going to tell Josie?"

"First, we have to find her, but I know where she might've gone." Sage rested her hand on the handle but didn't open the door. "She deserves the truth, same as you. She needs to know that you're her biological father."

The door opened on its own. Josie stood on the threshold. Tears ran down her cheeks and her voice trembled. "Mom? What's going on?"

"Thank goodness you're safe. I was so worried about you," she said. "Let's get inside and we can talk."

He assumed that Josie had heard everything Sage said—including the fact that he was the young woman's father. Michael still leaned on her shoulder. He limped into the house, watching his daughter.

Josie met Michael's gaze. "Hey."

It wasn't much, but it was a start. "Hey."

Josie asked, "You want some tea or something?" Then her eyes went to his side. "Oh my God, did you get shot? You're bleeding."

"Not shot but stabbed." It hurt to talk.

Josie slipped her shoulder under his other arm. "You two have to tell me what happened. I heard glass breaking and looked out the back window. I saw Corrin and knew something wasn't right. But the pain meds made me loopy and I couldn't think straight. I went to your room, Mom. You weren't there, so I hid." She wiped away her tears, but they kept coming. "I saw Corrin's body at the bottom of the stairs and then... Mom, I remember what happened."

"It's okay," said Sage, her voice soothing. "I'm here now and you're safe." She paused a beat. "Let's get Michael to the living room."

The house was still dark, but they made their way through the gloom. Windows let in enough light that Michael could see the sofa. He eased onto a cushion, his body hurting everywhere.

An ambulance pulled up next to the door.

"You stay here. I'm going to get the EMTs," Sage said to Josie. "I'll be right back."

She ran from the room.

He could feel Josie's eyes on him.

He looked at her. "You okay?"

"I heard what my mom said. Is it true? Are you my biological father?"

"I am."

"I guess I have you to thank for my kidney."

He shrugged. A sharp pain filled his side. "It was the least I could do."

"You saved my life." She inhaled and sat in a nearby recliner. "So where do we go from here?"

"I'd like to get to know you better," he said.

"That'd be nice."

Michael wasn't sure what it meant to be a father—especially to a child who was already grown. More than that, he'd spent his whole life avoiding relationships. He'd learned that love hurts.

Now he knew better.

The pain was worth the payoff.

But had he learned his lesson too late to make a difference with Sage?

In the hour since the EMTs had taken Michael to the hospital in Encantador, several things had happened. Dr. Garcia, the medical examiner, collected Corrin's body. Josie was taken to Bruce's house and was settled into bed. A search party had been sent out to find Decker Newcombe. It included several of the ranch employees and deputies from the sheriff's office, along with a troop from Search and Rescue.

So far, no trace of Decker Newcombe had been found.

Sage stood on her porch as Mooky gave his report. "It's hard to think that anyone could survive getting shot and falling into the creek with the water as high as it is. But Decker's survived worse. He's like a damn cat with nine lives."

"Thanks for telling me about Decker." But there was more that she wanted to know. "Any idea how Michael's doing?"

"Last I heard, he's still at the local hospital. Medevac couldn't come and get him because of the weather. And the local ambulances were out on other emergencies. He'll get sent to San Antonio eventually. For now, he's stable and comfortable." Mooky paused. "Can you stay at Bruce's for a bit? At least till your house gets cleaned up and the power lines get fixed."

Sage supposed she could stay at the foreman's house. But for now, she had someplace else she wanted to be.

The drive to the hospital took thirty minutes. Each mile traveled brought her closer to Michael and more certain of what she wanted. There were only a few cars in the parking lot, and she found a spot near the front door. The waiting room was empty, save for an aide who sat behind a desk.

They looked up as she entered. "Can I help you?"

As if she'd just run a long distance, Sage was breathless. Then again, it had taken decades to get to this moment. Life wasn't a sprint, she reminded herself, but a marathon. "I'm looking for Michael O'Brien. Is he here?"

"He's still in the ER waiting for transport. Room ten." The aide pointed. "Take that door, then it's down the hall and on the left."

"Thanks," she called over her shoulder, already opening the door. She found room ten and stopped on the threshold. Michael was hooked up to both a heart monitor and an IV. His complexion was pale and a bruise ringed his left eye. His chin and cheeks were covered with stubble and still, her heart skipped a beat at the sight of him.

He looked up. Their gazes met and held. "I was hoping you'd come." He reached for her, and she slipped her palm into his hand. "All these years I've been alone because I thought I didn't want to fall in love again."

"You don't?" she asked, kneeling next to his bed.

"The thing is, I've never stopped loving you."

Sage placed her lips on the back of his hand. "I love you now more than I loved you then. Who knew that was even possible?" She paused. "What happens now?"

"Wherever life takes me, I want you at my side."

She laid her head on their entwined hands. "Michael, there's no place I'd rather be."

Epilogue

Seven months later

The day was cloudy and unseasonably cool for South Texas. A dais had been set up in the parking lot of the newly renovated building. Across the street was a gas station and the post office. A flashing light hung above the road.

Aside from the makeshift stage, chairs for over three dozen people had been placed in rows. They were all filled. Media vans were parked at the back of the lot. The news crews had their cameras set up to take video of the grand opening.

Michael stepped up to the podium and addressed the crowd. “Thank you all for coming today. My name is Doctor Michael O’Brien and I’m the director of the Forensic Lab for Rural Policing.”

Behind him was the newly renovated one-story cinderblock building. A state-of-the-art lab had been born from a former bar and tattoo parlor. Sure, Michael was at the podium, but he couldn't take credit for being in front of the crowd. "I'd like to thank several people. First is Sheriff Maurice Cafferty." Mooky stood and waved at the crowd. "Sheriff Cafferty has been our local law enforcement partner from the beginning. Undersheriff Kathryn Glass will have an office in our lab—continuing our partnership." The Undersheriff was also on the dais. She stood and waved as well.

Michael continued. "I'd like to introduce you to our staff, who were instrumental in helping us seek funding and support for our newest effort. Dustin Halls is our lab tech, and my daughter, Josie Kruger, is our lab assistant."

Josie had recovered fully from the injuries sustained in the attack. For now, she was taking classes online. Being in Mercy meant she was able to work. Her time at the lab would count as clinical hours for her med school application. He hoped the time was well-spent. Josie would make a hell of a doctor. Then again, he was her dad and more than a little proud and biased.

Months earlier, Sage had spoken to Vance. She'd been honest and let him know that Josie had been told the truth about her paternity. Since then, Michael had spoken to Vance, too. Honestly, he was glad that Vance had been willing to create a home with Sage all those years ago.

Now Michael and Sage were creating a family with their daughter. Sure, it was a couple decades late. But it had all been worth the wait.

He returned his attention to the present moment. Dustin and Josie stood and waved at the crowd.

Michael took a sip of water and continued. "We have federal law enforcement partners as well. Supervisory Special Agent Jason Jones made it possible for the lab to move into this facility. He also helped us obtain a grant from the FBI's Rural Law Enforcement Initiative." Jason nodded at the crowd.

There was one more person on the stage who had yet to be introduced. "Finally, I have to thank my fiancée, Sage Sauter. Without her, none of us would be here today. It was Sage's idea to create this center."

After convalescing at the Double S Ranch, Michael knew he didn't want to move back to San Antonio—or any other city. He also knew that he still wanted to work as a forensic pathologist. Decker Newcombe was still at-large. Even after Decker was found, there would be other killers and other crimes.

"It happened one day when I said I wanted to stay in Mercy forever but needed a big hospital for my job. She asked me why that was. I gave her the most honest answer in the world." He paused. "It's all about the funding." There were several chuckles from the crowd. "It was then that Sage said, 'Let's find the money.' I thought she was joking. Obviously, she was not."

She stood and the crowd began to applaud.

Michael clapped as well. Once the crowd had quieted, he asked, "Is there anything you want to say, Sage?"

Standing in front of her seat, she spoke. "I love this community. I love my family. And I love you, too, Michael O'Brien. This lab is going to be an important part of life in Mercy and the surrounding communities. Having the facility here will mean jobs. It also means we can get justice for those who have lost their lives and the families who mourn them."

Michael still stood behind the podium "That was so well said that I have nothing else to add. I'm done with my remarks. Josie and Dustin will lead the tours. You can follow them."

It took only a few moments for everyone to file inside the lab. Then it was just Michael and Sage. They met in the middle of the dais, and he pulled her to him. "You did good today. I'm proud of you."

She laid her head on his chest. "I'm proud of you, too."

"Is it true what you said?" he asked.

She drew her brows together, a look of confusion on her face. "What did I say?"

"That you love me?"

"Of course, I love you."

"Good, I just like hearing you say it."

"Oh, you do?" She placed her lips on his. "I'm glad, because you're going to have to listen to me tell you that I love you every hour of every day."

"What about at night?" he asked, teasing.

"Then, too. I talk in my sleep."

Michael kissed her again. "I'm glad we found each other again. This time it will be forever."

"Forever," she said, wrapping her arms around his neck and drawing him closer. "And always."

* * * * *

Don't miss Ryan Steele's story,
The next installment of Texas Law
Jennifer D. Bokal's new miniseries for
Harlequin Romantic Suspense.
Coming soon!

And look for Isaac's story,
Texas Law: Undercover Justice

Available now, wherever Harlequin books
and ebooks are sold.

COMING NEXT MONTH FROM

HARLEQUIN

ROMANTIC SUSPENSE

#2247 PROTECTING COLTON'S SECRET DAUGHTERS

The Coltons of New York • by Lisa Childs

FBI special agent Cash Colton divorced his wife, Valentina, to keep her away from his dangerous job. But when his latest investigation brings him back to her and their—surprise!—twin toddler daughters, he'll reckon with a serial killer out for vengeance...and protect the family caught in the crosshairs.

#2248 THE COWBOY NEXT DOOR

The Scarecrow Murders • by Carla Cassidy

Joe Masterson would do anything to keep his young daughter safe, even give up his life and identity. But keeping his beautiful neighbor Lizzy Maxwell in the dark about his witness protection status threatens their fledgling attraction. Until the criminal he sent to jail escapes and vows retribution...

#2249 DEADLY VEGAS ESCAPADE

Honor Bound • by Anna J. Stewart

With no memory of his identity or past, army investigator Riordan Malloy must rely on the kind woman who rescued him from a sinking car. But Darcy Ford isn't sure if the handsome man she's helping—and falling in love with—is on the run from danger...or a murderer on the run from the law.

#2250 DOWN TO THE WIRE

The Touré Security Group • by Patricia Sargeant

Not many people get the jump on cybersecurity expert Malachi Touré, but Dr. Grace Blackwell isn't a run-of-the-mill hacker. She's convinced Malachi's latest client stole her valuable research. He'll help the beautiful researcher uncover the truth... and spend passionate nights in her arms. But is Grace the victim...or the villain?
